The Schombürgk Line

by

John Clifford Gregory

The Schombürgk Line

This is a work of fiction. Although set in authentic historical times and places, and including historical figures among its characters, the story described here is by in large imaginary. It is not intended to represent events as they actually unfolded.

Printed by CreateSpace, an Amazon.com Company

1st Edition

First printing in February, 2014

ISBN-13: 978-1495400599

ISBN-10: 149540059X

The cover design consists of the *Oil Portrait of Grover Cleveland* (1891) by Eastman Johnson. Overlaying the portrait image are the flag of the Republic of Venezuela, the Union Flag of the United Kingdom of Great Britain and Ireland, the flag of the United States of America (as appearing in 1895) and the battle flag of the Confederate States of America (1861-1865). All images reside in the public domain ; no permission is required for their use.

In memory of my incredible father, John Gregory, and in admittedly late-found appreciation for his love and leadership.

Acknowledgements

This is the first of—I fervently hope—several progressively superior works of historical fiction centered on the Gilded Age of American history. While time was short and resources were sparse, friends and family were incredibly supportive, as were the scholarly and creative infrastructures to which I have access.

I am extremely appreciative to my mother, Margaret Lee Gregory, for teaching me to love the English language and the calling of the wordsmith. Like me, Mom can sometimes come off as pretentious in speech; yet, in both of us, it grows from a reverence for our beautiful mother tongue and its myriad powers to inform and inspire.

Thanksgiving for friends can not be overstated. From church friends to former mortgage industry colleagues, I am blessed with many individuals who continued to encourage me when this project stalled. Among this group were those who invested financially: David Tardio, Fadi Hanna and Sarah Bobell have staked their resources on the success of this novel and I am humbled by their confidence.

I am likewise grateful to the awesome staff of the Wyckoff (NJ) Free Public Library that tolerates my obnoxious presence day in and day out. The assistance rendered by the reference librarians and circulation specialists is invaluable and I will spend the days left to me extolling the vital role of public libraries in the cultural lives of our communities.

The peer-review editors at authonomy.com give excellent suggestions on plot, structure and formatting. This is a fabulous resource for those who must self-publish on a shoestring; likewise for those who want a shot at a conventional book deal.

"It is impossible that a nation of infidels or idolaters should be a nation of freemen. It is when a people forget God that tyrants forge their chains."

--Patrick Henry, addressing the Virginia Assembly, 1784

"Those who promise us paradise on earth never produced anything but a hell."

--Sir Karl R. Popper, *The Open Society and Its Enemies*

"All the ends of the earth will remember and turn to the LORD, and all the families of the nations will bow down before him, for dominion belongs to the LORD and he rules over the nations."

--Psalms 22:27-28 (KJV)

He gripped the brass handles with what remained of his strength. Kneeling by the reddish-brown, mahogany casket, he could feel the increasing pressure of gravity on his substantial girth, as his weeping turned to sobbing, and then to bawling. The loud, steady clack of the train's wheels over the rail joints made for reassuring white noise, and he was confident nobody in the adjoining car could hear him. Upon attempting to lift his bulk to a standing position, however, the president of the United States collapsed on the floor with a loud thud.

Though morbidly obese – to both the amusement and contempt of his countrymen – Grover Cleveland was always as physically strong as an ox. In fact, his stamina was the stuff of legend. His current immobility reflected not frailty, but forty-five minutes of intense emotional purging. Memories – fond and not so fond – came flooding back as he spent some solitary time with the corpse of his dear friend and advisor. Cleveland had not expected to experience such gut-wrenching pain when he first suspected the imminent death of his comrade-in-peace. Of course, it was always Walter Gresham's way to downplay problems and soothe anxieties. Such a serene demeanor made him an ideal secretary of state. It also made him the perfect confidante and sounding board.

Cleveland made another attempt at rising, this time extending his arms over the top of the coffin, as if holding on for dear life. The door to the baggage car suddenly opened, admitting two aides. The president was unsure if they had heard him fall as they helped him to his feet. "We thought you would only be a few minutes, sir," one of them said softly, "so we were getting concerned." "When do we get to Chicago?" Cleveland asked in an unusually raspy voice. "Over two hours, yet," the other aide answered. As he needed the time to polish his eulogy, the president returned to his stateroom and dropped his 290 pound frame into the plush cushions of his lounge chair. He shut his eyes, awash in memories.

Fast friends they were. In spite of active Republican service from the War Between the States through Reconstruction and beyond, Gresham realized in 1892 that if reform was ever to take hold in the body politic, it would be at the chubby hands of this former Democratic president. Appointed to the federal bench by President Ulysses S. Grant, Gresham went on to serve President Chester A. Arthur as Postmaster General. Using this position to harass the corrupt Louisiana Lottery Company, he also authorized the creation of postal money orders. After a short time in the Treasury Secretary's chair, Gresham accepted an appointment to the Seventh Circuit Court of Appeals. His ongoing alienation and dissatisfaction with the Republicans crossed a threshold when the party dumped President Chester Arthur in 1884 in favor of James Blaine. As Gresham saw things, Arthur was a political hack-turned-statesman; Blaine, just an all-time hack. The disastrous term of Benjamin Harrison – coupled with a history of bad blood between the Republican president and Gresham – sold the judge on returning Cleveland to the White House.

In the once and future president's estimation, Gresham had crossed over on principle. For that – not to mention his judicial temperament, impressive background and the wisdom of his years – Cleveland named him the 33rd Secretary of State. Agreeing informally with Mrs. Cleveland to help her smooth Grover's rough edges, the secretary called forth all of his inherent warmth and modesty to earn the trust of his president. It took only weeks. Both men prized political honesty, though Gresham bathed his candor in honey, while Cleveland immersed his frankness in quinine and vinegar.

The two of them opened Cleveland's second term by shelving former President Harrison's illegitimate and immoral Hawaii annexation treaty. Because of new tariff rules, American sugar growers in Hawaii thought it best to plant their crop on American soil. A few Protestant missionaries also saw benefit in annexation. Executing step one of their plan involved removing the Islands' reigning monarch from her throne and installing their own regime. Step two called for immediate negotiations with the U.S. toward the goal of making Hawaii an American possession. The coup was unofficially, but unmistakably, backed by U.S. naval forces docked at Pearl Harbor for the receipt of coal. Queen overboard, the provisional "government" quickly negotiated an agreement with the Harrison administration. Fortunately, Cleveland and Gresham took power before the Senate ratified the document –which it surely and overwhelmingly would have. The new president's action was a wet blanket to the burgeoning class of young nationalists and a growing number of sympathetic Americans.

"Do they understand my position?" Cleveland asked Gresham one evening over a bottle of bourbon. Both men understood that annexation would come eventually, but the manner of the acquisition was as important as the islands themselves.

"Hold to your principles, Mr. President," Gresham advised. "If it is wrong for a man to pick the pocket of another, how much more grievous is one country stealing the land from a sovereign nation. The core of the problem is this restless generation coming up that is intent on competing with the European powers. We best find an outlet for all this energy."

Grover Cleveland knew that was correct, but he bristled at having to coddle jingoes like Senator Henry Cabot Lodge, who labeled every act of international restraint as cowardice.

"We're lawyers." Gresham continued. "Let's make the case against premature annexation in the annual message. I'll put my man over at State to work on the matter right away. The language will be ironclad. It should put the whole matter to rest." Gresham leaned back confidently, stroking his salt-and-pepper beard.

Cleveland gulped his drink and shifted his expansive body to reach for a cigar. Biting the tip he responded, "Anything to shut Cabot up. Teddy Roosevelt, too."

Gresham was right. The Hawaii issue was hardly an issue after Cleveland submitted his constitutional obligation that December. The president particularly appreciated the secretary's personal sacrifice – absorbing countless attacks from the jingoes – in terms of congressional relations. Cleveland himself did not have the patience to sell a position that was – to him, anyway – already self-evident and unimpeachable. Yet Gresham would confront the most pompous blowhards in the Capitol, and endure their berating and self-aggrandizement with agreeable equanimity. Through it all, the administration's policy prevailed, though Gresham's reputation took a severe beating. Political realities prevented the Queen from completely resuming her authority, something for which Gresham had argued vociferously. But even the chief executive could not take that step. A democratic republic would look hypocritical if seen installing a monarch.

His willingness to take the heat for his president made Gresham invaluable. Beyond his duties at State, Gresham spent many hours advising the president on domestic matters, cementing his loyalty. When he began, however, to evidence pleurisy in early 1895, Cleveland played the ostrich. As continued denial became impossible, he did concede one thing to his loyal lieutenant.

"We can't do this without Boyle, Mr. President. Promise me you'll keep Dustin in his position."

Cleveland, who knew why Gresham was asking, affected bravado. "*You* keep him on. You're not going anywhere, old man."

"Promise."

"OK", the president returned, his voice choking up.

Opening his eyes, President Cleveland put down his written tribute and gazed at the passing countryside from his private rail car. He surrendered to nostalgia, thinking of his youth. The Reverend Richard Cleveland was known to preach on the Holy Spirit. In Psalm 51, King David prayed that God would "take not your Holy Spirit from me." That source of peace and confidence was David's greatest treasure, according to the sickly minister. By contrast, Richard's somewhat heretical son Grover placed his confidence in a few trusted friends and advisors. As they dwindled, particularly with the death of Walter Gresham, the younger Cleveland might have reconsidered this heresy. He was also compelled to re-evaluate the fallible, human objects of his trust. Events would move "the Big One", as he was known among mid-level staffers, to forge an invisible alliance with an unfamiliar and politically hazardous partner.

1

July, 1895

Dustin Boyle painfully removed his feet from atop the large, age-worn, oaken roll-top desk, allowing gravity to send them to the floor with two loud claps. Violently shoving the document he had just digested into one of the many nooks and pigeonholes, he slowly stood up and cursed its author out loud with every expletive at his disposal. Immediately, his better judgment seized him as he stifled his remaining choice words, restricting them to the confines of his mind. The walls had ears in the State, War and Navy Building, and any emotional exclamation on his part was bound to affect his career. Yet nobody was more deserving of his invective at the moment than William Scruggs – leaving out Lincoln, Grant and Sherman, of course.

Dustin walked to the tall and stately window of his office and gazed down lustily at the Executive Mansion, standing proudly in the stifling humidity of Washington, D.C. So much evil has emanated from that place, he brooded, but the opportunity draws near to turn it about, and make the house worthy of its greatest occupants: Jefferson and Jackson. The limply-hanging flag at the top of the edifice struck him as symbolic of the country's lack of vitality and purpose. Thirty years had elapsed since the War of Northern Aggression but, like the lead imbedded in his inner thigh, its effects continued to irritate and insult. Yet, for all of the misery inflicted on him, his family and his compatriots, Dustin never gave in to resignation. Like an industrious ant, he was always one to start rebuilding a devastated hill.

Men like William L. Scruggs, however, wanted to raze what Dustin Boyle lived to build: a country that respected states' rights and tended to its own affairs. A planter's son, and once an aspiring agriculturalist himself, Dustin and his father had both foreseen the demise of slavery on the horizon. Many a night during his early teen years, the two would sit on the veranda – blanketed by the sultry Louisiana climate – and talk about the changes being wrought by mechanization. Fewer hands would be needed; the Negroes would have to go find jobs – perhaps rent some land from the Boyles. Either way, they would be on their own. The Yankees had understood this inevitability, too, but their desire to subjugate a whole region of the country was not to be contained, Dustin firmly believed.

No matter. Three decades hence, Dustin was embedded in the Yankee capital, working a plan that would exact justice. Without sword or gun, his design would be executed subtly, by the very government into which he had inserted himself. He was right on schedule, now occupying the role of Counselor-without-Portfolio to the United States secretary of state. He had come a long way since his own 1863 surrender to Union forces, who were none the wiser about the full extent of his service to the Confederacy. Lucky for them they had overwhelming numbers and resources, because they could not have won it on brains, he selectively remembered.

Dustin returned to his desk and retrieved the tract, hoping he had misread the contents. The bold letters on the pamphlet cover said it all:

British Aggressions in Venezuela, or THE MONROE DOCTRINE ON TRIAL

By

William L. Scruggs,

Late Envoy Extraordinary and Minister Plenipotentiary of the United States to Colombia and to Venezuela

Scruggs wanted to make an insignificant boundary dispute between British Guiana and Venezuela into a grand conflict, upon which the United States of America must impose a solution. Dustin did not doubt Scruggs was being compensated handsomely for his trouble by the Venezuelans. It certainly was not the first time. Nor did he believe that the ambassador would shortchange his benefactors. If anything, Scruggs was meticulous, as his introductory salvo demonstrated:

> Fortunately, however, the extent of those settlements is not a matter of mere conjecture; for their boundaries are very clearly indicated, as we shall see further on, by an unbroken chain of historical and documentary evidence extending

back over a period of more than two centuries.

At issue was a resource-rich swath of land lying between the Orinoco and Essequibo rivers over which Venezuela and Great Britain had been squabbling for decades. Boyle cared little about fights between "tea-drinkers and bean-eaters," as he called them. More than anyone, he could confirm the contemptuous indifference of the English. That they had steadily encroached upon their neighbor's countryside came as no surprise. Having stood at the receiving end of their arrogance in times past, Boyle would not contest Scruggs' assertion of a land grab. But that was really not the point.

The tract, now having circulated for nearly a year, was stoking a smoldering interventionist impulse across the country. National morale was low as the United States was enduring a third year of economic depression. While the second Cleveland Administration was only assuming power when the financial panic began, its resolute policy of a strictly gold-based currency became the symbol for hard times everywhere. Farmers, laborers and – worst of all – southerners were the hardest hit, as credit markets shrunk and jobs evaporated. Dustin resented the political bent in many of the president's men. Bourbon Democrats all, they tended to favor rich investors over wage-earners. He was grateful that at least his current position did not require him to flatter these plutocrats. At the same time, he dreaded the influential men seeking to gin up anti-British outrage in order to divert attention from lean times at home.

Boyle agreed with President Cleveland on most international issues, but could not warm to him as a man. Part of it had to do with the intentional isolation imposed on Dustin: he had spoken with the chief executive just three times, and then only briefly. Yet most of the disenchantment was rooted in Dustin's impression of Cleveland as someone who had never really suffered. Though a professed War Democrat, young Grover had chosen to avoid service in the Union army, paying an immigrant to assume the risk. Such a policy – while legal in the Union – was unheard of in the south, and would be a mark of shame if ever discovered, Dustin told himself. Like many hard truths he preferred to ignore, the Confederacy had actually adopted an identical policy when it instituted the draft.

After serving as a self-educated lawyer for the codfish aristocracy of bankers and railroad men, Grover Cleveland enjoyed a rapid rise to the presidency in but a few years. To Dustin, the president never had to contend with the rites of passage common to great leaders: academic achievement, military service or legislative accomplishment. True, he had developed a parsimonious reputation as Mayor of Buffalo and Governor of New York, but his terms were abbreviated by successive political promotions. Even the sordid Maria Halpin scandal of his past was not enough to halt Cleveland's nearly instantaneous ascendency.

Right now, however, personal distaste could not be indulged. The president was sensible when it came to foreign relations. Dustin knew that when presented with all the facts, Cleveland would decide correctly, his rumored peevishness over British intransigence notwithstanding. But powerful forces were at work to translate his present annoyance with the U.K. into a policy of confrontation that might result in a full-fledged war, and Scruggs was playing to those interests. The first problem was the Big One himself. Though President Cleveland was instinctively non-interventionist, he reacted angrily to any perceived bullying of the weak by the strong. Only a powerful appeal to his lawyer's mind would blunt his rage.

The next obstacle was the growing movement of jingoism in the country. Its advocates were influential and well-heeled, and were actively disseminating the Scruggs pamphlet to the widest possible readership. Countering the jingoist onslaught would require the Administration to close ranks behind a policy of strict neutrality – with or without the arbitration sought by the U.S. Short of direct attack by British forces, military options were to be rejected. This policy must be sold to the president and his cabinet at the soonest possible occasion.

Which presented the most fundamental challenge: Gresham was dead.

Although his rise within the government was a testament to his intelligence, work ethic and finely honed political instincts, Dustin would never have attained his current level of influence without the good graces of Walter Quintin Gresham. The late secretary of state had plucked him from a more obscure role at the Navy Department to serve as a chief troubleshooter and filter for the many worthless policy proposals that percolated up through the department bureaucracy. Dustin's own ambitions fueled his exemplary performance in the job, once earning a presidential audience for his withering critique of the Hawaiian annexation proponents.

As the months passed, however, Dustin began giving his all – quite against his own will – out of genuine affection for the older man. Gresham sensed a need in Dustin for acceptance and respect, though the counselor always exuded proud self-sufficiency. The Secretary lavished his aide with encouragement and confidence, and usually took Dustin's advice. This was not shallow flattery: his questions could be incisive and difficult to answer, perhaps reflecting the wicked cross-examinations Gresham was getting from the president himself. Dustin sometimes thought the Secretary was grooming him as a potential successor, working in perfect accord with his own designs for higher office. But the relationship went deeper than political considerations.

Despite youthful good looks accentuated by emerald-green eyes and a carefully groomed mop of sandy-brown hair, Dustin Boyle was an aging bachelor with few friends in Washington. With no friends, actually. His reckless combat reputation – earning him near-mythic status among fellow Confederate veterans – made him an embarrassment among Democrats in the capital city, even southerners. Accordingly, invitations to social functions were scant. Also hotly rumored among former rebels was Boyle's clandestine service to the doomed Richmond government. CSA operatives were not accorded the blanket amnesty given to soldiers. Political embarrassment was sure to stick if the administration was proven to have hired a war criminal. To contain this scuttlebutt, the Cleveland Administration kept Dustin largely under wraps, excluding him even from most official functions. His active war service cemented his isolation in still another, more intimate, way: during close-quarter fighting, a well-placed minié ball from a Union-issued muzzleloader had denied Dustin any hope of marriage or progeny.

If genuine sympathy for an apparent loner was a motive, one factor made Gresham's friendship most extraordinary – the Secretary was a former Union general. He would routinely bring Dustin home for dinner, the two reminiscing about their respective war histories – Gresham exhaustively, Boyle selectively. Gresham bore no ill will over the war. He had seen good men shoot at each other before. Lifetimes of differing experiences and mentors often drove them into opposing camps. Though Dustin's policy evaluations and advice were coldly analytical, Gresham had sensed a romantic idealist living deep inside the ex-rebel soldier. Drawing him out became a near-obsession for the older man, whose efforts met with limited success. Gresham had been wounded during the March to the Sea, limping badly ever since. Dustin admitted to having been shot at Shiloh and Seven Pines, and walked ever since with an awkward gait, but would share no details of his injury beyond its mere existence.

Still, Dustin could not help but warm up to the Secretary. After all, Gresham was resented by congressional Republicans for jumping ship and joining a Democratic administration. He further angered his old partisans by reversing the attempts of the previous administration –

aligned with Yankee businessmen – to annex Hawaii. Having served as his point man in that fight, Dustin came to admire Gresham's adherence to the letter of the law and the doctrine of non-interventionism. His native soil might be Indiana, Dustin thought at the time, but Gresham's spirit was born in the heart of Dixie. It was in the aftermath of the Hawaii affair that Dustin began to open up with Secretary Gresham, talking about personal memories of his revered father, an old flame, his closest friend, and life on a sugar plantation. It felt good to trust somebody again, even if it was the former Postmaster General who scotched the Louisiana Lottery with typical Yankee high-handedness. Had Walter Gresham lived, he may well have charmed the vengeance out of Dustin Boyle. Alas.

Considerably less charming was Gresham's successor, Richard Olney. Intellectually sound, professionally competent, and philosophically in harmony with the Cleveland foreign policy, he must have occurred to the president as a logical choice. Dustin was not so sure. Intelligence and wisdom were of two different species. While loaded to the brim with the former, Olney was possessed of a pride that wounded easily. When so injured, he tended toward impulsiveness, as evidenced during his recently completed duty as Attorney General. The overbearing and ham-handed response to striking Pullman workers in 1893 was an ugly episode that Dustin suspected was all Olney's doing. The dispatch of federal troops into Illinois, in the face of pleading protests by that state's governor, had a disturbing familiarity to it. President Cleveland, always and forever an advocate of federalism, was not naturally disposed to using the army to impose order in local streets unless persuaded that pandemonium was imminent.

Olney, however, was insulted by what he perceived as the American Railway Union's belligerence and the incendiary language of its leader, Eugene Debs. The union had called for arbitration between workers and management but was rebuffed with extreme prejudice by George Pullman. Although Debs himself was practically a pacifist, he did find confrontation an effective attention-getter. A boycott and strike ensued. Having spent much of his career representing railroads, Olney could not remove his advocate's cap even while serving as the nation's chief law enforcement official. Thus did he advise the president that national anarchy was inevitable if military muscle was not applied. In spite of labor and management both trying to avoid violence, the government ignited it and left blood flowing in Chicago's streets. Olney was satisfied nevertheless: the union was broken.

Interesting, Dustin thought, how the newly-minted Secretary has done an about face on the issue of arbitration. With the Pullman crisis, he wanted to shoot first and negotiate never. He now liked the idea of mediation, as did the Venezuelans…as did their American tool, William Scruggs. From the insipid tract:

> All standard authorities are agreed that
> when the territorial acquisitions and
> foreign relations of a nation threaten the
> peace and safety of other states, the right
> of intervention is complete. It then
> becomes a moral duty to interfere to

> prevent the threatened mischief, rather
> than wait till the mischief is
> accomplished and then interpose to
> remedy it.

Not content to leave the issue to personal interpretations of morality, Scuggs pulled out the cannon:

> Such a controversy, involving as it does
> principles so vital to autonomous
> government on this continent, can hardly
> fail to deeply interest the American
> people. Moreover, since the contention
> has assumed a phase in open conflict
> with American public law, and with an
> international status in South America for
> the maintenance of which the United
> States stand solemnly pledged, it has
> ceased to be a matter of mere local
> concern, and has already become a grave
> international question.

There it was. Scruggs knew all the right strings to pluck. If the U.S. failed to stick its nose in this affair, it would be essentially repealing the Monroe Doctrine and surrendering the hemisphere to Europe once again. This argument resonated in Washington, Dustin knew. He acknowledged – with some difficulty – that Scruggs was sincere. Like many diplomats Dustin encountered, Scruggs was in love. Immersed in exotic overseas cultures, ambassadors often came back talking like envoys to – rather than from – the United States. But men like William Scruggs were oblivious to the domestic political forces gathering steam. His earnest plea for arbitration could be exploited by warmongers. Indeed, Scruggs concluded his tract by alluding to the prospect:

> Still, if England should finally decide upon this course, and under the flimsy pretext of a boundary dispute of her own seeking, and which she has hitherto obstinately refused to adjust upon any just and reasonable basis, she should persist in her efforts to extend her colonial system within the territory and jurisdiction of an independent American republic, that fact would be but an additional reason, if any were necessary, why the United States should reaffirm, and maintain at all hazards, the principles of the declaration of 1823. The only alternative would be an explicit and final abandonment of those principles; and that would involve a sacrifice of national honor and prestige such as no first-class power is likely ever to make, even for the sake of peace.

War was not acceptable to Dustin Boyle. The country was not prepared for a conflict with the world's dominant navy. This was not 1812. Soldiers and sailors, their families and the depressed economy would all suffer irreparably. Not to mention his own plans for a southern political renaissance.

His father has been a reasoned voice of caution when rebel fever was gripping the South in 1860. Yet the appetite for violence – when coupled with a seemingly righteous cause – had a momentum that plowed reason into the ground. History was repeating itself, he feared. Dustin had to nip this movement in the bud before the Teddy Roosevelts and the Henry Cabot Lodges buffaloed the Cleveland Administration into a wasteful international conflict.

He would have to approach the issue on two fronts. He sensed Olney was gravitating to an aggressive position from which he would not be dissuaded. Anything Dustin advised would likely solidify the Secretary's intransigence, given his seething resentment at having to retain a Gresham holdover, a Johnny Reb no less. Leapfrogging Olney and taking his case directly to the president would be difficult. Cleveland's political advisors were intent on picking Dustin's brain in private, while publicly ignoring his existence. Word of a meeting between the two men would put the president back in the same defensive posture relative to Union veterans that marred his first term and hurt his first attempt at re-election. Dustin would become a person of interest and reporters would start digging. It was too soon for such investigations. To deliver his message therefore, he would have to work covertly, outside normal business hours and beyond regular channels of communication.

Secondly, he would penetrate the British Embassy. Their typical air of contempt was pouring oil on the fires of war. Fire and war were inseparable to the former Cavalry officer. Everything the North touched caught fire and burned, it seemed. He literally so hated fire that he only burned coal on the coldest winter nights. Dustin jotted down a few notes and the embassy address. It was time to call in a favor and give some people a chance to demonstrate gratitude. He knew that the British did not want to fight with the U.S. over the Venezuelan question. Pride, however, clouds good judgment and nullifies the best of intentions. It had to be exposed and exorcised before their war ships set sail.

2

The stern admonition of Mr. James Bulloch in 1863 still echoed in Dustin Boyle's mind:

"This will be our only meeting. The Yankees have agents all over this city, watching me and my associates. Should they see us together a second time, you will have earned their unwanted attention. Do not write my instructions down, but commit them to memory now. Too many of our plans have been scuttled by loose paper. That's why you were not identified to me in advance."

At once calm and urgent, Bulloch immediately impressed Dustin a consummate professional.

"We're losing this war, Major. Nothing short of a miracle will save us, and that is what I have been ordered to make happen, a miracle."

"Understood."

Any other man of five foot and eight – with a pallid complexion, to boot – would fail to intimidate the youthful, and now storied, war hero. But Dustin gradually began to absorb the full measure of Bulloch's imposing personality and razor-sharp mind. He needed sailors. Ticking off vessel specifications from memory, the one-time merchant ship captain and U.S. Navy lieutenant dictated precise qualifications for each billet to be filled.

"I am returning to Liverpool presently, and you will have no resource in London other than your own wits." Sensing Dustin's unease about locating willing seamen, he added: "You commanded soldiers, correct? Answer me this: What do they do to when there's nothing to do?"

With that, James Bulloch rose from his chair and left the dreary eatery at which they met without as much as a nod in Dustin's direction.

Dustin pondered Bulloch's question. Of course there were many hours, days, even weeks of inactivity during the days that Dustin led men into battle with the Yankees. Dustin recalled the dismal realization that chivalry and restraint were not universally practiced by his compatriots, especially during times of idleness. In fact, a great many confederate soldiers were akin to the enemy in their vices, if not their politics. Perhaps Bulloch was on to something.

Of all the weaknesses Dustin encountered among the men in his charge, gambling ranked highest in frequency. Poker, faro and chuck-a-luck were pervasive card games in encampments, where other games of chance included horse racing and raffles. Since money was rarely seen, articles of personal property – clothes, knives, jewelry and food – were the common spoils for the victors. Dustin was raised by his parents to behave with the utmost rectitude. He saw this activity as more a disease than a pastime. Still, if this illness had conveniently crossed the ocean, he reasoned, that – along with his anticipated cache of pounds sterling – would serve as his best recruiting tool.

Dustin walked back to the window and gazed again at the structure that Washingtonians liked to call "the White House." Cleveland just couldn't be considering hostilities, he just *couldn't* be. War would ruin everything. During Reconstruction, Dustin had seen war orphans and widows struggling under the haughty dominance of a powerful and victorious aggressor. Were the upper tiers of the administration so blind as to not see that if the U.S. intervened with guns then she *would be* the aggressor?! If, by a miracle from heaven, the United States gained victory, a whole slew of heroes would come home. These men would be natural competitors against Dustin's vision for America's future. No, this conflict must be defused as immoral and ill-conceived. It would take a bigger issue than some gold deposits between two rivers to rise to the level of a Monroe Doctrine concern, the Scruggs tract be cursed.

Dustin quickly snapped out of his ruminations as the 10-foot high door swung open and the 34th Secretary of State entered the office with Nathan Oberstreet, his First Assistant and – in Dustin's estimation – toady. "Evening, Boyle." Richard Olney carried several bound documents under his arm. His salt-and-pepper mustache was matched by a carefully-combed and very short haircut. He wore a purple coat and gold waistcoat with matching trousers, a rare ensemble of busy hues for a Cleveland man. Walking over to Dustin's desk he slapped one on the surface with a smack that echoed off the walls for several seconds. "That's for your review, per the policy worked out by my predecessor and the president." Oberstreet remained silent, but worked hard to emulate the disapproving glower of Olney. The Secretary continued, his voice now rising: "You can review it to your heart's content, but know this: I'll not change a word of it, not one word!!" With that Olney turned on his heel and strode from the room, Oberstreet in tow.

Olney chafed at having to inform his superfluous advisor every time he made a policy pronouncement. His resentment was not lost on Dustin. The two men were wary of one another since Gresham's descent into pneumonia, his final and fatal opponent. Olney began functioning as Secretary, with Cleveland's baleful approval, during Gresham's final days. At first, he was polite – even deferential – to the Counselor. Upon the late Secretary's interment, however, Olney lost no opportunity to apprise Dustin of how little his opinion mattered.

Dustin walked to his desk, sat down and opened the leather binder. It took only moments for his heart to sink.

"Welcome back. Your trip, Señor Scruggs, was to your liking, no?"
"Your people gave me a smooth sail and the best of everything. I thank you, sir."
President Joaquin Crespo pulled out all the stops for influential guests, even before they arrived at the presidential palace in Caracas. From the carriage to the train to the boat to the presidential palace, William Scruggs was treated to luxury and abundance: champagne, fresh

fruit, jumbo shrimp. As it should be, he thought. He spent too many years in this part of the world to miss the fact that Americans were accorded the respect of brother-protectors. The capitals and salons of Europe, regardless of their civilized pretensions, could take a lesson from his host in Caracas.

"My American friends tell me that your manly defense of our interests is gaining favor in your country. I hope your government pays attention to it," Crespo observed.

"I guarantee you, General, that my government is thinking of little else at this time," Scruggs assured him, with a generous dollop of smugness. "Patience with Great Britain is already diminishing at the highest tiers of authority. I doubt we will welcome 1896 without this matter being fully settled in favor of the Venezuelan people."

"You do not believe it will come to shooting?" the Venezuelan probed curiously.

"That I can not say with definitiveness. Rest assured, though, that you have a staunch ally to the north, one that will make whatever sacrifices are necessary to preserve the integrity of this hemisphere."

Having resumed power after a revolution in 1892, the president wielded absolute authority within Venezuela, spending money freely and eliminating opponents with equal copiousness. His black frock was ornamented with gold epaulets, a multi-colored sash and numerous medals with which he awarded himself. Tailored smartly to complement his scarlet and gold trousers, it would surpass most dress uniforms in the United States military in terms of elegance. To Crespo, these were but working clothes for a man of his stature. With his coarse black hair and neatly groomed whiskers, he looked every inch a president. To his disappointment and resentment, however, that stature was not acknowledged across the oceans, or even in the U.S., for that matter. American newspapers were full of the boundary dispute, dropping the names of Salisbury, Cleveland and Olney. Neither Crespo nor his ambassador merited such citation, it would seem. Even the error-prone surveyor Schombürgk received more ink, a vexing reminder that only foreigners could help Crespo raise his profile. The Germans – already confronting Great Britain in other parts of the world – had invested in Crespo's regime, albeit much to their financial anxiety. The Americans, on the other hand, were a harder sell. William Scruggs, however, was becoming the diplomatic peddler who might just close the sale.

For his part, Scruggs had more than earned the generous stipend afforded by Crespo. Early in the year, he had persuaded a friendly congressman to introduce legislation calling for U.S.-led arbitration of the Venezuela Boundary Dispute. The measure not only passed both houses, but was signed by the normally provincial President Cleveland. Since then, the nettlesome Walter Gresham passed away, a more reasonable successor was installed and the American president himself appeared to be growing more favorable to Scruggs legal position on the conflict. That alone was a testament to Scruggs' abilities, earning him his handsome remuneration from the Venezuelan government. Losing his ambassadorship because of his own financial gift to Crespo back in 1892 made his present fee collection all the sweeter. The two men understood each other. With dark, wavy hair and beard, Scruggs could pass for Crespo himself were it not for his intense blue eyes and the prominent lines on his face. Their interests, though, were less than identical. Scruggs wanted to revive his reputation as the premiere American diplomat south of the border. Crespo, for his part, had indebted his country beyond his ability to recompense its creditors. He knew his days were numbered unless he could take hold of that gold between the rivers.

"Some of us were disturbed when you left your diplomatic post here. We thought we lost a trusted friend. It seems, however, that your friendship is even more valuable to us with you back in the United States."

Scruggs sipped the rum he was served, and fixed a confident gaze on Crespo. "Señor Presidenté, you have no idea."

Despondent, Dustin finished reading Secretary Olney's remonstrance and placed his hands atop the document, his fingers tapping nervously. Olney bought into the whole Scruggs argument, hook, line and sinker. The gist of it was that if Britain were to make a claim to the tract lying between the rivers, it would have to get the approval of the United States. The language left the United Kingdom little room to maneuver: submit or fight was a fair characterization of Olney's position. Dustin thought the president might approve it, if only as a bluff, to light a fire under the Tory government of the Marquis of Salisbury. After all, this issue had simmered during Cleveland's first term, eight years earlier. The president was not a warmonger, but neither would he be a pushover.

Dustin's brief mission to London for the Confederacy taught him that the Brits had their own sensibilities. His mind again flashed back to the arresting smell of fish when he arrived by steamship at the East End; the seedy pub at which he met the Confederacy's chief spy and shipbuilder, James Bulloch; and the large roll of pounds-sterling Bulloch gave him to recruit English naval officers. It was a heady experience for the Louisiana sugar heir, who could still recount every sight on his long walk from the docks to his temporary headquarters in Kensington. With a high degree of satisfaction, Dustin sent word to Bulloch in Liverpool that he had recruited a full contingent within a few nights. Most were restricted to shore pending disciplinary hearings for one infraction or another. They were all eager to cast off, none receiving much respect or money while confined on land.

When the *CSS Georgia* sailed for open sea in1863, Dustin knew that none of the men he saw off that day had any love for the Confederacy. Each had a selfish desire they wished to feed. Nothing much had changed in 30 years. For all the British pretensions to chivalry, he firmly believed that if the Venezuela matter was to be resolved peacefully, the United States had to make it worth Her Majesty's while. Recalling the young navigator he plucked from the jaws of death by killing the officer's attackers – pimps whom the youthful and promiscuous sailor had stiffed – Dustin was sure the appropriate incentive could be found to induce the U.K. to sit down for arbitration. After all, was not indebtedness the foundation of foreign policy? The foundation of human interaction?

Olney would be departing Washington for his home on Cape Cod in a few days. It gave Dustin some room to operate and execute his plan. Despite the oppressive temperature, he could feel the advent of a cold sweat. Exposure of his anticipated activities would have dire consequences. The next few months would possibly define the country…and definitely determine if Dustin Boyle had a future in it.

<u>3</u>

The salty, briny freshness of Cape Cod air was therapeutic for the president, ever since he retreated there to recover from his secret surgery over two and a half years before. Julys in Washington were unbearable, but here at Gray Gables there was no sweeter month. The sun glistening against the surface of Buzzard's Bay provided a needed shot of adrenaline to his spirit. Purchased during the interregnum between Cleveland's two presidencies, the estate had all the solitude of isolation without any of the inconvenience. With numerous marshes and estuaries nearby, it was perfectly situated to suit this duck-hunting, deep sea-fishing executive.

War Secretary Daniel Lamont had accompanied President Cleveland and his family to the Cape on this trip. Serving as Cleveland's right hand during the New York governorship and the first presidential administration, Lamont appreciated the weighty assignment of managing America's army, but would not yield his old role of presidential protector to anyone. The two had shared too much history for Lamont to just abandon his chief upon promotion. While he got along well with the First Lady, an unspoken rivalry existed between the two since the Clevelands' East Room nuptials in 1885.

The president's vacation schedule differed from his regular routine in that he only put in a full day's work as opposed to his usual fifteen to sixteen hours. Marriage had tempered his legendary industry somewhat, and he now liked to finish with enough daylight to get in some fishing before dinner. There would be no games of cribbage after dinner on this day, however. The Clevelands (Lamont included) would be receiving an additional visitor in the evening: the Honorable Secretary of State – and Cape Cod neighbor – Richard Olney.

Quite well-known in legal circles, Olney was a still political question mark when he met Grover Cleveland. He had been a most persuasive advocate for corporate interests before the president placed him in the Attorney General's chair (where he remained a most persuasive advocate for corporate interests). His disastrous counsel during the Pullman strike was offset by his day-to-day competence and diligence. Cleveland appreciated the Boston lawyer's attention to detail and indomitable self-confidence. Unfortunately, to Daniel Lamont anyway, these assets blinded the president to Olney's short fuse. The Attorney General would do better to yell, pound the table or punch the nearest subordinate when offended, Lamont thought. Instead, Olney's emotional outbursts took the form of court orders and troop deployments, neither of which served the president politically.

At the same time, Lamont appreciated Olney's belief in at least some American assertiveness internationally. Gresham had his good points, but the late Secretary's temperament was all too often that of a judge prone to rule against his own country. While Lamont was no jingo, he thought Gresham's hyper-isolationism was actually fueling that nationalist movement and its irresponsible militarism. A military man himself, Lamont was concerned about the skeletal army in his charge, believing that Greham's continued influence on Cleveland would have suffocated the American forces beyond resuscitation. The War Secretary needed time and treasure to fortify U.S. land forces to defend the country's interests. Gresham's way would deny him the funds to adequately equip and mobilize American troops.

On the other hand, Olney's way was the enemy of time, if his rumored snit about Venezuela lead to shooting in South America any time soon. The army was woefully unprepared for such a conflict, and sentimental references to overwhelming odds against American forces during the Revolutionary and 1812 wars were misleading. David may have successfully slain Goliath with a slingshot, but how often had that battle strategy been replicated?

The naval outlook was brighter. If the president's well-intentioned outreach to the South had any bright spots for Lamont, it was the appointment of Hilary Abner Herbert to be Secretary of the Navy. The 16-year veteran of the House of Representatives knew instinctively how to soften up a reluctant Congress in order to gain significant increases in naval appropriations. Herbert demonstrated how a bi-coastal United States was under-protected without a new class of modernized warships, which he was now in the process of building. Lamont could look at Herbert with both admiration and envy. His talents acknowledged, Herbert still had one ugly blemish: he brought Dustin Boyle to Washington.

Lamont had always suspected Dustin of vindictiveness. For all the careful language in his analyses and memoranda, Dustin's consistent theme centered on keeping America weak. An odd stance for a combat veteran, Lamont thought, unless that veteran was intent on humiliating the army that once defeated him. From his perch at State, Boyle could stanch the flow of dollars to the army by convincing Cleveland that such investments were unnecessary or even dangerous. As much as he suspected Olney's temperament, the new Secretary was a necessary ally against Gresham's living legacy. This meant burying any differences with Olney over timing, and convincing Cleveland that the British were intent on expanding their holdings in South America. After all, it very well could be true.

Justus Boyle had raised his son to pursue excellence in everything. From his primary education with private tutors to his college years to his military service, Dustin expended all his efforts to make his father proud of him. Justus was different from the other landowners in St. John the Baptist parish. He was future-oriented. Not only did he perceive the impending obsolescence of slavery, he valued the potential of each and every slave in his possession. "Law and culture dictate that we care for them and engage them usefully, Dusty, but we should never forget that they are made in the image of God." Dustin took some satisfaction that his father was not a boor toward his slaves, as were many of their neighbors. Owning one of the largest sugar plantations in Louisiana, Justus delegated authority generously to his servants, much to the annoyance of the succession of white overseers that he inexplicably employed.

From Dustin's earliest memory, Caleb Webb had served as foreman and unofficial overseer of the Boyle farm. His father invested great confidence in this capable man, befriending him and consulting with him on all major decisions. Caleb, in fact, taught Dustin the fine art of growing sugar cane at a young age, even serving as a second father to the boy. Upon receiving a deep laceration from a typically razor-sharp cane leaf at his knee, a 6-year old, sobbing Dustin was taken up in the arms of the big colored man, and delivered to Caleb's wife , Lizzie, to dress his wound. The foreman held the child in his lap, singing an old spiritual in his comforting bass voice. "You're going to be just fine, Seedling," Caleb said, using his usual moniker for Dustin.

On most plantations, the foreman always reported to the overseer. Not so on Boyle lands. Caleb had carte blanche to call on Justus, often being welcomed on the veranda with a strong handshake and a friendly arm slung around his shoulder. Dustin treasured those scenes in his memory: the two men he loved the most showing brotherly affection to one another. Not so fraternal was the planter's relationships with the overseers, who often resented this violation of unspoken protocol. Dustin could not remember exactly how many overseers had been let go during his childhood and youth, but he did remember the one who managed to survive.

Richard Trueblood was an old school tyrant who relished corporal punishment and verbal abuse. Given Justus' views, Trueblood's retention was puzzling. On one occasion, teenaged Dustin rebuked the snaggle-toothed man for kicking a female slave felled by unbearable heat. He subsequently informed his father of the cruelty. How surprised he was, then, to encounter Trueblood's defiant smirk just a few days later. Justus simply explained to his confused son: "Things are not always as they seem, Dusty."

The tolerance accorded the overseer did not conform to Justus' progressive management of his sugar concern. It was a leadership philosophy in which Dustin took great pride, and stemmed – he believed – from Justus' deep religious faith and love of humanity. It made the son furious when militant abolitionists would denounce the South for its peculiar institution. Men like Justus Boyle were committed to the welfare of their slaves, and were preparing for their eventual release. White northerners could indulge in false indignation because most of them did not know any Negroes. Dustin knew them intimately. "When I own this land, Caleb, we'll work it together and make us a fortune!!" young Dusty would promise the foreman as they sat astride a sleek, black Boyle mare, surveying the daily cultivation.

"I like how that sounds, Seedling. We'll have a fine time."

The partnership was never to be, however. A fatal fire in Caleb's cabin put an end to that dream. The loss of his best friend hardened Dustin's outlook. The Christianity he learned at his mother's knee evolved into a cynical Deism. *God may or may not exist*, thought the teen going off to war, but *I am on my own.*

That same self-dependent mindset held true nearly three decades later, as Dustin brainstormed ways to circumvent his superior. Running a hand through his short layer of sandy-brown hair, he devised an effective argument to use with the president – if he was ever able to get to the man. Leaving his office and walking down the wide, ornate corridor – replete with etched moldings and marble busts – he entered the State Department's elegant library, and made a beeline toward a large, cavernous, dimly-lit room to find one of his few allies in the department.

"Are you closing up, Jake?"

Jacob Stansfield's homely visage soon emerged from the darkness. In truth, it was beyond homely. His facial skin permanently ashen, it bore three bayonet scars and a permanent scowl.

"What do you need, Dustin?"

"I want to see Secretary Gresham's official journal from last April. That was archived, correct?"

Stansfield's emaciated body came into full view. "No doubt. But Olney and his stooges are coming through here all the time now. They grab documents and walk out without signing for anything. My careful record-keeping is all for naught."

Dustin nodded in sympathy. "Understood. Do you have time to look for it? It's very important."

Stansfield winked a bloodshot eye, turned on his heel and disappeared into the blackness. For all Dustin knew, he and Stansfield could have been firing upon each other during the war. Wounded several times in battle, Stansfield was a reluctant warrior. He had been arrested during a draft riot in 1862, and was subsequently mustered into the 108th Infantry Regiment out of Rochester, New York. Once afield, he had no choice but to fight, if only to stay alive. Yet he never supported the war. Having no use for slavery, Stansfield nonetheless thought states had the right to secede. Accordingly, he placed blame for the carnage squarely on the shoulders of President Lincoln and the Republicans…and voted Democrat ever since.

After the war, Stansfield – a lawyer, like Dustin – was unable to find steady employment, so applied for a military pension. The petition was vetoed by none other than President Grover Cleveland early in the first term. Fortunately for Stansfield, an old school chum was elected to Congress that same year, and successfully persuaded State to employ his constituent and friend. Given his marred appearance, Stansfield was put in charge of the murky executive archives, sentenced to toil amid aging documents and correspondence. The archives was a depressing cave that stood in stark relief against the staid opulence of the rest of the library.

Though having fought for opposing armies, Dustin and Stansfield were kindred spirits: each saw one side of the Civil War as evil and the other as foolish. They both bore permanent reminders: Stansfield's, for all the world to see; Dustin's, a perpetual private torment. Most importantly, each man worked in imposed semi-isolation. It was natural for them to bond to the degree they did.

After what seemed to Dustin an eternity of inhaling mustiness, Stansfield re-appeared with three large charcoal-gray binders, marked with an alphabetic code that only he could decipher. "It would seem he was busy last April, Dustin."

Dustin carefully filled out Stansfield's ledger, knowing full well that Olney's people perused it during their after-hours espionage, eager to entrap any and all with evidence of disloyalty. He wanted Olney to know that Gresham's legacy was not dead, and that the late Secretary would have his say on Venezuela, if only from the grave. "Thanks, Jake. Have a pleasant evening."

"After that request? I'm going to be up all night, wondering what you're up to."

"Have to stay one step ahead of the jingoes, friend. You can understand."

"Godspeed. They breed like rabbits and infest like rats. You know that."

Dustin gave a wave as he left the archives for another storage room. Up one flight of stairs, this room was restricted to certain personnel. The door was locked, as always, and only Dustin and the Secretary held pass keys. Since Olney's ascendency, however, he suspected many copies were made. Many, many copies. Actually, Dustin was surprised the lock had not been changed.

Entering the Map Room was an experience diametrically opposed to visiting the executive archives. The room was flooded with sunlight, even during the early evening hours of summer. The ornate carving on the molding and high ceiling gave it a majesty that rivaled the unfinished monument to the despicable tyrant that was incrementally rising on the eastern bank of the Potomac. This room was Dustin's sanctuary. Early in his time at State, Gresham had authorized him to research and implement the establishment of a new unit: Office of the Geographer. Understanding the world and its resources, landscapes, and passages was key to formulating sound policy, the two men agreed. Compiling and organizing a library of maps and gazetteers was the first stage of the project and – observing his own work – Dustin could not be more pleased with the outcome.

With little time for self-congratulation, Dustin immediately located several maps covering the disputed territory between British Guiana and Venezuela. Taking a stool at one of six sloped reading desks, he spread out the first map, a topographic representation of the northeastern region of South America. Although without a future as a ladies' man, Dustin was nevertheless too vain for spectacles, inheriting a dazzling pair of emerald-green eyes from his father. He consequently at all times carried in his coat pocket a large magnifying glass, which he withdrew as if a pistol. He quickly located the disputed topography, noting a broken line extending from the mouth of the Rio Amakura to that river's source in the Imataka mountains, then running along the mountain ridge to the source of the Acarabisi creek, following the creek to the Rio Cuyuni. The line was coterminous with that river right up to its source at Mount Roraima. This was the delineation formulated by the surveyor Robert Schombürgk in 1835. Although not defined in the agreement conveying the colony from the Netherlands to the U.K., the Schombürgk Line became the rock upon which the British stood against Venezuela, whose own territorial claims would – if accepted –have shrunk British Guiana by two-thirds.

Although Dustin empathized with Venezuela, he thought the Schombürgk Line was the least noxious of several bad options. The South American state's refusal to recognize it, according to Gresham's notes, gave the British permission to ignore it, as well. The problem was that Great Britain was now assuming *more* territory, west of Mr. Schombürgk's demarcation, deeper into Venezuela's claim, prompting the Latin American country to petition the U.S. via William Scruggs. The recent discovery of minable precious metals in the region had doubtless brought the long-simmering disagreement to a boil. Secretary Olney's remonstrance to the British government, which he was obviously taking to Cape Cod to show the president, was menacing in tone and uncompromising in substance: refusal to engage in American-led arbitration would be viewed by the United States as a bald-faced land grab, in contemptuous defiance of the Monroe Doctrine. Taking the sting out of the Olney document would be challenging. If the Brits disavow the Schombürgk Line, where is the basis for negotiation? What is to stop the shooting.

Again thinking back to his short time in London, Dustin reflected on what manner of men comprised the largest and fiercest navy in the world.

Military men were poorly regarded in Victorian England, though Navy men tended to fare better in the court of public opinion than their army counterparts. Unless serving in a royal ceremonial post, officers were largely ignored and, sometimes, reviled. Their off-duty time, therefore, included few opportunities to regale civilians with tales of combat heroism and derring-do. Many of them instead gravitated toward other social outcasts and assorted misfits. The cement binding these diverse untouchables was a potent concoction of alcohol and cardsharping. Once engaged with one another, they were soon divided over any number of variables – cheating, perceived slights and, delicately put, insufficient funds. Violence was not uncommon and lives were occasionally exacted in lieu of cash proceeds.

Finding recruits was all too easy. Every East End beer shop Dustin could locate had the familiar sight of blue frock and white waist coats worn by commanders and lieutenants. Other elements of the populace were also present. For the first time in his life, he witnessed actual prostitutes soliciting business with neither fear nor shame. Bookies – homely and bloodless – circulated, taking wagers on fistfights, dogfights and horse races. Here, government bureaucrats and less-educated craftsmen found a perverse fellowship in the service of their common demons, whose appetites far exceeded their assets.

Among these souls, Dustin had managed – in one long night – to glean a competent core group to man the Japan, soon to be re-christened the CSS Georgia. Some were broke, but still others were eager to return to the sea – a refuge where they found purpose and acceptance. In need of a navigator, Dustin questioned his most recent recruit. The young officer could only think of one: a lieutenant who was currently furloughed while under investigation for running his previous vessel aground intentionally. Why jeopardize a career with a stunt like that? "He bore the captain a grudge," the new recruit reported dutifully. "The grounding finished the captain's career."

Dustin learned further that the officer in question liked to live dangerously, both in battle and at rest. Identifying with this instinct, he thought interviewing the lad was worth the effort. The Confederate navy was at a strategic and economic disadvantage that could only be offset by guts. Given the desperate times, emotional stability was desirable but dispensable. Obtaining a list of the man's favored haunts from the other officers, Dustin realized that this embattled navigator lavished his earnings not on chance, but sure things. Resolved to show no sign of revulsion, the son of a respected planter and state legislator – and Episcopal vestryman – was headed to his first brothel.

Rolling the maps up, Dustin had no illusions of the carnage in store should this border issue blow up. Gentlemen on the outside, maybe, he conceded, but the Brits still carried the pagan ferocity of their Nordic, Celtic and Anglo-Saxon ancestors when it came to acquiring assets. His aim was to convince them that the wealth on which they set their sights could be theirs at the low cost of a little swallowed pride.

4

President Cleveland, as usual, ate twice as much as his guests, while finishing his dinner in half the time. While his young wife brushed crumbs from his ample belly and walrus mustache, he turned his attention to the Secretary of State, smiling for the first time all evening.

"I knew there was a reason I picked you to succeed Gresham. Old man, that remonstrance hits right between the eyes. You gave me a twenty-inch gun to point at those Anglo-bullies. How the deuce can they ignore that?"

Although Frances Cleveland had managed to cultivate in the president a new refinement, he usually left that sensibility back in Washington. Gray Gables was his refuge and he possessed no inhibitions about talking business at dinner…in mixed company, no less.

Richard Olney swallowed a dangerously large piece of haddock in order to respond quickly. "It needed to be stated clearly, Mr. President, no holes barred. I hope you will authorize transmission at the earliest possible date," he urged, hoping Cleveland would forget the protocol established with Walter Gresham.

"Well,…"

"Why don't we finish up here before you men tend to the world's vibrations. Unless you seek the female perspective," the First Lady suggested. The president cast an appreciative glance her way, and then veered off into a comparative discourse on duck hunting in the Adirondacks and on Cape Cod. Olney finished his dinner in a slow burn. He was this close to shipping the document to U.S. Ambassador in London were it not for Cleveland's unfinished qualifier, an interjection he fervently hoped would not include the name of Dustin Boyle. Now, he might lose a day or more. In the interim, the jingoes would be indicting the president – and, by extension, Olney – for spinelessness in dealing with the arrogant Brits.

It was no secret that Cleveland was in trouble with the party. The populists were painting Bourbon Democrats like him as enablers for corporate combinations. The administration's dependence on J.P. Morgan to replenish the country's dwindling gold supply cemented that image in the minds of many disaffected Democrats in the south and out west. A successfully executed confrontation with the U.K. would offset his domestic political woes with a diplomatic – or military, if need be – triumph. Sadly, Olney's friend based precious few policy decisions on political considerations.

Olney felt a heavy hand on his shoulder. The president cocked his head toward the front porch, indicating that the Secretaries of State and War should follow him out. Three rattan chairs were pre-arranged to face one another, a bottle of brandy and three snifters on the small table in the middle were waiting for them. Lamont did the honors, after which Olney began swirling the beverage around in his glass. Impatient with silly rituals, Cleveland gulped his portion in one swallow, holding out his glass for a re-fill. He then pulled three Reina Victoria cigars out of his coat pocket and passed them out.

"You're afraid I'm going to second-guess you on the remonstrance. Am I wrong?" Cleveland's blue eyes were twinkling, as they always did when he successfully read the body language of friends and foes.

"It's just that time is of the essence here, sir. I'm eager to let the Brits know where we stand relative to the Monroe Doctrine, and the sooner the better. I think Dan is with me on this."

Cleveland looked to Lamont, who nodded, but said nothing.

"It may surprise you to know, Dick, that I want you to get it to Bayard without delay. He is to deliver it to the Prime Minister at the first available appointment. Now are you satisfied?"

He was indeed. The president's vote of confidence was a ringing endorsement that liberated the Secretary from Gresham's posthumous shadow. It would also put an end to the journalistic provocations in the newspapers of William Randolph Hearst, the jingoes' chief scribe. Best of all, it relegated Dustin Boyle to honorary status, like some of the ornate White House furniture that nobody was allowed to sit upon. To think that it happened here, in his beloved home state. If he could not get rid of his Counselor, the next best thing was to let him sit in an office and politically decompose.

"I appreciate that, Mr. President. I'll wire Oberstreet to transmit it by diplomatic pouch first thing in the morning. Since I'll have an early day tomorrow, might I take my leave, sir? Much to do."

"Thank you for coming tonight, Dick," Cleveland said.

Lamont gave a semi-friendly wave to his colleague, who hurried back into the house to collect his wife.

"So?"

"You know I have no use for Hearst and the rest of those drum-beaters, Mr. President. Still, it appears that world leadership is being thrust upon us in spite of ourselves. You're doing the right thing. You really are."

Cleveland puffed on his cigar wistfully. "What's the point of being elected, or re-elected, to anything unless you stand for something? I thought about having that lawyer…what's his name?"

"Dustin Boyle," Lamont replied with pursed lips.

"That's right. I thought about getting some input on this whole thing, but the facts here are indisputable. If the U.K. does not agree to arbitration, and we do nothing, we may very well be ceding more of this hemisphere to Europe. How could I hand the next man to occupy this office a neutered Monroe Doctrine?"

"You can't,,,and shouldn't, especially if the next man is you."

"Don't know, Dan. A third term breaks a hallowed tradition"

"It would be a second *consecutive* term. I think you're not doing anything radical by standing for election in '96."

Looking at his boss, Lamont realized how much the man had aged during his four-year exile between terms. Grover Cleveland claimed that retirement suited him, but Lamont knew self-deception when he heard it. If the Big One liked just two things, they were: 1) Being president, and 2) Complaining about being president.

The president continued to puff as the wheels of his mind turned. The side of him that hated politics wanted nothing more than retirement. At the same time, he so wanted to see the victory of sound money and tariff reform while still in office. He was sure of their correctness, but the policies were taking their time bearing fruit. Perhaps another term would win him vindication. Unfortunately…

"Maybe not, but the populists in the party hate my guts. Your political pugilists would have to do some pretty fancy footwork to win me another nomination. I'm not going to cringe before political demagogues, you know."

Lamont smiled. "Give it some thought. Remember this, though: cringing before the British will give the demagogues that much more ammunition. This Venezuela matter must be resolved in our favor if you are to have a chance."

"Let's wait and see," Cleveland responded, "what happens when they find themselves before the barrel of Olney's 20-inch gun."

The life of a senator was perfect, thought 45-year old Henry Cabot Lodge of Massachusetts. A descendant of the Pilgrim Fathers, the waspish Lodge took pride in his heritage and in his leadership ability. In the Senate, he could work as much or as little as he pleased. He could make himself invisible for issues that either bored or threatened him. At the same time, he could grab the nation's attention with his gift of oratory for those subjects that inspired. America's rightful assertion of international interests was his all-consuming passion these days, it seemed. To be sure, Manifest Destiny was an important benchmark to be reached; but it was only a step, not a destination.

As his valet carried his bags to a waiting carriage, Senator Lodge observed his image in a full-length mirror. So many of his colleagues were slobs, he thought. His gray cutaway might strike them as too formal for travel, but they lacked the cultivation in matters of appearance and bearing. Benjamin Tillman came to mind – the one they called "Pitchfork" – the boorish southern Democrat who did not have the manners to wear a glass eye where the original had been lost. Such neglect made the man's already homely face into a hideous one.

Politics made for strange bedfellows, though, since Pitchfork was performing a valuable political service.

While Tillman may be an ignorant farmer, he was a thorn in the side of his fellow Democrat, Grover Cleveland. The corpulent chief magistrate alienated many over his insistence on retaining gold as the sole basis for the value of money. Southern and western farmers, crushed by debt, would stand to gain some relief if silver had been thrown into the mix. The president got his way on gold, however, and Tillman promised his South Carolina constituents that he would confront the man and "stick a pitchfork in his fat ribs." Opening up another front against Cleveland could only benefit Republicans, Lodge was sure.

It was time to go. Lodge had a stauncher ally than Pitchfork Tillman to cultivate. This man was an old friend and fellow Republican. Until recently, they saw each other almost every day. Now, his compatriot worked in New York, and Lodge was on his way to enlist his assistance. While impulsive and at times overly verbose, his friend was a brilliant strategist who shared the senator's beliefs about America's place in the world. Adding to that his boundless energy, this man was well-equipped to motivate the timid and soft-headed. National leadership would be his one day, with the indispensible help of Senator Henry Cabot Lodge.

Although Venezuela was deeply indebted to Germany, the latter reluctantly financed President Crespo's corrupt regime as a counterweight against British influence in South America. The dictator knew this, and availed himself of German largesse at every available opportunity. Ignorant, though, he was not. He knew the Kaiser would put a brake on the gravy train sooner or later. It made winning the boundary dispute all the more crucial. If the gold reserves were as ample as his scouts had observed, Crespo could pay his obligations and then some. He could even arrange for more generous lines of credit from other European powers; perhaps even the United States. After all, relations were warming up. Although William Scruggs gave himself full credit for the amity, Crespo knew that his biggest ally was the pneumonia that killed Walter Gresham.

The late Secretary of State was one of the loudest American critics of the Venezuelan government. Had Gresham lived, President Cleveland would now be completely unmoved by the land grab perpetrated by the United Kingdom. Though aware of British encroachments, Gresham did little other than forward notes to American ambassador Thomas Bayard in London, asking him to gently prod the British on arbitration. Bayard had a global reputation as an anglophile, and should never have been trusted with the task, Crespo believed. Between Gresham and Bayard, Venezuela had no recourse but to call in Scruggs and exploit American public opinion. It was an expensive investment, but it seemed to be working. The actions of Secretary Richard Olney demonstrated that Venezuela would not be ignored. Crespo only hoped that Walter Gresham could see it—suffering in torment, hopefully—in the next life.

Scruggs had hit a raw nerve in the States when he tied the matter to the Monroe Doctrine, that odd political statement from decades ago. As he explained it, it was meant to guarantee the independence and sovereignty of all the nations in the western hemisphere, and to prevent further European domination. Crespo was sure the U.S. exempted itself from the doctrine's proscriptions, yet he would not object. Venezuela needed a rich and powerful patron and Germany's benevolence was running short. The good news was that Crespo conceived an idea that would stoke American sympathy for Venezuela while retaining the good graces of Kaiser Wilhelm II. It would not be easy, but it would pay off handsomely.

In short, he would get the British to shoot first.

5

August, 1895

The large and ornate doors at the Embassy of the United Kingdom of Great Britain and Ireland bore the red, blue and gold coat of arms of the Royal House of Hanover, the ancestral line of the reigning monarch. A handsome footman appeared and ushered Dustin into the vast front hall of the embassy proper. Large and flattering oil paintings of royals adorned the walls; shimmering and immaculate marble floors reflected the plush red carpet covering a grand staircase; tropical plants in expensive vases were strategically placed to express tasteful British understatement amid the grandeur. The footman led Dustin into a small anteroom off of the hall, where he sat on what looked like an antique love seat large enough to fit Henry VIII and a couple of wives. As his escort exited, Dustin listened to the 11 low, guttural chimes of the large grandfather's clock exuding majesty and gravitas. This environment set another wave of memories loose in the once and present clandestine operative.

One irony in the pursuit of the rogue navigator was that it brought Dustin to the more reputable areas of the West End of London. Handsome townhomes and gaslight lamps adorned the newly-paved streets, populated by well-to-do gentlemen and women in silk gowns. Alongside respectability, however, was the seedy underworld of the dysfunctional. Most of the locations on Dustin's list were taverns and dance halls in the vicinity of Haymarket, the crowded avenue running between Picadilly Circus and Pall Mall. Finding the nooks, crannies and corners that hosted dubious maidens and their customers was more difficult than he anticipated. After visiting Kate Hamilton's Night House, the Argyll Rooms and Highbury Barn in search of the elusive officer, Dustin was amazed at the stonewalling he was getting from employees and patrons. The world of harlotry had its principles, so to speak, and would not voluntarily reveal the whereabouts of its most frequent denizens.

As he approached the Portland Rooms – a structure with a stately brick face that belied its internal goings-on – he suddenly heard the very name of his quarry shouted from an adjacent alley. Briefly touching his breast pocket to confirm the presence of his Derringer, Dustin moved cautiously into the dark cavity to discover the source of the bellowing. Three men, their backs to him, were shouting epithets at a fourth, whose body was obscured by the phalanx they had formed around him. Two were landing blows upon the victim savagely, while the third was moving in with what looked like a wooden-handled Bowie knife.

That was the last scene Dustin could recall as he now stood over three dead bodies: two flowing blood from wounds inflicted by his own hunting knife, a prize possession forged for him by Caleb years before. The third thug lay motionless with a bullet to the forehead. Dustin could then see the battered naval officer trying to stand up. Not knowing why he had acted so impulsively off the battlefield, Dustin was slow to hear the young man's pleas for help.

Back in the moment, Dustin heard the comforting sound of tea decanting from a pot. Looking up, he was dumbstruck to see an attractive, smiling, young Negro woman, her bright green eyes matching his own. He was stunned. Immediately considering the unthinkable, Dustin just as quickly banished the idea. He knew of planters in his youth who would visit their females to augment the herd. His father was not among them, though. Justus Boyle always respected the family structure. Concubines were not found among Boyle hands.

"What do you take in your tea, Mr. Boyle? " The servant – like Dustin – had obviously honed her speech to near-perfection, without a trace of dialect. "Uh, three lumps and milk." He was about to involuntarily say "please" but caught himself. She handled the spotless and ornate silver tea service with effortless dexterity, indirectly reminding Dustin of Hortense, his mother's cook who was notorious for dropping cups and dishes. Were it not her delicious edible creations, Hortense would have been exiled to the fields. This woman, though, exuded competence in every movement. She was of medium height, thin but not emaciated, and bedecked in a long, black cotton dress covered by a smartly-starched white apron. Under the head cap, her carefully bundled black hair gave off a reddish glow when illuminated by the gas light.

"Mr. Alderson receives so many visitors from the government, often late into the night. You must have a very busy position, Mr. Boyle."

"Very busy", Dustin muttered, summoning every ounce of his will to keep from staring into her eyes.

"Do you know Mr. Cleveland?" she inquired.

Marveling that this Negro servant would dare converse with him – as with an equal – Dustin stammered, "Y-yes…uh…, not well, but yes. I do."

"He never visits the Embassy, I'm told. Oh but he just had a family addition, did he not?"

"Yes, Mrs. Cleveland gave birth to Marion on July 7th."

She set a place for the tardy Alderson, picked up the tray and began to depart. Stopping short, she turned about and asked, "Do you have children, Mr. Boyle?" That inquiry always hurt, no matter the source.

"You ask a lot of questions", Dustin countered with an edge in his voice.

"Oh, I do apologize. American dignitaries so interest me. Enjoy your tea. Mr. Alderson should be with you straight away."

Straight away. She fully embraces the British culture, he thought. As she turned to leave, Dustin called after her: "Can I ask *you* a question?"

She turned to face him, neither hesitant nor uncertain. "Indeed. I do not keep count," the maid fired back with a delightfully wry expression.

Dustin could not help but smile back. "Are your people from Louisiana?"

Her minimal smile broadened into a winning grin. "If 'my people' are my family, then no. I was born right here in Washington. Nodding to the tea service, she added wryly, "But the sugar might have hailed from those parts. Good evening, Mr. Boyle." As she departed, Dustin could feel the temperature drop in the room. The lighting from the chandelier seemed dimmer, too.

Satisfied that the servant was not a relation, Dustin sipped his tea. Never before had a Negro – outside of Caleb – spoken to him with such informality and directness. Dustin was, at once, put off and intrigued. Didn't these Brits school their Negroes in proper decorum?

As if on cue, Nigel Alderson bound into the room like a ham actor in a stage play. Chubby and bespectacled, he barely resembled the Nigel that Dustin had known three decades earlier. Balding on top, he let his graying hair grow long on the sides, reminding Dustin of Benjamin Franklin. Clasping Dustin's hand in two of his, Alderson welcomed him with as much pretense as he could conjure: "Dustin, my lad, seeing you reminds me that once I was young. You still appear to be only of 19 years yourself!" the fat man gushed.

"I'm sorry to call on you so late, Nigel. It is important that we speak with as few eyes and ears nearby as possible."

Alderson's face betrayed just a hint of panic. "Don't give it a thought," he said cordially. "Sit, shall we?"

"I noticed you employ a Negro housemaid in your official parlors?" Dustin fished.

"Oh yes, Sarah. Well to be truthful, old boy, she's a laundry maid by day, but she is so devilishly efficient at everything. Of course, she is not…*suited* to maintain the public floors during working hours, so we use her to serve goblins like you, who insist on keeping the rest of us from our beds," Alderson said with a wink.

About to recount their conversation, Dustin instead kept silent, assuming Sarah would be harshly disciplined for her forwardness.

"Does the work of three white domestics without the constant blathering," Alderson continued. His expression turned sly. "Did her presence offend you? After all, the war ended many years ago, as did Negro enslavement. They have to earn a wage, you know."

"I am hard to offend these days, Nigel. My own presence at the State Department would appear to bring more insult to this city than a Negro pouring tea at its largest diplomatic post."

Alderson looked down ruefully at the tea service, pulled a silver flask of whiskey from his coat pocket and poured it in his cup. Dustin extended his emptied cup to receive the same, hoping it would lubricate a difficult conversation.

"Frightfully sorry about Gresham. What did the old chap die from?" Before Dustin could respond, Alderson changed the subject. "You know Landis was here often during Gresham's time, going on about you. 'That son-of-a-Boothe', he called you. He'd say 'That son-of-a-Boothe is up to something. He's got the boss thinking like a Reb!'"

Kenisaw Mountain Landis had been Gresham's private secretary. An unrepentant Republican, he needed no reason to distrust Dustin. Yet the Secretary's obvious affection for his counselor gave Landis plenty of additional cause to despise him. Landis expressed his loathing by ruthlessly enforcing the unofficial policy of keeping Dustin quarantined.

"Ken departed soon after Secretary Gresham's funeral. Seems he hates all Democrats, not just Southerners," Dustin reported dryly.

"You're both fish out of water, in a sense," Alderson offered, delaying the inevitable conversation he did not want to have.

"Nigel, we need…"

"Say no more. I failed you in '63. I know. You must understand that my government was playing its cards close to the vest regarding your civil war. They were supporting the victor, whichever side that turned out to be. Noise about an alliance with Jeff Davis was only a contingency, not a conviction. Forgive me. I was just a bloody, low-level bugger in those days. I did not know the rules." Having purged, Alderson leaned back, exhausted.

Amused that Alderson was getting his lies mixed up, Dustin was grateful that the Emglishman had at least remembered a debt to him. Lowering his voice, he played along: "Nigel, I didn't come here to rebuke you. I was as ignorant as you were about the situation. Little did I know, as I sailed to England, that President Davis had already given up on any affiliation. It was all vanity, the whole business."

"A couple of green pups, the both of us," Alderson observed with some relief. "But I was dead in earnest when I told you that I owe you my life. I'm ashamed that I was unable to come through for you."

"It's not too late."

Alderson began to stiffen. "Venezuela?"

Dustin nodded. "Salibury's cold shoulder is firing up the war camp in this country, Nigel. You must have seen the Scruggs screed. "

"Blast, Dustin, how do reasonable men give credence to such a rag?! The Monroe Doctrine? He must be jesting."

"As a rule," Dustin explained, "President Cleveland has not responded to jingoism. But the events here are yielding different results. Had Secretary Gresham lived, I would not be here tonight. Olney has seized the Monroe Doctrine to fan the president's temper white hot."

"But why does he care about such a small parcel? The last thing Her Majesty wants is to rule over those Venezuelans. At issue here is boundary integrity—not conquest." Alderson's previous humility had evaporated as he assumed the role of government mouthpiece. "British Guiana will not be shrunken to satisfy some gold-digging wogs."

Dustin wondered if Sarah had overheard this uniquely British racial slur. Then he wondered why it mattered.

 Alderson was now pacing, jabbing his index finger upward, while intoning the London-approved script. He was neither intellectually gifted nor in any way disciplined, but Alderson could deliver a stem-winder. Much like the

Yankee demagogues who flooded into the south during Reconstruction, Dustin thought, Alderson was now bathed in righteous indignation without ever having reflected on right or wrong.

"Her Majesty's government is unwavering in defending the rights of her subjects in South America!" Alderson triumphantly concluded.

"You're quite a powerful speaker, sir," Dustin said, quoting Dickens. "It's a wonder you don't go into Parliament." Alderson smiled and sat back down, panting heavily and smugly assuming that there was nothing more to be said of the matter. The secret to success, he always told his trusted associates, is to tickle the ears. When this art is mastered, poverty is vanquished. He had indeed made a stable career as a flatterer and toady. True friendship, on the other hand, was alien to him.

"Why don't your ministers make those excellent points in arbitration, as my government is recommending?" Dustin offered.

"Submitting to arbitration is tantamount to supine surrender. It suggests the boundary is fluid and invites further encroachments by those barbarians. Not only that, but it tempts the neighbors of our other possessions around the world to engage us in similar frivolous disputes."

Growing irritated, Dustin parried: "Frivolous is in the mind of the encroacher, Nigel. Nation-states can not absorb territory and resources without accountability. Britannia may rule the waves, but she does not control the world…nor should she!"

Alderson was ready for that. He had heard the charges of British arrogance *ad nauseum*. They were always leveled by the jealous and inferior. "Who pulled out of the Samoan protectorate, Dustin? More to the point, who continues to keep Samoa under her thumb? America and her bloody Teutonic partner, that's who. We gave up our position in the Pacific. 'Rule the world.' Rubbish!"

Dustin remained silent for a few moments as Alderson caught his breath. He had gone too far with his last remark, he realized. An analyst rather than a diplomat, Dustin understood how unsuited he was for this task. At the same time, he took careful note of Alderson's reference to a European rival.

"Fair enough, old friend," he resumed. "I didn't come here to argue moral principles. I am a messenger. The message is that sentiment in my government and throughout this country is growing in favor of greater aggressiveness abroad. I do not share in this sickness. But its presence can not be denied. Granted, the Monroe Doctrine is not an international treaty. But among Americans it is a venerated principle upon which opportunistic men will stand in their lust for war. I've seen this type of contagion before, from without…and within."

Alderson, once again at room temperature, listened with one eye on the clock. Dustin was not his last appointment for the evening. "What would you have me tell the ambassador? Or have him tell the prime minister? To cravenly capitulate to American threats?"

Dustin mentally noted the nearly identical rhetoric of the jingoes with that of the British ruling class. "Think of it in this way, Nigel: agreeing to arbitration will save immense quantities of blood and treasure, which you can then direct against, as you call them, our Teutonic partners." Rightly suspecting that British anger at Germany was a greater motivator than her indignation over arbitration, Dustin reminded Alderson of Her Majesty's troubles in South Africa, where Germany was lending support to the rebellious Boers.

Alderson leaned forward conspiratorially. "Blood is more easily replaced than treasure. From our vantage point, there is abundant treasure between the Essequibo and Orinoco rivers. Since it is our land, we will exploit its resources. Venezuela has no case. Q.E.D., arbitration is unnecessary."

Alderson may have morphed in appearance, Dustin thought, but not in character. Frustrated by the Englishman's parroting, he took an uglier tack: "Fine, Nigel. We will then need to settle our personal affairs more crudely. You will recall an incident in 1874 regarding an improperly documented shipment of textiles from Manchester that found its way to Mobile? How you needed a lawyer to certify its legitimacy? When this lawyer investigated the contents, he concluded that the goods were stolen and that the shipper paid a large courier fee to an anonymous facilitator in the British Foreign Office. Rather than exposing the fraud, the lawyer—out of friendship and upon a promise of percentage—vouched for the questionable cargo at great risk to his own standing with the Bar, and arranged for speedy release of the materials by Customs officials. I want my cut, Nigel. Five-thousand pounds-sterling will be sufficient."

Alderson blanched. His ventures were never undertaken with the expectation of exposure. He had but one recourse. "I'm of modest means, old boy," he lied. "But perhaps you will consider alternative forms of compensation." Even after 30 years, Dustin recognized the tone of temptation. Ignorant of Dustin's physiological condition, Alderson assumed every man was as concupiscent as himself.

"No doubt your girlfriends are fetching, Nigel, but I invest for the long term. Since both our currencies are backed by your gold, I'll accept either. Five-thousand pounds-sterling should suffice for saving the skin of such an important champion of British policy."

His back against the proverbial wall, the attaché yielded. "Blast, man, I'll do as you ask!!" Alderson sputtered. "You must know I will just be rebuffed, and probably lose any influence I have. Then what good am I to you?"

"I'm not asking you to go empty-handed. If Britain agrees to mediation under American auspices, I can guarantee you that your resources will be safe for exploitation." Dustin expected the next question; the answer, however…

"How?"

"Nigel, a southern nationalist does not get to the upper tier of the Yankee government without knowing a few things. Trust me. Even the jingoes have no use for Venezuela other than as a pretext for war. If you fellows can make a show of cooperation, this whole dispute is soon forgotten and," Dustin added, "we will be squared, you and I."

"Why not go through your Ambassador Bayard in London. He can take that promise directly to the PM," Alderson offered, hopefully.

"Three reasons. First, Bayard favors British interests more than the Queen herself. Second, he is a former Secretary of State and will, out of courtesy, want to clear all of his correspondence with Olney. Finally, I am not authorized to make such a promise. But – and this is the most important thing, Nigel – I am fully capable of delivering on it."

6

Walking back to his rooms, Dustin forgave himself for the lie: he had no inside advantage if arbitration were to be agreed upon. He was spending his own personal capital faster than he could earn it, he knew. What else could he do? Desperate times, desperate measures. Alderson's allusion to the U.S. Ambassador in London was troublesome. Were Bayard to get wind of Dustin's maneuvering, he would assume it was all done at Olney's direction, prompting a wire to the Secretary asking him to please advise. The mission compromised, Olney would then have the requisite ammunition to have his counselor fired.

Dread discomfort entered Dustin, and he stopped in his tracks. Turning about, he could swear he saw the hooded cloak of the Grim Reaper, sans sickle, in the distance. The glow from the street lamps was weak, but the eerie image made him shiver as he resumed his march home, now at an accelerated tempo. Previously, he had only despaired over the unlikelihood of his mission's success. Presently, he was brooding over the danger. War had many vested interests in this city, some of which may want to get a jump on the bloodshed. Since the beginning, doing business with Nigel Alderson had always carried the risk of kill or be killed.

"Can you lend me some strength, friend? I think those bloody buggers broke my leg."

It was not Dustin's way to interfere in private disputes, much less so fatally. His bad leg ached, but he was intact otherwise. The other man's white waistcoat was streaked with blood, the same of which flowed copiously from his nose. He staggered to his feet nonetheless.

"I guess the leg is OK. You saved my life, sir. Thank you."

Dustin forced his thoughts to return to the present: "Are you Lieutenant Alderson?"

"Call me Nigel. Yes, that's me. Whew, I thought I was a gonner. Who are you, and why did you save me like that?"

"I need you to serve on a warship being launched in a couple of days."

"You're an American!!!" Alderson shrieked in disbelief. The mop of red hair atop his skinny frame softened his angular features and pale complexion. "I knew I was in dutch with the Admiralty, but never thought they would exile me abroad," Alderson said breathlessly, stanching the blood with his sleeve.

"I'm Major Dustin Boyle of the Confederate States Army. I'm here to assemble a crew for a warship, and we need some British officers. I need a navigator of your ability."

Alderson smiled, revealing three gaps where, minutes before, teeth were rooted. "You want me to fight in the American war? Major, I owe you my life, but my future is with the Empire. Are you aware that I am restricted from sea duty until I am cleared by a tribunal?"

"I've been informed regarding your status. What will it take to clear you of the charges against you?"

Alderson sat himself down on a crate, continuing to dab his nose. "Friends. Half the crew supported the Captain of my ship – he would have killed us all, mind you, through incompetence – and the other half came to my defense. I need people to vouch for my character to tip the scales in my favor."

Gesturing toward his fallen victims, Dustin asked, "Why were these men about to kill you?"

Alderson flashed an embarrassed smile. "I have a weakness for the ladies, chum. Sometimes I buy what I can't afford. I didn't know she had a bully."

"Bully?"

"You know, a pimp. I usually only stiff the freelancers."

Alderson's life may have been spared today, Dustin thought, but his days are numbered if lust clouds his judgment this way. "You said you needed friends. How are you going to make any when you do business like this?"

Alderson shrugged.

"Hear my proposal: you serve on the CSS Georgia – alongside a Confederate and British crew – and you will return with ten British officers ready and willing to save your career. You will also be paid handsomely," Dustin *added, handing Alderson an envelope thick with currency. "A token of good will, up front."*

Alderson caressed the package. "You're going to lose that war, you know." He then brightened. "But, like I said, I owe you my life. I'll do it. May I call you Dustin?"

"I would be honored, Nigel. Let's attend to your condition, first."

Arriving at his chambers at the Hotel Washington on 15th Street opposite the Treasury Department, Dustin nervously lit two lamps, thankful for summer, when hearth-lighting was unnecessary. He was either afraid of fire or just depressed by it. Reminding him of the burned-out cities of his native South, he lit a fire only the coldest winter nights. Maybe he was afraid of it, after all. Stripping off his clothes, Dustin lay down in his bed, his body exhausted, but his mind racing. All he would need was the slightest hint of cooperation from the U.K. The president would not dispatch troops if he saw a glimmer of hope. Nevertheless, Dustin would pursue a parallel course with his own government. He could not bet all his cards on the likes of Nigel Alderson.

Drifting off to sleep, he reviewed his grand plan, recalled his father's wisdom and envisioned the embassy maid with the striking green eyes.

Rafael Mendoza was roused from slumber with the tip of a soldier's boot against his cheek. He despaired that the eight-month nightmare he had endured was continuing. Sleep, as hard as it was to come by, was a sweet refuge from the misery of his life. It was still dark, but the soldier's lantern revealed the dank, moldy walls and the army of mice and cockroaches that were his permanent roommates.

"Get up, you rat, and follow me!" one of his jailers ordered.

"What time is it? Where are you taking me?"

"Ha. Many questions from a despicable rodent. Keep quiet and get moving."

Wearing his dingy, soiled prison issue of ragged clothes, he staggered toward the light at the opening to his putrid cell. In the equally putrid corridor, he found his dreaded tormentor, Captain Victor Patiño. The officer was commanding a detachment of guards to assume formation, which they did with some difficulty.

Venezuela is in some trouble, Mendoza thought, if the prison gossip is true and the British are preparing to attack.

Patiño got in the prisoner's face. "What was your occupation, rat?"

"I am an engineer. You know that."

"*Were* an engineer!" the Captain roared back. "And we know that it was only your daytime vocation. Evenings were spent in intrigue, were they not?"

"I am innocent of any crime…"

The Captain's iron backhand connected explosively with Mendoza's face, as the prisoner, losing consciousness, sank to his knees. The burly officer was brutally strong and his knuckles felt like bullets hitting the prisoner simultaneously. Mendoza was then doused with cold water and pulled up to standing posture by his unkempt black hair. The foul breath of Patiño assaulted his nostrils.

"Rats can make no claims in this court, you disgusting informer. Were it not for my good graces, you would be dead by now." The officer's nostrils flared and his eyes were scarlet, as though full of evil. Almost immediately, however, he softened in demeanor.

"You can prolong your days, you know. We have need of a man with your skills. If you apply yourself, Rafael, you might even win your release," Patiño tempted.

Not believing it for a minute, Mendoza saw seven men, prisoners all, filing in behind the disorganized phalanx of soldiers. He knew most of them. They were illiterate, detained for petty crimes, and not imprisoned for political reasons as he was.

"These men will assist you when brawn is called for," the Captain offered.

"What will I be doing?" Mendoza asked, still lightheaded.

"There are wagons outside waiting. You will be instructed upon arrival."

"Where?"

"I do not work for you, rat!" the Captain erupted, returning to his menacing behavior.

Taking his place at the head of the line, Mendoza and his fellow prisoners proceeded down the corridor, exiting beneath a full moon. The fresh air was welcome relief from the stench of the jail in the outskirts of Ciudad Bolivar, and Mendoza inhaled deeply. Shoved by guards onto the wooden bed of the unstable wagon, he then helped his weary and malnourished comrades into the rickety conveyance. *If these men are brawny*, he thought, *I would hate to see weaklings*. They could, nevertheless, be useful allies.

After horses were attached, the soldiers mounted their own steeds and flanked the clueless band of convicts. After strenuous effort, the wagon pitched forward toward wherever. Mendoza had enough experience with the Crespo regime to know that gratuitous hints of freedom usually ended with a bullet to the head. While he was unsure of the destination, he knew he must seize any opportunity to escape.

<u>7</u>

September, 1895

The Prime Minister was pensive as he studied a South American gazetteer in the spacious Cabinet Room at the British Foreign Office. Despising the cramped quarters on Downing Street officially designated for him, he chose to work at the Foreign Ministry's headquarters on King Charles Street. Since he was doubling as his own Foreign Secretary, it was a fitting arrangement.

"We still have ships and marines at the ready in the region?"

"Since the spring," answered his First Lord of the Admiralty, who was peering over the PM's shoulder at the topographic maps. "Three warships and 400 marines remain since the incident with Nicaragua."

"Why they want a row over this matter is beyond my powers of comprehension. It affects their interests not a fig. Why do they get so warm over such a trifle?"

Robert Cecil, the Marquis of Salisbury, had – like Grover Cleveland – earned a return engagement as the head of government after his Conservative Party had suffered a brief exile. Unlike many of his partisans, Lord Salisbury was sensitive to the delicate balance of interests among the aristocracy and the masses. Born to privilege and loyal to the peerage, the Prime Minister nonetheless appreciated the growing political clout of commoners. He rarely made a decision without reflecting on the consequences for them. Such a deliberative personality was reflected by a burdened countenance and thinning hair, which was more than compensated for by a majestic brown beard with a few flecks of gray.

Salisbury's attention returned to the document the two men had been discussing. The pages spread out on the green leather surface of the double-pedestal mahogany desk, the remonstrance sparked uncharacteristic anger in the prime minister. "This is a bloody insult to Her Majesty's rights and responsibilities, Goschen. What if we chose to regulate American borders with Mexico? Or side with her indigenous populations against her government? For all his bloviating, Olney gives no meaningful grounds for submitting to American arbitration. I venture to say he is simply appeasing the Visigoth movement now active in the United States. Calling his bluff would be a fitting response to the whole business."

Clean-shaven with a full head of snowy-white hair, the Viscount George Goschen seemed an odd choice to lead the mightiest navy in the world. Like Salisbury, he was Oxford-educated, well-born and well-bred. Of German lineage – a pedigree that forced him to take a conspicuously hard line in the conflict over lands in Africa, lest he be accused of divided loyalties – Goschen was a successful banker and financier prior to his political career. Content to leave the day-to-day management of Her Majesty's fleet to the seafaring professionals, Goschen carved a niche for himself as an advisor on the economic repercussions of naval and military strategies. The gold discovery between the rivers excited the monetarist inside of him. His very public stance against Germany over the rebellious Boers, however, gave him pause about committing additional military assets to another continent.

"You may be right, Prime Minister. At the same time, the communication from Pauncefote in Washington would indicate that American mediation may play to our favor."

Salisbury shrugged. "Landsdowne and the other ministers think it is a hollow proposal, designed to give the Americans time to mobilize their forces, such as they are," he observed contemptuously. "On top of that, we have no certitude as to the credibility of the source from which Pauncefote bases that representation." The PM had a hunch about the source, believing his doubts to be well justified.

"True," Goschen countered, "but Lord Pauncefote has demonstrated superior judgment in the past. We should not dismiss his opinion out of hand."

"I am by no means impugning his competence, George, but history demonstrates American guile. We have two defeats at the hands of their inferior armies to prove it."

Goschen adopted a reassuring tone. "Your caution is commendable, sir, but we are not yet at the point of urgency. I would recommend that we let this matter stew for a season. American forces will in no wise improve over the next month or two. Meanwhile, we can better divine whether Mr. Cleveland's intentions are represented by

Secretary Olney…or by Lord Pauncefote's mysterious informer."

After an extended mulling, Salisbury finally spoke. "So there it is, then," the Prime Minister agreed. "We shall rest this matter on a shelf for a while, and see what comes of it. Do you wish to remain for my visit with Bayard?"

"I should get along. I am not nearly as astute as the Marquis when it comes to American guile," Goschen said dryly, with a twinkle in his eye. "By all means, forward my benevolent regards to the ambassador from the United States of America."

Henry Lane enjoyed the life of an academic. Few things interrupted the long stretches of serenity and the pleasant routine associated with the professoriate. Somewhat nervous and shy by nature, his anxieties had been flamed to a boil by his service in the War Between the States, as he had learned to call it. The exposed innards, severed limbs and slow deaths were frightening enough. But the 52-year old scholar was still most haunted by the screams and caterwauling from his wounded compatriots. The piercing cries for help and for mothers, from young men who – minutes before – were oozing bravado, were burned into his brain. He had envied his college mate who maintained icy composure in the heat of battle. When Lane asked him for his secret, the curt answer was: "You take too much time to think, Hen. It will ruin you." No small wonder that his friend went on to become a lawyer.

Teaching at a women's college was particularly gratifying because there were no young men to remind him of his maimed and dying soldiers. Girls were less rambunctious, too. They were there to learn; he, to teach. Recalling his graduate school days at Yale – "the belly of the beast" his father called it – Lane still felt the sting of practical jokes and snide references from his fellow collegians. "Y'all can't pay in cotton, Colonel," was the usual taunt when he purchased his lunch in the dining hall. When speaking in class, he was subjected to men sneezing the word "Appomattox" during his orations. Never overtly assaulted or attacked, Lane realized that northern men had a passive-aggressive, if unforgiving, way of putting him in his place.

Shaking off these memories, Lane walked across the Wells College campus in anticipation of the coming term, when the grounds would again be teeming with proper young ladies who completed their assignments and listened dutifully to his expositions on the reign of Charlemagne. With a wife and four docile daughters at home, Lane's life was perfectly sublime. Fending off specters from the past was his only battle now.

 Crossing a lush green lawn, he approached Old Main, the academic and residential headquarters where his comfortably-cramped office was located. The stone and brick edifice was a pleasant cocoon in which to conduct research and tutor his young charges. Entering the building and passing through the reception room, Lane was suddenly intercepted by an aging, diminutive administrative type, her hair in a tight bun and her gaunt face weathered by decades of central New York winters.

"Excuse me, Professor, but this telegram arrived for you several days ago. I apologize, but there was no one available to deliver it to your house. The messenger said it's from Washington, DC," the clerk added with excitement.

"Thank you, kindly, Miss Kennelly," Lane responded, hoping to hide his growing feeling of dread. "I'm sure it is a routine matter."

Double-timing it to his office, Lane shut the door and cleared a place for himself among the stacks of books and manuscripts. His hands were shaking as he broke the seal and unfolded the message. Maybe the general amnesty declared by President Andrew Johnson was not so general, after all. Maybe his war service was finally catching up with him, as many a nightmare had prophesied. Swallowing desperately to restore moisture to the inside of his mouth, he finally focused on the contents of the transmission:

MXT344   ORIG WASHINGTON DC

HEN –(STOP) – IN NEW YORK FOR BUSINESS ON 10/21 –(STOP)—
MEET AT THE GILSEY HOUSE 29TH AND BROADWAY FOR A LATE
SUPPER? –(STOP)—EIGHT PM—(STOP)—PLEASE ATTEND—(STOP).

DUSTIN BOYLE
                6:18PM

HENRY LANE
WELLS COLLEGE
C/O AURORA NY TELEGRAPH OFFICE

Dustin Boyle was like a brother/protector to Lieutenant Henry Lane, CSA. From their training days forward, the two men commanded units side by side – or, more accurately, front and back. Lane was always hesitant in combat; Boyle, impulsive. It was always reassuring when Captain Boyle went first because there were a good many Yankees already dead by the time Lane and his men arrived on the scene. Unlike Dustin, Lane had no taste for Union blood and – after his friend was transferred to Richmond following an injury at Seven Pines – the future professor exploited the administrative confusion that was ubiquitous in the CSA. Riding right up to the edge of a Tennessee melee, he turned left and kept riding, surrendering to Union forces days later, and subsequently enrolling in the Louisiana State Seminary of Learning. In less than a year, Dustin would arrive to resume his own education.

The two were friendly, if not friends. Dustin loaned Lane money to make a tuition payment. He visited Lane in the hospital when Yellow Fever almost took his life. After the two parted, and Lane had sojourned north for graduate study, Dustin – a newly minted lawyer – had assisted with the disposition of the Lane family estate. He never asked for anything in return, but Lane had difficulty believing in Dustin's altruism. There was abundant selflessness to the man, but little warmth. Always suspecting that a giant favor was coming due, the professor now realized that the moment was at hand.

General Ezekiel Swanson was practically walking on air as he read and re-read the message just wired from the War Department. A natural swashbuckler, the blondish six-footer held himself erect at all times, his gray eyes darting like those of a bald eagle in search of prey. A proud servant in the profession of arms, Swanson was at his best in a fight. Pity that he served in an administrative role in Washington for the duration of the War Between the States, he would frequently torment himself. He remembered the many evenings when President Lincoln would pace the floors at the War Department waiting for the latest battle statistics. Swanson paced, too. While Lincoln's anxiety was directed at ending the war, Swanson's was aimed at getting into the thick of it before it ended.

It was not to be. After the end of hostilities, the sinewy major was sent south to enforce Reconstruction, where he encountered a resentful, but defeated, population. From there, Swanson received command after command – and multiple promotions – in the Indian wars, serving in posts from the Dakotas to New Mexico. At first, the combat was exhilarating, and Swanson excelled at crushing the warrior bands and tribes that dared stand in the way of Manifest Destiny. After a while, though, the thrill wore off. Like the vanquished rebels in Dixie, the native populations were beginning to give up: their attacks were less ferocious; their war cries, less menacing.

With Indian country pacified, the general had his fill of the west. A native Bostonian, he yearned for an assertive projection of American force abroad, as envisioned by his home state senator, Henry Cabot Lodge. His troops were as good as any in the world, Swanson believed, and he would prove it at the earliest opportunity. Naturally, the wire from Washington was like a shot of adrenaline. Not only did it instruct him to consolidate his cavalry regiment – then spread across three territories – in preparation for movement east, it also directed him to ensure his troop numbers were at authorized strength, a rare level of readiness during the prior decade. The general knew that the Venezuelan boundary argument would boil over eventually. This was everything he was waiting for. The fact that the transmission appeared over the name of Secretary Daniel Lamont was gravy.

 Laying out seven uniforms side by side, Swanson began inspecting each with a keen eye for flaws. Appearance matters, he always said, and the arrogant Brits would soon learn that Americans could match them in both strategy *and* bearing. As today would be a working day, he donned the most utilitarian of his uniforms, highlighted by a khaki fatigue blouse. Were it not for the gold stars on the collar, he might have been mistaken for an enlisted man. Appropriately so, he thought. Swanson mixed easily with the noncoms in his command, earning their respect by occupying forward positions; humping with infantry when a wounded soldier needed his horse; and digging burial plots for his men. He also had ambitions. True, he had missed out on the heroics of the mid-century. He was every inch a general, though, and was sure he could hold the reins of executive power more effectively than the Democrat who bought his way out of the war.

A confident knock on the door was followed by the entry of his aide-de-camp. "Begging the General's pardon, sir: Company D has just arrived from New Mexico and awaits the General's inspection."

"Very well, Lieutenant," Swanson said, slipping on his boot. "Summon Colonel Simms to my quarters. I want a few words with him and then we will review his troops together."

"Sir!" The lieutenant snapped a salute, pivoted on his heel and departed with flawless execution.

Swanson admired what he saw in the looking glass. With a war victory in his cap, he would be unbeatable in 1900. All he needed was the war. And Lamont's backing to run it.

<u>8</u>

Mendoza had nodded off; for how long he was unsure. He knew dense jungle when he saw it nonetheless. Obviously many days had passed since the sojourn began. By now the sun had risen and the heat of the day was ramping up. Summer was approaching in South America, but it made little difference in Venezuela's equatorial climate. From the look of his face, arms and hands—and those of his compatriots—the tropical insects native to the area had been feasting for some time. The wagon rambled forward, lethargically but consistently. Ahead, in the distance, he could see Captain Patiño and a sergeant on horseback, advancing the party. An additional guard rode with rifle in hand on either side of the wagon, and a third pulled up the rear, driving a second horse-drawn wagon. That conveyance appeared to carry some familiar-looking heavy equipment, though Mendoza could not quite remember where he had seen it before.

A year before, Mendoza was supervising a dam construction project in Cojedes. It was there that he witnessed the wasted resources and copious graft associated with the enterprise. Many of the workers were unskilled, not to mention shiftless. Yet they were taking payments from government officials who stopped by from time to time in order to "monitor" the dam's progress. These gifts were over and above their agreed-upon wages.

Frustrated and suspicious, Mendoza took his concerns to a Caracas newspaper editor, hoping to spark an investigation. Looking back, he realized how naïve he had been. That very night, he was greeted at the entrance of his home by government agents who—in front of his terrified wife and two daughters—beat him to a bloody pulp before hauling him off. He had been subject to President Crespo's accommodations ever since.

The endless jungle began taking on a familiar look. The warp and woof of the landscape told Mendoza that he had been through these parts on prior occasions. A somnambulant anaconda paid no heed to the convoy passing its resting place on an imposing Aragueney tree, partially hidden by the trees bright yellow flowers. The concentration of yellow- and red-leafed Moriche Palm trees reminded Mendoza of an earlier expedition on behalf of the previous regime. He was spotting more jaguars, too, as they eyed the modest parade with interest. Heading directly toward the ascending sun was disturbing. There was a hostile power to the east with a reputation for ruthlessness, its pretensions to civility to the contrary. If Mendoza was correct, they were heading for the Rio Cuyuni, a river not only claimed by the English for British Guiana, but a fatally dangerous body of water in its own right. Mendoza's breath became shallow and his heartbeat quickened. They had to turn back.

As much as he tried to focus on his other duties, Dustin was severely preoccupied with Venezuela. He knew Alderson had transmitted his shallow pledge of favoritism to his superiors at the legation. Beyond that, he was in the dark as to how the British government would respond, or whether the embassy would transmit the information at all. His outreach to Henry Lane was also pending without even the guarantee of a response. The stress was eroding Dustin's health. He ate and slept poorly in recent weeks, plagued by the memory of the Grim Reaper.

Taking a yellowed piece of paper from his coat pocket, Dustin unfolded it and re-read what he had read at least a thousand times before:

Christmas Day, 1862

Dusty,

As I write, your mother has fallen ill with Yellow Fever, and is not expected to survive more than a few days. You may have heard that the land was confiscated by Yankee troops, divided and allotted to freed Negroes. None of them were our people, who themselves were dispersed when the Yankees invaded. My own health is precarious and we are presently living with the Monteaux cousins in New Orleans, in a dwelling much too small for the lot of us. Reports that you were wounded were troublesome but we rejoice that you are alive and little hobbled. I write to tell you how proud your family is of your courage, and to advise you to resume your studies as soon as hostilities cease.

My apprehension is that I may not see you again, son. You have been the delight of my life and you have a special calling to redeem our compatriots from what looks like many years of oppression. If God could charge a stammering Moses with such a task, how much more qualified is my noble and brave offspring. In this effort I know you will not fail.

Love always,

Your devoted father

Dustin had leaned on this very last paternal communication to keep him going as he climbed his way slowly to his present tier of influence...*noble and brave offspring...* The Moses reference was classic Justus. He was forever extolling the leadership power of Moses and King David to his son. Seven Christmases before that letter, when he was again praising these biblical figures as leaders of men, Dustin's mother interjected, "Don't forget Jesus, Dusty." Justus looked at his wife in disbelief. "Angelique, honey, all *his* men ran away."

Indeed, Dustin Boyle was groomed for courageous leadership and he would assume the mantle when circumstances were optimal. That glorious day, however, was in jeopardy unless the threatened war was thwarted. For now, he had to wait on others.

A barely audible knock emanated from his door. Jacob Stansfield peeked inside. "You busy?"

"Come in, Jake."

Pale, pasty and brutalized, Stansfield's homely face had taken on an urgent expression. "Olney's man – what's his name, Oberstreet – was at the archives snooping around, as usual."

"OK?"

"I heard him tell his assistant that troops are being called back from the southwest to prepare for hostilities in South America."

"Is that all he said?"

"Does he need to say more? Dustin, this thing is on."

Dustin felt dizzy as he sensed his grip on the situation slipping. "It was good of you to come by, Jake. I will speak with you soon," he said distantly.

"Are you alright?"

"Yes, Jake. I need some time to think is all."

"Think all you like, friend, but please do something. These lunatics are playing for keeps."

As the door shut, Dustin realized his strategy needed an additional prong. Besides getting to the president and influencing the British, he would have to slow down the military effort at home. Dreading the next few minutes, he left his office and moved swiftly over the black and white tiles that covered the floors of the corridors. Upon reaching the west side of the building, he descended two flights of granite stairs that were ornately flanked by cast bronze balusters, alighting at the entrance to Room 232, the official chambers of the secretary of war. Summoning all of his martial background, Dustin ceremoniously identified himself to the military clerk manning the outer office, requesting that he be announced immediately.

Surprisingly, it worked.

The high-ceilinged office with large windows on two walls was slightly intimidating to Dustin, as he was escorted in by the clerk. Lamont was standing at his desk, yelling into a telephone, a luxury for which Dustin did not rank highly enough. A War Department crest was emblazoned on the front of the secretary's desk. The secretary was of medium height, lean and balding. His dense chevron mustache softened the severity of his face, but his dark suit and black ascot tie made him look like an irate mortician.

"Just get it done," Lamont barked into the transmitter. "We'll never see additional appropriations if you keep fouling up!" Returning the transmitter to the cradle, Lamont sat and motioned Dustin to do likewise.

"Well, Boyle, they let you out of your cage, did they?" Lamont sported a wry smile and Dustin was glad he caught him in a good mood.

"With Secretary Olney still in Massachusetts, I thought I should bring a matter to your attention, personally, sir."

"Oberstreet or one of the others couldn't handle it?"

"It's a military matter."

Lamont arched an eyebrow. He knew Dustin was not satisfied to mind his own business, but the secretary was surprised he would be so forward.

"Well?"

"The rumor of troop movements is wafting through the corridors, Mr. Secretary. People are coming to believe that war over Venezuela is a forgone conclusion."

Dustin was fishing, that much Lamont knew.

"Whatever 'people' choose to believe, Boyle, troop movement and war are not *ipso facto* cause and effect. You know the man we work for. He is parsimonious with the people's treasury. With Indian country pacified, we are not just going to leave cavalry troops at loose ends out west. We will consolidate, then re-assign or disband as circumstances warrant. Tell that to your 'people'."

Dustin could see that Lamont was irked to know his secrets were leaking. He rubbed salt in the wound.

"My point is that if I can learn this information so easily, we have to assume the Brits can do likewise. And they will assume the worst, submissive Sioux notwithstanding."

Lamont leaned forward in challenge, his tone one notch short of belligerent."Alright then, Mr. Cocksure. Why then hasn't Pauncefote objected, through formal or informal channels?"

Dustin crossed his legs confidently, knowing that his information had thoroughly infuriated the Secretary. "Playing their cards close to the vest, perhaps? Why give them cause? Is it untenable to leave the troops in place until Venezuela gets resolved? We both know that arbitration will just end up with the same old Schombürgk Line."

"What makes you think we'll get to arbitration with the attitude those Brits are now assuming?" Lamont looked down at his lap and then at Dustin again. "Or do you know more than you let on?"

"Just what I hear, Mr. Secretary. And if I'm hearing it, and the Brits are hearing it, then so are the jingoes. They are no doubt salivating over this."

Lamont rose from behind his majestic desk, walked around to the front, and sat down in the wing chair opposite Dustin. He spoke softly and soberly. "You listen to me. Believe it or not, I admire you in many ways. You are smart and you are tough. As far as talent goes, there are few in this administration who can match you. But I don't trust you, and that jingo remark is one of the reasons why. That bunch has not the least influence over me – or the president – and you will not manipulate matters either. The troop consolidation will continue apace. It's too late to stop it. You have missed the boat, Boyle."

Dustin had another arrow in his quiver, but was not sure he wanted to shoot it prematurely. Perhaps just brandishing it a bit…

"I hope not, Mr. Secretary. Boats, after all, are where lives get saved. Good afternoon, sir." He stood ramrod straight, pivoted and exited the office."

Lamont walked to an oversized window and gazed out upon the clear day…yet saw nothing. Quaking on the inside, he now suspected that Dustin possessed knowledge of one of the most closely held secrets of the Cleveland Administration. How could he ever be dismissed? Or even put in his place? How was it that Gresham was directing foreign policy posthumously? Lamont felt the vein in his neck bulging in frustration. For sure, the secretary had never felt so vexed by an underling.

Lamont called his clerk, who scurried in dutifully with paper and pencil.

"Lieutenant, I need you to transmit the following orders to General Swanson." His eyes bore down on the diminutive assistant. "If this message leaks, you will serve out your commission bathing horses at Fort Leavenworth, am I clear?"

Dustin walked back to his office believing his arrow had hit its mark. His knowledge of President Cleveland's operation was something he had planned to take to the grave, but circumstances compelled him to drop the hint to Lamont. While the secretary evinced no reaction, Dustin knew a poker face when he saw one. Lamont would either have to accommodate him or, alternatively, have him killed. Dustin would not put the latter past the president's most loyal cabinet member, but guessed that slowing the troop movement would be the easier option. If London responded to Dustin's unauthorized overture soon, the whole issue would be just as soon forgotten. And soon it had better be, since he was running out of water to put out all the political brushfires.

And yet, secrets were his indispensible tools if he was to achieve the destiny that Justus ordained for him. As an attorney, he had parlayed his relationship with Nigel Alderson into a network of mid-level government trade administrators throughout Europe. Focusing on maritime law, he utilized these allies when defending ship owners against cargo claims, getting them to pressure port officials to either misrepresent or simply forget pertinent facts. Anyone doing business out of the Port of Mobile, Alabama knew Dustin's name, and thought twice before suing one of his clients. He made both himself and partner Hilary Herbert wealthy enough for the latter to pursue a political career and the former to grab tightly on Herbert's coattails.

The rest was history, but the next chapter would also require coattails. Herbert had no further aspirations than his current billet as Navy secretary. If Dustin was ever to attain the presidency, he needed to build a strong record as secretary of state that would demonstrate his talent and dispel any suspicions about his past. Given his uneasy relations within the Cleveland Administration, it seemed expedient to cultivate ties with the anti-Cleveland wing of the Democratic Party—the populist faction that chafed against the president's gold-buggery and parsimony.

Such a candidate now possessed a seat in the U.S. Senate, following a dramatic stint as a governor. His eloquence was legendary and his admirers were legion. Under the right circumstances, he could make a smooth transition to the presidency in 1896 and serve one term. Dustin determined that after four years it would then be safe to—in maritime jargon—dump his ballast.

The stars had to line up just so for all this to occur. War with Britain would definitely disrupt their formation.

Richard Olney sat staring at the landscape as it morphed from the rocky northeast to the flat, sandy mid-Atlantic. He was returning to Washington in triumph, having set the Cleveland Administration on a policy of vigorous hemispheric defense. Sipping a cognac in his private rail car, he savored the president's confidence in the official remonstrance, and imagined the terror the document was striking in the hearts of the British Tory leadership. Well-deserved, too, he thought, given the decades-long pattern of ignore and delay to which London had been adhering. Maybe force is what is needed in this matter. Talk is fruitless when only one side does so.

Concluding the long-running Venezuela Boundary Dispute with firm American resolve would breathe new life into the Cleveland presidency, Olney believed. With his fortunes ebbing within the party, the president needed a big issue to attack and dominate. Once victorious, Grover Cleveland would dwarf his enemies in the Democracy and receive a fourth consecutive nomination. With another term, Olney could then establish himself as an international statesman and, once retired, could command unprecedented fees for his law practice. The presidency itself was not beyond the realm of possibility either.

He was never sure, however, that the president's confidence in him was absolute. Approval of the remonstrance was heartening, but Olney knew that Gresham would have chosen a different approach…and that Cleveland would have agreed to it. His own supreme confidence wavered since assuming leadership at State. He could not always tell who his friends were and his top assistants—loyal to a man, save one—were doing their level best to root out the more treacherous employees of the department. Still, Lamont's wire from the morning was unsettling.

Dustin Boyle had issued no negative response to the remonstrance, likely knowing it would do no good. Just as probable was the fact that he would use his knowledge of the president's surgery in '93 to prevent any military action from commencing in the event of diplomatic stalemate. How could he have known? It made no sense. At any rate, the problem of Dustin Boyle would be the Secretary's first order of business when he arrived back in the capital. Ignoring him did not work, nor did threats. Olney decided he would have to be more imaginative. He needed to maneuver Dustin into a compromised position to neutralize the counselor's current advantage.

In the mean time, he would give Dustin plenty to do in order to make him feel secure. For starters, Dustin could assist in drafting the foreign policy sections of the president's annual message to Congress, to be delivered in December. Though Olney had no intention of using any of it, the contribution would flatter Dustin into thinking he had influence. Once off his guard, Olney was sure, Dustin would make an error in judgment and expose the secret that he—and many other middle-aged, wifeless men like him—harbored.

9

October, 1895

"Where are all my blessed bunnies?" The Commissioner of the New York City Police Department arrived home to his comfortable brownstone without the usual avalanche of hugs and kisses from his many offspring. Suddenly, scurrying feet were audible from the parlor, along with antiphonal shouts of "Papa's home!" Theodore Roosevelt crouched low, assuming grizzly posture for his unsuspecting chards. Upon their arrival he let out an ursine roar, batting the two youngest with his pretend claws. The older boys ran to his rear and climbed onto his back, as the pile of Roosevelts collapsed into a giggling heap. "Usually, you children get the jump on me as I enter," Teddy said breathlessly. "Why the delay?"

"Company, Papa," answered his oldest— the adoring, if rebellious, Alice. Though she was too old for the traditional arrival roughhousing, she ran to him and helped him up. Embracing her father, she queried, "Can we stay up late while you talk?"

Finding it always difficult to deny this winsome girl who was turning into a striking woman, he evaded: "Did Lodge arrive, that old Brahmin? Where is he?" As if on cue, Senator Henry Cabot Lodge appeared, Edith Roosevelt on his arm. A son of the Mayflower, Lodge exuded the elegance of wealth while retaining a puritan simplicity. He was always scrupulously groomed – as though receiving a daily haircut and beard trim – and immaculately attired.

Roosevelt kissed Edith and turned to Lodge, wringing his hand vigorously. "Good to see you, old man," he said in his usual high-pitched, clipped manner. "I keep meaning to visit with you in Washington, but my duties here keep me pretty busy."

"No apologies required, Teddy. You're doing good work here, but I suspect you'll be back in Washington soon enough," Lodge reassured him. "Edith has been telling me of the unusual hours you keep. I feared I might miss you altogether."

"Not at all. When I learned of your impending visit, I re-ordered my priorities," Roosevelt replied with a wink. "Let's go to my study and get down to brass tacks, shall we?"

"Papa!" Alice exclaimed, plaintively.

"Later, dear," Edith affirmed. "Your father and Senator Lodge have serious matters to discuss. They would not hold any interest for us." Alice shot Edith a defiant glare before stomping up the stairs. Roosevelt was always grateful to his wife for her willingness to play the wicked stepmother role, allowing him to retain hero status in the eyes of his first-born.

"Thank you, Edie. Now Cabot, let's have at it." He led the patrician Bostonian down a short corridor into a study that struck Lodge as more of a natural history museum. Like Roosevelt's familial home in Oyster Bay, the room was cluttered with stuffed fauna and books about fauna… and books about stuffing fauna. The two men sat side by side in red, leather-backed arm chairs, a ring-necked pheasant under glass gracing the table between them.

"There's some positive noise emanating from the State Department, Teddy," Lodge confided. "Seems the new man is willing to take a stronger position with the British over Venezuela."

Roosevelt probed: "Who's your source on that, Slim? Is this a serious change in policy? Or just a lot of hooey from the yellow-bellied crowd?"

"Olney drafted a remonstrance against all the foot-dragging across the pond. In short he's telling Salisbury to make haste with arbitration or prepare for another drubbing by American forces. I'm astounded, I tell you!" Lodge continued excitedly. "Could you imagine Gresham ever demonstrating that kind of backbone?"

Roosevelt smirked at the mention of the name. Though the late secretary's courage in battle during the War Between the States was to be applauded, his record as a diplomat was much less laudable. He seemed always to err on the side of spinelessness. Most vexing was his tendency to promote feckless policies as virtuous. His unsuccessful attempts to restore the Hawaiian queen were outrageously humiliating, as was his complete lack of support for the courageous Cuban revolutionaries. While never saying so out loud, Roosevelt believed Gresham's death occurred not a moment too soon. Still…

"Has Cleveland OK'd this document, Cabot?" The president and Roosevelt had alternately sparred and collaborated since the latter's days in the New York State Assembly. Governor Cleveland had good bona fides when it came to government reform and resisting corrupt influences. Roosevelt always thought of him as a man with whom he could do business, an opinion confirmed by his own retention at the Civil Service Commission after Cleveland's return to the presidency.

Yet the man was parochial. He was neither educated nor well-traveled. In fact he had never set foot in Washington until the eve of his first inauguration. His principles worked well enough in Buffalo and Albany but America was a world power, or at least should be. Cleveland was content to let the barbarians of the world run roughshod over the civilized classes, so long as the conflict did not penetrate U.S. borders. How could the man not understand that staying out of these fights actually invites aggression? Perhaps Gresham's cowardly pronouncements were really just part and parcel with the president's isolationism.

"That I can not say," Lodge replied, "but I do know that it was drafted at his request. I think His Corpulence is finally getting annoyed with Her Majesty."

Roosevelt adjusted his pince-nez glasses. "High time, I tell you. How many insults must we endure before the Big One takes offense?"

"The point, Theodore, is that momentum is building for strong and decisive action. Scruggs' pamphlet is enjoying national circulation and acclaim. We now have at least a reasonable secretary of State who does not shrink from every conflict. We're building support among southern Democrats in Congress who resent the British banks. May not be the best reason to back intervention, but I'll take it. Above all, the Commander-in-Chief is getting hot under his 20-inch collar!" Lodge summed up.

Roosevelt flashed his toothy grin. "This is an opportunity for us, then. We're heavily outmatched but we have geographical advantage. As I see it, Cleveland is putting some blood back into our flaccid navy, albeit too slowly. But the army lags even farther behind." He was standing now, in all of his pedantry. "Granting that English warships will be free to fire upon our eastern cities at will, we can still amass the men and munitions to take Canada and hold her until the British yield to our demands. I stand ready to raise a fighting regiment for just such a purpose."

Lodge suppressed a laugh. His friend was no more suited to lead a band of warriors than Lodge himself, the senator silently surmised. Despite Roosevelt's long stay in the Badlands of the Dakotas – roping and branding cattle, bagging wild game and confronting bandits – his voice and bearing were those of an eastern dandy. What hard-scrapple infantryman would pay him any heed?

"Teddy, had we been serious about strengthening our naval forces back during Cleveland's first term, we would not need to consider Canada."

"Agreed, agreed. Your speech on the Senate floor back in March convinced all men of good will of the necessity of naval primacy."

"Well," Lodge continued, "I'm hoping that this fight with Britain will not only serve to defend our interests in this hemisphere, but also provide an unforgettable lesson to this administration on preparedness."

Roosevelt bristled. "So let's get on with it. Momentum is all well and good but swift action moves nations."

Lodge sympathized with Roosevelt's impatience, but wanted the British to push Cleveland beyond the point of no return. Any more agitation on the part of Lodge or his partisans – slandered with the name "jingoes" – may well push the stubborn Grover Cleveland back into the camp of gutless Greshamism. Lodge then changed the subject: "Do you hear from Cecil these days?" he asked his old friend.

"Rice? Not lately. I assume he's lying low while this matter festers." Cecil Spring Rice was the secretary to the British legation in Washington and had forged close friendships with both Roosevelt and Lodge. As close as they were socially, Rice was a sealed container when it came to the machinations at the embassy. But Lodge was fishing.

"It behooves us to know as much as we can about London's attitude and her purposes," the senator intoned. "If we can confirm her intransigence into the near future, the administration will have no choice but to mobilize. As taciturn as Rice is on official subjects, he may let things slip if we catch him unawares."

Commissioner Roosevelt shook his head. "Not Rice, old man. He has an iron will. His integrity is set in granite. You know that."

"Perhaps." The Senator was silently conceiving. "Is he an anomaly among the legation…or typical?"

"Meaning what?"

Lodge sighed. "If the Prime Minister is feeling the heat on this boundary dispute, he is doubtless corresponding with his people over here. If he has little concern – as we suspect – then he fears no serious American response to his land appropriation between the Orinoco and the Essequibo. It follows that Ambassador Pauncefote and his staff are blissfully confident of American inaction. That sanguine attitude might be easily betrayed by a lesser man than Cecil Rice."

Roosevelt caught on: "So we want a weak man – who is also a credible diplomatic source – to convince the Big One that the Brits care not a lick for the Monroe Doctrine or American prerogatives!"

Lodge nodded approvingly at his friend and sometimes disciple. "A weak man is a weak link."

"That's a capital idea, Cabot, but a tall order. Finding such a man is nearly imp…"

Commissioner Roosevelt suddenly stopped his frenetic pacing. His mind jumped to his current job, far from the rarefied world of international politics under discussion. His present duties were honorable but pedestrian. They brought him into contact with the underside of humanity, replete with rape, murder, theft, drunkenness and vagrancy. And that was just among the constables in his charge.

He was equal to the task of changing all that, however. Above the mantel in the crowded study was a large pencil drawing of a police club – heavy, menacing, but easy to use and devastatingly effective. The Commissioner was intent on equipping each and every officer with "a big stick" before the year ended. A tool but also a symbol, the new and improved night stick would demonstrate that the law is violated at the criminal's peril. Progress in reforming the department was slow, but bearing fruit. The cops knew they were now being watched. Graft was on the decline. Sunday liquor laws – unpopular with the working class and immigrants – were nonetheless being enforced. Fake doctors were now apprehended and prosecuted for their quackery. Illegal gambling rings were promptly disbanded.

Yet there was an insidious cancer on the island of Manhattan that would not recede despite the most ferocious attacks by Roosevelt and his men. The flesh trade was alive and well in New York. As outraged as he was that women (and men) would dishonor their bodies for lucre, Roosevelt reserved his most intense contempt for the pimps and madams who greedily took their cut with seemingly no risk at all. Also galling was the seeming resignation to the situation on the part of the public. Trying to eradicate prostitution in the City of New York without public support was tantamount to draining a swamp with a teaspoon. The commissioner soldiered on nevertheless, sending in undercover plainclothesmen to catch the solicitations in the act and to sniff out hidden brothels. He would make as many pay for their crimes as best he could. He hated when any got away.

"Impossible?" Lodge inquired. "Is that what you were going to say?"

By Jove!" Startling his friend, Roosevelt swung around and leaned in close. "Cabot, do you really think you can obtain constructive information from someone so soft-headed and selfish?" he asked hopefully.

"I wouldn't trust divulged information from any other sort."

"Mind you, I will not be party to anything untoward," Teddy declared piously.

"Who's asking you to? What's on your mind, Theodore?"

"We apprehended a man. Twice. Last winter, I believe. Each time he was in the company of several young women who were known to us as harlots for hire. While under surveillance, he was paying each of them on the street to accompany him to *Washington* for assignations. He was arrested on the spot. It turned out that he was a British diplomat and, according to custom, we released him unpunished. Four or five women, Cabot!"

"As if we don't have enough of that in Washington already," Lodge observed. "What's his name?"

"A thoroughly disreputable, drunken and portly fellow. Homely, too. He never would have passed muster with *my* Civil Service Commission."

"Very good. What's his name?"

"Of the most despicably soft and selfish character! An out-and-out reprobate!!"

"Theodore! His name?"

"Let's take a stroll over to headquarters and look him up. I'll ask Edith to hold dinner."

Sarah Corbett knew from her mother's shared memories that oppressors perverted the work ethic to maximize profits and minimize their own exertion. Slaves were always exhorted to apply themselves to their assignments, sometimes by means of the lash. Yet the more sophisticated landholders held out the mirage of freedom before their slaves, to be rewarded at an undetermined time in exchange for an unlimited measure of effort. Still, none of that mattered to this first-generation free woman. She viewed industry as the great equalizer. While work was a curse under slavery, it was a blessing in liberty.

Beginning her day before dawn, she donned a plain, gray dress – baggier and much less elegant than her upstairs uniform – and white apron with head cap. Even before her breakfast, Sarah began the herculean task of sorting the enormous piles of laundry left in her care. Each article was to be scrutinized, categorized by fabric, identified by stain and logged into a mammoth register. Stains and grease spots were set aside for special treatment while the remaining linens and clothing were heaped according to material: white linens, body linens, sheets and collars in one pile; colored cotton fabrics in a second; fine muslins; woolen materials; and heavy, more durable items in the fifth heap.

Sarah went at her task as though performing heart surgery – with total concentration. Hers was a story of upward mobility within the restrictions of Negro womanhood at the close of the 19th century. Her mother escaped from a Virginia plantation in 1862 after being forcibly impregnated by the overseer. By her own wits and the grace of God, she managed to travel from Culpeper, Virginia to the nation's capital by foot and stolen horse. The war had exacted enough of a toll that fewer men were available to intercept runaways. Having once overheard the father of her baby cursing the freedmen's organizations then mobilizing in Washington, she delivered herself to the steps of Asbury Church, a hotbed of refugee support and activism. Sarah came into the world within those very walls while her mother found a community that taught her to read and secured her a cleaning position at the Freedmen's Hospital. With her meager wages, she found a dwelling for her two-person family near the hospital. It was filthy and infested…but it was hers. As soon as Sarah was seven, she accompanied her mother to work and learned the difference between disadvantage and helplessness. Here she encountered the decrepit, lame and lunatic. They had neither foremen nor overseers, yet were in bondage nonetheless.

From her youth Sarah resolved to make the most of every opportunity as long as she possessed working limbs, faculties and mind. Her mother died of consumption on her

13th birthday. Devastated, Sarah nevertheless remembered her oath. Through her friends at Asbury Church, she obtained a laundress position at the U.S. Soldiers' Home, an asylum for aged and permanently crippled veterans. After three years on staff, she was assigned to tend to the laundry at Anderson Cottage, a summer retreat on the Soldiers' Home grounds for Presidents Buchanan, Lincoln and Hayes. By both good fortune and design, her handiwork caught the eye of Mrs. Lucy Hayes, who immediately took a liking to Sarah. The servant girl was at once serious and winsome. Best of all, she was abstemious, a trait highly valued by the First Lady known pejoratively as "Lemonade Lucy".

As time passed Sarah was getting hints by Mrs. Hayes that she would be hired to work at the Executive Mansion, a coveted assignment. Those intimations, however, were nullified by the President himself, who resolutely stuck to his pronouncement of serving only one term. While Sarah awaited her next favorable circumstance, Mrs. Hayes recommended her to the wife of the Honorable Lionel Sackwille-West, Envoy Extraordinary and Minister Plenipotentiary from the United Kingdom. The diplomatic mission in Washington would soon be an embassy, the outgoing First Lady advised Mrs. West, and you want the very best servants for your official residence.

The position was proffered and Sarah had been there ever since. She had to temper her usual vivaciousness for the understated English, but she was treated with kindness, admittedly of the condescending variety. Although other Americans were on the household staff, Sarah was the only

Negro and political necessity required the new ambassador – Lord Julian Pauncefote – to exploit her efficiency without upsetting cultural norms. To that end she lived by day in the basement laundry rooms, her own sleeping quarters adjacent to them. When Nigel Alderson requested her presence upstairs for certain evenings, the ambassador deferred to the judgment of the nocturnal attaché.

Sarah loved the ornate and formal rooms of the embassy's main floor. And she loved interacting with important men from the U.S. and British governments. From the time her mother got wind of Asbury Church as a refuge for runaways, she instilled in Sarah the importance of keeping her ears open. The lesson was not lost on the girl. At every chance, she positioned herself within earshot of conversation. The strategy was as exciting as it was enlightening. Suspecting that Alderson was up to something crooked, she was surprised to encounter Mr. Dustin Boyle in his web. Sarah trusted her own instincts. This was an upright man, an idealist and – at bottom – a sad man.

Alderson's usual guests were often drunk, disrespectful of their surroundings and loud. Other than a few seconds of raised voices, Dustin Boyle was soft-spoken and serious. She knew he was a southerner at first glance: sitting erect while looking completely comfortable, completely self-possessed. She rarely saw that posture among northerners. Also revealing was his conduct toward her, as if the inbred attitude of racial superiority was struggling with his similarly inbred Southern chivalry. The reference to Louisiana just confirmed what she already knew.

Despite the violent treatment her mother suffered under slavery, Sarah gave Dustin the benefit of the doubt. Most likely, he supported the injustice of his native region. Yet he struck her as a good man with regrets, a man who needed to confess sin but, for whatever reason, could not. His involvement with Mr. Alderson would come to no good, she knew that much. That man was up to something beyond the usual duties of an attaché. Her inquisitiveness – though often earning her a rebuke from the Housekeeper – led her to learn much about how the embassy operated. Among the many tidbits she absorbed was that attachés were representatives of particular government ministries back in London. There were attachés from the War ministry, the Exchequer, the Admiralty and the Board of Trade. Yet Alderson never identified his government sponsor, nor did his evening conferences have any official air to them. Mr. Boyle was in danger, and liaisons with the mysterious attaché would only increase the hazard. Her mind told her to tend to her own affairs, but her heart could not leave the Alderson-Boyle relationship alone. With steely resolve, she planned to uncover the secrets the very next time she was summoned upstairs.

10

"Señor Captain!" Mendoza shouted. "I must speak to you, sir!"

Patiño turned his horse about, glaring with hatred. Raising a hand to halt the procession, he trotted his horse back to the prisoners' wagon.

"You do not summon me, you filthy little stoolpigeon!" He brandished his sword, pointing at the nervous engineer. "Next time you address me like that, I will decapitate you. Am I understood?"

Mendoza always counted himself as a scientist first. He was not, he assured himself and others, given to superstition or theological passions. But Patiño tested this self-image. The man was pure evil. In spite of himself, Mendoza prayed for supernatural protection against this embodied demon.

"I am sorry to delay you, sir," Mendoza said, his voice quaking. "But I believe a navigational error has occurred. I have been to this region before—several times, actually—and I must warn the Captain that we are coming perilously close to the Schombürgk Line, if we have in fact not crossed it already."

The officer looked at the clueless prisoners, then back at the engineer. He laughed wickedly and conceded, "Your memory is sharp, Mendoza. We are approaching the fake boundary line, but what of it? We do not recognize it, and lately, neither do the stinking British."

"My point exactly, Captain Patiño. The British are claiming the boundary is west of the Schombürgk Line which, by their interpretation, puts us in British Guiana even now. Should we not turn back?"

"So now the rat has turned chicken. I hope you can decide what species you are eventually, Rafael. Until then, there is work to be done. We are only a few hundred yards from our destination. Perform your assignment, perform it well and we will take you back to your chicken coup." With a snort of contempt, he returned to his lead position.

Suddenly, an aggressive jaguar emerged from hiding, hissing at Patiño and the forward party. Its sleek, tawny coat and rosette markings formed a beautiful counterpoint to the stocky feline's powerful jaws and lethal paws. The men backed their horses up nervously as the cat advanced, old and sick, perhaps, breaking the usual behavior pattern for its species. Patiño ordered his lieutenant to dismount and dispatch the animal with his sword. After a muted protest was rebuffed by the captain, the officer timidly got off the horse and brandished his blade, slicing the air furiously. After a seemingly endless dance of parrying, thrusting, bobbing and weaving, the jaguar grew fatigued and retreated into the forest.

Though he briefly thought of making a break for it, Mendoza figured that any attempt at escape would end in apprehension and torture. He was also intrigued. Strange,

Mendoza thought. The Victor Patiño he knew would have simply shot the animal on sight. Why the extended swordplay and wasted time? Was the captain as hesitant in reaching their destination as his prisoners? What possible purpose was there to this expedition through the forest?

Patiño signaled for the convoy to proceed, and galloped on ahead. Mendoza was sure he worked a project here. As they came to a clearing, the terrain became flat and open. Straight ahead was an expansive river bank.

"Mi Madre!" he muttered under his breath while tugging anxiously at his unkempt mustache.

He knew where they were. This was the Rio Cuyuni that Mendoza had surveyed the previous year for mineral deposits. The project had lost two men. The shallow edges of the river bed dropped off suddenly to depths of 30 feet or more. Teeming in those depths were the most lethal piranha on the continent. Still, it was illogical that the men would be taken all this way just to be fed to the fish. Then, in a flash, it dawned on him: President Crespo was going to take the gold, and use expendable personnel to do it. Moments later, he confirmed just how dangerous this trip was.

Looking across the vast expanse of grassland to the right, he could see a small unfinished garrison of stone and wood on the distant horizon. That fortification must have been erected recently, Mendoza decided, squinting to make out detail. What looked like cannon embrasures were cut in the walls of the fortification, though no guns were visible.

Above the edifice flew the Union Jack.

Patiño must be insane, Mendoza thought. He was going to get them all killed.

The train south was late and the connecting carriage ride was interminably slow due to inclement weather. After 20 hours of travel, his destination finally came into view. Unfortunately, he would have to head back to Washington right after his meeting if he was to be at his desk Monday morning without provoking suspicion. Dustin approached the large, federal-style house at the top of Arsenal Hill. From this perch, the Governor's Mansion hovered over Columbia, South Carolina. The white edifice, ornamented with black shutters, was fully electrified, and Dustin was grateful to see lights on after midnight. Although the former governor figured into Dustin's long-term vision, his immediate assistance was also essential.

A Negro houseman in crisp white serving jacket and black bow tie greeted Dustin without a smile. "Right this way, sir," were his only words as he lead him into a small drawing room amazingly similar to Nigel Alderson's preferred meeting place at the British Embassy. The furniture, however, was decidedly early-American, and said to have belonged to former Governor and Declaration of Independence signer Edward Rutledge. Senator Benjamin Tillman had been mildly annoyed at the delay until he beheld the image of the South's most fearless warrior, the choicest fruit of the white race in Tillman's way of seeing things.

"Can I believe my eye, or has Major Dustin Boyle graced this threshold?"

"I'm so sorry to disturb you at this ungodly hour, Governor," Dustin apologized, using Tillman's preferred title, though he had just completed his first year as a U.S. Senator. States' rights men were not eager to trumpet the federal offices they held. "Events are moving so quickly, I needed to speak with you before the Senate convenes next month."

"Come in, son, come in," Tillman said, showing him to an overstuffed chair. The Governor's Mansion reminded Dustin of his Louisiana home, and he half expected Caleb to show up with the latest batch of harvest statistics. Dustin and Tillman had agreed upon the house as a contact point for fear the national press corps—and the Lamonts and Olneys—would stoke a public scandal should they be seen together in Washington. Tillman's gubernatorial successor agreed to host the senator upon request, more out of fear than love.

"I keep a farmer's hours, wherever I may be, and I expect to rise in about three and one-half hours. But if this matter is urgent, I am at your service, sir."

"You honor me, Governor, with your tolerance," Dustin flattered, as the men took their seats. "You were elected only a year ago, and already you are a man of influence in the upper chamber. The respect you command from your colleagues brought me here."

"You exaggerate my impact, young man. If I had any real influence, that old bag of beef you work for would be standing trial in the Senate." Tillman—a Democrat—was a leader of the swelling anti-Cleveland wing of the party. Although he was the same age as Dustin, his prematurely graying hair and superior political stature led him to address his prized political advisor in a paternal manner.

"I understand your sentiments, Governor. I believe the president knows that his number is up politically in '96. I am concerned about something more pressing, though." Dustin leaned in closely toward Tillman. The senator was even homelier than he remembered. It was almost as though the South Carolinian went out of his way to repulse people. "The boundary issue between Venezuela and Great Britain is coming to a rolling boil, as you must know."

"I'm following the whole thing with great interest."

"Then you must know the absolute wreckage that military intervention will bring about. This is the War of Northern Aggression all over again, using our young men as cannon fodder for British guns in order to impose a warped vision of justice."

Tillman stared at Dustin knowingly, but said nothing.

"I am working to convince the president not to resort to arms in trying to resolve this. But I know that if Congress declares war, he will feel duty-bound to prosecute it, regardless of where he stands on the matter personally. That's why I came to see you."

Tillman gave Dustin the once-over, then turned his head 90 degrees to the side before speaking. As with portraits and public addresses, the senator preferred that people see his profile during conversations, thereby concealing the vacant socket where his left eye once resided.

"Major, you honor me with your very presence, much less your support for my presidential bid next year." He rose from his chair and stood, looking at the floor. "You can be assured, sir, that I will name you secretary of State, as we discussed, after quietly securing that pardon you require. It's a travesty that such a measure need be taken, since you were entirely in the right."

"I appreciate your confidence, Governor. But if this war is ignited, it will change the entire political landscape. Your candidacy may be obscured by a host of returning and ambitious veterans. If the Brits win, which is probable, the Republicans will ride back into 1600 Pennsylvania Avenue on the charge of national humiliation. If we manage to repulse them, which is hard to fathom, one of the generals—Ezekiel Swanson, most likely—will be all but crowned, and they are all Republicans, anyway."

"Major, you and I represent the hardworking farmers of the South, who are being shackled to a slave economy while being denied the right to slaves. The goldbugs and corporatists who currently hold sway over this administration keep money expensive, adding more weight to the debts that are crushing our people. Ours is the only race fit to maintain an American civilization, and we are destroying ourselves. The quest for empire will just exacerbate this trend. This is why I set my face to running."

Dustin felt more secure as Tillman lectured. It was a small price to pay for such an important alliance.

Tillman continued: "You know where I stand on empire. I was with you on Hawaii, and stand with you on Cuba. We can not bear the burden of supporting inferior races. And the jingoes will have us subsidize every indigenous brute and half-breed they can find."

Dustin suspected this concession was a mere preface to refusal. "But?"

"There is a difference here. This is about gold. The British have too much and this administration is bent on keeping gold the singular basis for our money. Were you proud to see that pile of blubber in the White House bowing and scraping to those corrupt Wall Street bankers, all so we could put more gold back into the treasury? It was all so unnecessary. If silver—or the white producers in this country—have any future, we must put an end to British acquisition. As it stands now, Baron Edmund de Rothschild practically owns our government."

Dustin knew Tillman had a flair for exaggeration, which added to his considerable political gifts. His reference to the London banking tycoon reflected his nativist resentments. Surely, though, he had to see that there was more than one way to skin a cat.

"Governor, when you are president, you can assert these values with England, and use trade and tariff policy for leverage. We have to get you there, first," Dustin implored.

"You fought admirably in the War of Northern Aggression, my friend. But I fought during Reconstruction. I laid my life on the line when all was lost, so we could consolidate white rule as is meet and proper. I battled Negro militias and Union blue bellies, and have the notches on my guns to show for it. Then, I fought my way to the top of the South Carolina Democratic Party, rebuking corruption and cowardice at every level. I was the governor. Now, I am a United States senator on his way to the presidency, with your help."

Dustin began to panic. "Will you help yourself, and denounce the war camp on the Senate floor?"

"I am dead in earnest, Dustin. It is all vanity if we continue to allow British banks to dictate our monetary policy. A president so shackled is nothing but a shameful symbol of impotence."

Dustin winced at the imagery. He was confused by Tillman's obsession with the gold standard. Couldn't he understand the futility of a war over the Venezuelan boundary?

The unrivaled demagogue's right eye narrowed into a glare during the long silence. Then, "I'll make the speech, Major."

Hugely relieved, Dustin exhaled enough anxiety to fill a dirigible.

"I just wanted," the Senator continued, smiling now, "to give you a foretaste of 1897."

Ben Tillman did not go back to bed after Dustin left him. Instead, he paced back and forth for hours, the wheels in his head relentlessly turning. The major had good political instincts and an immaculate background. In Tillman's mind, Dustin's recruiting assignment in England only burnished his credentials: more than a pardon, he deserved a medal. In any event, a prospective president intent on restoring Southern political fortunes should be grateful to collaborate with this brave and intelligent warrior.

One flaw, nevertheless, was glaring. This encounter confirmed a suspicion Tillman harbored, but would never admit to himself: Dustin Boyle's heart was not in it. Whatever his history, whatever his pronouncements against the Yankees, Dustin was not committed to the principles of white Southern agrarianism. He simply wanted to be president...after Tillman, that is. His motivations seemed increasingly murky, but one thing was clear: the Confederate hero had written off white supremacy, if in fact he had ever adhered to it. Tillman would have to secure Dustin Boyle's loyalty on a less solid foundation. Yes, he would deliver the speech.

And expect payment in kind.

11

"Mr. Alderson speaks highly of your abilities," Dustin told Sarah as she again poured the tea. He was growing used to her distinctive manner. "You must feel honored to have earned his confidence."

The servant shot him an amused look while quickly tending to an imperfection she found in a spoon.

"I'm always gratified when my effort is recognized, Mr. Boyle," she said, shining the implement with concentrated fury. "Honor, though, is not something I seek or expect for my work here."

Deep in his guts, Dustin believed her. They could give her a crown and scepter and she would not change in outlook or attitude, he was sure. He saw in her, strangely, both hungry ambition and complete contentment.

Sarah changed the subject. "When do you think this Depression will end?"

Taking his turn to look amused, Dustin adopted a patronizing tone: "You ask the questions a banker asks. I think you're safe from our dismal economy."

"I do not doubt my ultimate safety, Mr. Boyle. I ask for your sake more than mine."

"My sake?" She was an enigma for the ages, Dustin decided.

"Yes, sir. The Democrats' fortunes are ebbing the longer it lasts. What happens to you if the Republicans get elected next year?"

As surprised as he was at Sarah's knowledge of current affairs, he had to confess that he had not given the Republicans any thought. He was consumed with Tillman getting the Democratic nomination. Running on an anti-Cleveland platform in '96, the party could capture popular discontent while retaining the White House.

"I'm not too worried. I've got plenty of money." Dustin instantly regretted that comment. It sounded smug and—for whatever reason—he wanted her to respect him. He was about to amend it when Nigel Alderson made his standard grand entrance.

"Late again, I know. Terribly sorry, Dustin, but my many duties keep me in a perpetual state of tardiness," Alderson said, extending his hand.

Dustin could see Sarah's dark eyebrows arch in surprise at Alderson's explanation.

"Don't give it a thought, Nigel. Thank you, as always, for fitting me in."

Standing behind the British diplomat, Sarah looked in no hurry to leave. Alderson looked back at her and then again to Dustin, saying with a laugh, "She would sit in on every meeting if she could."

Dustin gave her a half-smile as Sarah retreated, shutting the door quietly behind her.

"I had to take desperate measures since last we met, Nigel."

"More desperate than what we're doing now?"

"Indeed. Troops out west were being called back from their outposts, presumably for the purposes of mobilization."

"Outrageous! We've not even responded to Olney. What did you do?"

"Let us just say that I convinced the military authorities to slow down. But the decreased tempo will not endure indefinitely."

Alderson leaned back, evincing a troubled expression. Dustin continued.

"You see, by not responding, your government is—after a fashion—responding in the negative."

"Oh, gammon and spinach!" Alderson sputtered dismissively. "You Americans must learn to delay gratification."

Coming from Alderson, that remark reeked of comic irony. Dustin suppressed a laugh and came to his point: "You need to lean on the ambassador a little harder, Nigel."

"You did not spend enough time in England, Dustin. We make rational decisions based on careful study. We take pains not to be impulsive."

"This issue is decades old, Nigel. There is no moisture in the pot left to simmer. We need a response from Lord Salisbury *post haste*."

"I have to pick and choose my battles, old boy."

"Can you speak with Lord Pauncefote tomorrow?"

After an uncomfortable pause, Alderson shrugged. "I suppose I must, but can make no promises as to the result."

"Do your utmost, Nigel, please. I can not hold back the legions when the emperor orders them to march."

Alderson nodded impatiently and stood. "I have business upstairs. You will hear from me soon."

Dustin was mystified as the attaché hurried from the room. Sarah returned to the doorway, apparently intent on fishing.

"So many appointments so late in the evening. What do you make of it, Mr. Boyle?"

"I can not comment, I'm afraid. I do not know. Unfortunately, I have an early morning, so must take my leave."

"I will show you out, sir." Heading to the door, Sarah added, "He needs a friend like you. I think he is troubled in his spirit."

Dustin was struck by her language. Nigel Alderson impressed Dustin as all flesh and no spirit. Could this washerwoman have any idea of the inner workings of a professional diplomat?

"Ours is a professional relationship, Sarah. Mr. Alderson does not share his hopes and dreams with me."

"Would you welcome it if he did?"

He looked at her quizzically for a long while. Was she sincerely concerned with the welfare of a man with whom she shared no history, no blood and no aspirations? To care that much would surely be dangerous for this clueless servant.

"He can find better confessors than I. Good night."

As he left, Dustin had a bad taste in his mouth. Alderson's agreement to hasten an answer from the ambassador was offset by a lack of presence. His mind was elsewhere and that was a problem. As always, Nigel Alderson was becoming a full-time job.

Sarah watched him descend the steps and make his way to the street. It is Dustin Boyle who needs a friend, she was told. She was born for such a time as this.

The 15-year old lieutenant, looking every inch a man, dismounted from his midnight-black Morgan horse and strode purposefully toward the veranda of his familial home. The many months spent at the Louisiana Seminary for Learning and Military Institute buffeted the young officer into an imposing physical and intellectual specimen. After a warm reunion of tearful embraces with his mother and sisters, Dustin Boyle basked in his father's pride and

*admiration. It was a moment of sheer elation. The two
retired to Justus' study for a discussion between men.*

*"You do honor to our name, Dusty," Justus assured him. "I
just wish it had not come to this. Your troops go into this
war at a severe disadvantage."*

*"As did Washington and the Continental Army, Daddy.
Right usually wins out," the son predicted confidently.*

*Justus' green eyes sparkled and his white mane was like a
fleece conferring all manner of wisdom.*

*"I can only hope, my boy, I can only hope. You have
excelled at school to such a degree, I am saddened
nonetheless that you have to interrupt your education."*

*"The Seminary is closing, probably for the duration of the
war, which should not be long."*

*"I suppose that's best for all concerned. Have you said
farewell to Caleb? He's been asking for you."*

*"I stopped down at the cabins first. Sanford told me that
Caleb and Lizzie were having some 'married' time. Well, I
know what that means, so I told them I would visit with
them before I left tonight."*

*Justus looked puzzled for a moment, then resumed his
fatherly advice. "However things turn out, you have a
future in this state. Avoid heroics, if you can, but eschew
timidity as well. We want you back here with your body—
and your reputation—unharmed."*

"That is a narrow path to tread, Daddy. Don't most men fall off one side or the other?"

"Not Boyles, son."

"I'll do my best, sir."

"I can ask no more of you, Dusty. While I think the Fort Sumter attack was a mistake, and this war premature, I am still proud that you have volunteered. Think of it, my son a lieutenant at the age of 15. Reports I received from your instructors told me you excel in every discipline. It is no wonder that you are the youngest officer in the Confederate States Army."

"I doubt many of my brother officers had such a fine upbringing as I," Dustin told his father with a sincere and full heart.

Justus began to mist, then cleared his throat. "Let's dine, Dusty. One last family dinner for a while."

"Yes, sir. Afterward I'll ride over to Caleb's."

Justus paused, looking at the floor. Raising his head, he smiled wryly and said, "I know a pretty young lady who might like to see you first."

Priscilla Girard was the object of Dustin's young love. A shapely strawberry blonde at once exuding innocence and allure, Priscilla treated Dustin like Sir Galahad: a handsome and brave knight willing to slay all oncoming dragons. Her desire for him stirred him at the level of instinct and he found it difficult to detach from her when so excited. Detach, however, he did because the Boyle name was synonymous with virtue in St. John the Baptist Parish.

Now grinning back at his father, Dustin said, "That is true. I reckon Caleb can wait."

Dustin despised himself ever since for allowing hot-bloodedness to override friendship and fraternal affection. Caleb was dead by the time Dustin returned that night.

Nigel Alderson dismissed the footman for the evening, choosing instead to receive his distinguished guest himself. "Congressman, you are as punctual as you are painstaking. Can I have my girl get you anything before we get down to business?"

"English food is horrid, Nigel. Let's just get to the main course, shall we?" the legislator countered in a flat, Midwestern accent.

"As you wish, sir," Alderson deferred, gesturing to the staircase.

The congressman was, like Alderson, somewhat pear-shaped, topped by an unruly mop of auburn hair. His clothes were respectable but not first-class, perhaps the only suit he owned. Yet he never failed to deliver when it came to compensation. Men like this helped Alderson to live in the civilized manner to which he was accustomed.

Once on the second floor, Alderson opened a door revealing a narrower set of stairs leading to a less ostentatious part of the embassy. They finally came to a non-descript door where they parted company. On his way back downstairs, Alderson made a mental note to remind Lord Pauncefote of Dustin's outreach, and of the increased urgency in answering.

If the two of them—Alderson and Boyle—could broker a peaceful solution to the boundary dispute with Venezuela, he could go from unappreciated attaché to perhaps becoming an ambassador himself. With his very own embassy to play with, Nigel Alderson could one day afford a peerage and a seat in the House of Lords. Those who today scorned him as a lightweight would then have to eat their words.

Perhaps his appeals for peace would be more persuasive if he were an out and out pacifist, like Henry Lane. In fact, the blood and horror of war never weighed heavily on Dustin Boyle. He had seen eager young southern patriots surge fearlessly onto battle fields, only to return – if they, in fact, survived – traumatized and haunted. As a young officer and leader of men, he desperately wanted to relate to his soldiers, to be their hero and a confidante for them. It was no use. To so many of them, rattled and sobered by carnage, the loud reports of cannon and musket fire constituted a dreaded call to terror and doom.

To Dustin, on the other hand, those same thunderous claps were invitations to peace of mind, alluring siren songs of a world that made sense. He rushed into it headlong and immersed himself in the saturnalia of blood, expertly picking off Yankees with his father's Colt percussion revolver, or else lacerating them with his repetitively-drilled saber technique. The violence had a momentum all its own, as though unstoppable until only a sole survivor remained. Men from other regiments heard of his bravery and stood in awe. His own men, by contrast, concluded that he was unbalanced, an opinion once voiced to him by a dying comrade.

Outstanding commanders help their soldiers to use fear to their advantage. Dustin's handicap was that he could not understand fear in battle. To him, theaters of war were safe havens in a universe of injustice. Ruffians were dispatched in combat, the arrogant brought low. What sweeter justice was there than the flowing blood of bloodsuckers? Common sense dictated that if war was thrust upon a nation, that nation must prosecute it to its logical conclusion. Only fools choose caution when facing an enemy that leaves only death and impoverishment in its wake.

Few of his soldiers knew their teen-aged commander at Seven Pines. They were alienated by his bayou accent and unnerved by his lack of caution. Making matters worse was the alien Chesapeake terrain of peninsular Virginia. The low, flat coastal plain did not quickly absorb the torrential rains of spring, and many had to sleep on cold, wet ground in cold, wet clothing. Illness rivaled combat as a cause of death.

Ordered by General Joseph Johnston to lead his squad south along the saturated Chickahominy River bank in search of isolated Federal troops, Dustin was more upset by the anxiety of his own men than by the surprisingly large Union encampment they discovered at a distance.

"That's a mess of blue bellies, Captain. There's not enough of us to take them," shouted Sergeant Rufus Belding.

"Should we surrender, Belding? Is that your suggestion?" Dustin's tone was at once mocking and menacing. He wanted the man's friendship but would not abide cowardice.

Sergeant Belding was six foot two and 10 years Dustin's senior. Despite his greater experience, he made every effort to show the 17-year old captain respect, but was unnerved nonetheless by the boy's impulsiveness. Speaking through chapped lips and three remaining teeth, the longish brown-haired soldier moved his horse close to Dustin's and spoke softly.

"I only mean to suggest, sir, that a short retreat might buy us some time for re-enforcements. The Yankees haven't spied us, as yet."

Dustin looked into the experienced warrior's pleading blue eyes. His previously severe expression became benign and he even gave Belding a slight smile.

"So the cover of tall corn has concealed our presence and you believe we can make a quick escape with no Union soldier the wiser, is that it?"

"It's all I'm asking, Captain, just to come back with more men," Belding assured him with a tone of relief.

Continuing to stare into Belding's eyes, Dustin raised his pistol high in the air and fired a loud shot. The squad listened to the Union encampment then come to life. They stood frozen in terror.

Dustin turned his mare about and glared at the men he wished would love him: "It seems we have no choice now but to fight. Any man who runs from this duty will be shot. There are no cowards among us as long as I am leading you. "

As their modest squadron charged the larger contingent, the sound of feet and hooves crushing the corn stalks eclipsed the sound of gunfire coming from down river. As always, Dustin took the forward position and unsheathed his heavy saber from its scabbard, preparing to slice as taught by instructors at the Louisiana State Seminary of Learning and Military Institute. Without warning, a Union non-com on horseback approached him from the right side. Using a circular moulinet technique with his broadsword, Dustin confused his attacker before striking hard on the Yankee's shoulder, dropping him from his horse in a spray of scarlet. Continuing toward the Union gathering, he listened hard to confirm the fact that his men were behind him. What he did not hear, however, was the minié ball that grazed his horse and pierced him close to the crotch. As the startled mare threw him painfully to the ground, Dustin could hear the cheers of warriors when felling an enemy.

Before losing consciousness, he wondered whether that ovation was coming from the Blue or the Gray.

Like Seven Pines in 1862, the battles Dustin fought in 1895 were lonely ones. There were no confidantes upon whom he could rely. It appeared, again like Seven Pines, as though every party to the controversy was working against him. He would not be deterred, in any event. He would ride herd on Nigel Alderson even if it destroyed their friendship. The stakes were just too important.

12

Nigel Alderson liked living in Washington, especially during the Cleveland era. He related to the president's personality: not one to suffer fools, nor one to deny his appetites, if the rumors were true. Grover Cleveland would steer the ship of state intelligently, Alderson surmised, the current cacophony notwithstanding. More than admiring the administration, though, the hedonist-diplomat appreciated the perks the city offered to the political class.

His haunts in London were not the finest establishments, nor were they the seediest, and he followed suit in the American capital. Like the young Grover Cleveland of Buffalo, New York, Alderson enjoyed the raucous atmosphere of a German beer garden, though he loathed Germans. In fact, contrary to his ancestry, he came to like his beef warm and his beer cold. Also like the president, his frequent patronage led to substantial girth. But eating and drinking were only small attractions for the British attaché. One favored spot was Kozel's at 14th and S Streets, where he indulged his stomach, abused his liver and…

This autumn day was warm and business was slow, and Alderson surveyed the outdoor patio for any new points of interest. Other than some federal clerks out for mid-day relief from their ruts, only a few patrons loitered.

Then she appeared.

It took only seconds before he was literally stupefied. She was stunning. No, stunning was not strong enough. She made him light in the head. And she was looking right at him with her inviting blue eyes, brimming with interest. He knew that if she removed her hat and let down her chestnut-red hair, it would drop to her shoulders in the most wild and care-free style. She was medium-tall in height and perfect in every dimension. She would be a profitable worker, he was sure, but he could not imagine sharing her with another. Alderson returned her gaze and lifted his stein in invitation.

"Bridgette Maher. May I sit?"

"I didn't think you were waiting tables, dear."

She flashed him an incredibly winning grin, confirming to him that resistance on his part was futile. True, she was Irish, and by breeding and custom, Alderson hated the Irish. Their emotionalism, their superstitions, their religion and overall boorishness was all fodder for his ingrained contempt. Without British rule, they would descend into barbarism, he was sure.

But their colleens were another matter altogether.

"So, Bridgette Maher, what brings you to this establishment? Don't you people play with your little beads this time of day?" The words were insulting, but Alderson's expression displayed nothing but desire.

"Ordinarily, yes, Mr.___?"

"Call me Nigel."

"Ordinarily yes, Nigel, but my rosary has brought me nothing but disappointment lately. I keep running into Englishmen."

Alderson loved quick rejoinders. He hoped his giddiness would not be too evident. "I've not seen you here before. Are you new to Washington?"

"No, Nigel. I'm just looking for a better class of friends. I'm done wasting my time with men who are going nowhere." She displayed only the slightest trace of brogue. She struck him as somewhat educated…and tantalizingly defiant. Her flirtatious smile never left her face, as she recounted her voyage to America, and explained her very definite goals and objectives. She had her sights set on becoming the premier hostess in the capital, and would take whatever actions she deemed necessary to ascend to that status.

"Sounds to me like you want to be a lady of influence, Bridgette." He paused— fearing he should not offer too much too soon—but dove in anyway. "I'm the top assistant to the British ambassador," he fibbed. "I can introduce you to other important personages. Frankly, my dear, an Irish immigrant – a woman at that – will need a sophisticated patron to smooth her rough edges, if she wants to be of influence in this city. Who better than an English diplomat with aristocratic blood?"

Bringing her face near to his, she responded: "And who better to quicken the veins of a cold-blooded English aristocrat than a warm-blooded colleen from Kilkenny?"

Her hot breath broke any hesitation he had left. Ecstatic, Alderson believed he had hooked his best conquest and recruit yet. He was unconscious of the net enfolding round about him.

Henry Lane did not like New York. Its constant pulsating set his teeth on edge. The non-stop street traffic left more manure than the city workers could pick up in a timely fashion and the walkways were teeming with self-important financiers and their mindless clerks. Checking into the mammoth Gilsey House, with its 300 rooms, felt like committing himself to an insane asylum. After quickly depositing his change of clothes in his room, Lane descended six floors on the hotel elevator and headed for the tea room for a meeting he had already delayed twice.

He was annoyed by the newly installed electric lights in the tea room, believing them appropriate for a business office or a hospital, but not for a place of dining and civilized conversation. Taking a table that overlooked 29th Street, he sat down and lit his pipe, his hands fiddling nervously in the process.

"Goodness, Hen, you look like you're going to the gallows. Relax."

Henry Lane stood to greet his old comrade-in-arms and college mate. Dustin Boyle hardly changed, he thought, save for dark circles under his eyes and a careworn expression, despite the reassuring smile. He wore a dark brown suit and a tan bow tie, looking very official. Lane steeled himself for the ordeal.

"Dustin," he said breathlessly, shaking his hand, "you look like time stood still. Obviously, Washington agrees with you."

"You flatter both me and Washington. You look well, yourself. I imagine upstate is a pleasant locale for a scholar."

"I hope to remain and die there, my friend. It has been a place of healing and sustenance."

Dustin noticed Lane's expression as he spoke of his home. It was relaxing with every word, his voice transitioning to a more serene tone. Clearly, the professor did not want to be dragged to Manhattan, and may be hesitant to aid him. Dustin would have to beat around the bush for a bit.

"I run into some former brothers-in-arms down in Washington from time to time, Hen," Dustin remarked, lighting a cigar. "It's nice to find some sympathy among friends once in a while. I have the Yankee boot on my neck most of the time."

Lane's anxiety returned with a vengeance. He would not have this conversation. "I've closed that chapter of life, Dustin. North and South, Blue and Gray, we're all Americans now."

"Granted Hen, but you can't will the past away. The northern men I work for so alienated the Union veterans the last time in power that they have swung to the other extreme. Southerners in town have so inadvertently talked me up that the president's men fear I will single-handedly lose the election for the Democracy. All they want is that I work diligently for them—without reward or recognition."

That line irked Lane. He had come far from his own upbringing – morally and intellectually. In truth, he was ashamed to have been part of the slaveholder tradition, and wondered whether Dustin could hear the rich irony of his complaint. Still, what was he talking to former rebel soldiers about down there in DC? Was Lane's inauspicious exit from the hostilities known beyond himself?

"No, but you can move forward, Dustin. You're a talented man with the world as his oyster. Just don't get stuck in the 1860s."

Wise words, perhaps, but Dustin sensed an abnormal haste to change the subject. He probed.

"Well you certainly moved on quickly. I never figured out how you had completed nearly a year of schooling before I returned to college. What regiment were you with when you surrendered? We never spoke of this."

Henry Lane sat frozen, staring at Dustin's tan bow tie. His old colleague had him dead to rights, he believed. Why? Why was he making him squirm?

"You know I never had the enthusiasm for warfare that you exhibited, Dustin," he said, his eyes cast downward. "It was about duty, at first. Then I wondered to whom my duty was owed."

"I never had an enthusiasm for war, Hen. I was all about duty, too. My family opposed entry into the war, at least so soon."

Like Dustin, Lane was raised with notions of honor and chivalry. He never felt equal to them. He suddenly began to tear up and quake. "It's different. You responded to the call of battle with bravery and courage. I shrank from it, repelled by the unspeakable brutality."

Dustin knew he was a hero to many former Confederate soldiers. It gave him no satisfaction. He never felt heroic. But he saw where Lane was going, and prodded him to get there.

"So you withdrew…individually?"

"Say it, Dustin!" Lane cried. "I deserted! That's the purpose of this meeting, right? To let me know that you know that I am a coward!" Lane began sobbing cathartically, as though decades of shame were lifting.

As hard as he had tried to draw Lane out, Dustin recoiled at the remark. They were men of honor. To be a coward in the South was worse than rape or murder. He would never acknowledge it among his circle of acquaintances. Never. Nor should Henry Lane be blubbering in public.

"Don't say that, man! And lower your voice," Dustin hissed with intensity. His mind began clicking, as he constructed a rationale. "As far as you're concerned, leadership had evaporated, so you saw no choice but to go home. That is what happened, Henry. That is how you will remember it. Are we clear?"

Lane removed a handkerchief from his front pocket and blew his nose. "I thought you would hate me when you found out."

"I don't. You're an honorable man, and that is why I asked you to meet me here. Now compose yourself."

After Lane's emotional confession, Dustin knew he could get straight to business with little resistance. The two sat quietly as Lane gradually assumed a calmer demeanor.

"You read the papers, Hen. What stench is thick in the air right now?"

"War," Lane replied, dabbing his eyes.

"Correct. You didn't like the brutality in the War of Northern Aggression? Well, this war of American aggression will be much worse. The guns are more lethal now, the cannons more powerful and the enemy more ruthless. I need to stop this before it starts, Hen, and you can help me."

"I wish I could, Dustin," Lane explained, his composure recovered. "What can a simple historian do to stop the jingoes bent on mayhem?"

"I need a meeting with the most distinguished alumna of Wells College."

"Dustin."

"I mean it, Hen. You have the entrée."

"Me? You work for her husband, within a few hundred yards of where the woman lives."

"It's not that simple. I told you, Cleveland's men ticked off the Yankee vets in the first term, and I'm paying the price in the second. First of all, the president himself got out of the draft. When inaugurated, he returned the CSA battle flags and vetoed Union veteran pension requests left and right. The Grand Army of the Republic made political war on him and then he lost to Harrison."

Dustin let the history sink in for this southern-born historian, then continued his appeal:

"When they returned to the White House, they had to appoint southerners like Secretary Herbert. But my job with him had no policy consequences. When Gresham recruited me, I became something of a pariah to the political operatives. They keep me in a box."

Lane was looking more empathetic, Dustin could tell. It was time to close the deal.

"Had Secretary Gresham lived, he would have scotched this war talk from the outset. Mrs. Cleveland is my next best opportunity. But, I can not get in to see her without an invitation."

"A First Lady can't stop a war, Dustin. If she could, neither you nor I ever would have seen combat," Lane countered, alluding to Mary Todd Lincoln's rumored southern sympathies.

"I know that, but she can get me in to see the president. She doesn't know me, and I'm sure if I could talk with her for a few minutes, I could convince her that a meeting would be good for him."

Lane sighed with trepidation.

"Hen, think of how scared you were way back when. At least that cause was noble. This will be mindless bloodshed to appease the designs of madmen. Should the young men of today face terror for that?"

The professor pondered the question for a while. In contrast to all his frightened imaginings, Lane found this request from Dustin to be much less dreadful. "OK, Dustin. I'll see what I can do."

"Do you have access to a telephone?"

"Possibly."

"Take my card, and call me when you know something for sure. I fear my wires are being read before I get them. "

Lane extended his hand. "Thank you for forgiving me, Dustin. You've always…"

Dustin pre-empted any more talk of cowardice. "There's nothing to forgive, Hen. Nothing."

Sarah Corbett was not educated, but she could make deductions easily enough. On duty upstairs the previous evening, she was confronted with a large pile of bed linens placed right outside the door to her room the very next morning, long before anyone else would arise. It always seemed to be the case when she doubled as a maid: a pile of sheets placed by her quarters – as opposed to the drop station designated for the chamber maids – to greet her upon awakening. Was there a new procedure of which she was unaware?

Following her early morning routine, she walked down the narrow corridor from the laundry to the servants' hall, where the din was loud and chatty. Taking her place in the middle of the long banquet covered in a modest checked tablecloth, Sarah said a quiet prayer before digging into her sausages.

"You'll need a powerful prayer, love, to get those wine stains out of His Lordship's waistcoat," cackled Patrice, Mrs. Pauncefote's personal attendant. The whole room erupted in laughter, as household staff members gossiped about the drunken congressman who had collided with the ambassador at a private dinner the night before. Mrs. Temmerton, the housekeeper, shot a glare at Patrice that soon silenced her, and the rest of the room as well. Conversation soon resumed, albeit at a low hum.

Seated next to one of the chamber maids, Sarah inquired, "Pauline, did you make up any guest rooms yesterday?"

"I should say I did," Pauline answered in thick cockney. "Three of them. Don't make no sense, His Lordship and the

Mrs. going out on the town when they have guests in the house."

"That is strange."

"Not the first time, neither. Speaking of which, why are you stripping the beds, girl? Putting me out of a job?"

"No, Pauline, never. Somebody is leaving the bedding outside my door to collect in the morning."

Pauline's baby blue eyes widened to dominate her youngish, but gaunt, pink face.

"Ohhh, if old lady Temmerton finds out, one of us chamber maids will be begging on Dupont Circle. You know how she goes on about procedure. Don't say nothing about it, will you?" Sarah patted Pauline's hand in reassurance.

"I hear my name. Is there something I should know?" Mrs. Temmerton was now looking at the two women, as were the other servants.

"Uh, no ma'am."

"Sarah!"

"I mean, no, Mrs. Temmerton."

"How did things proceed last evening?"

"About as usual. Mr. Alderson's visitors, save one, are always preoccupied. I assume it's all official business."

"Sarah, as I have told you before, their business is their business, official or otherwise. Our job is to make them comfortable and make their dealings run smoothly."

"I love it!" piped up Marvin, the gardener. "These Yanks are so high and mighty. Let them see a colored girl working on the state floor. Won't see that at the French Embassy, I'll wager."

"Let Sarah upstairs during daylight, Mrs. Temmerton," echoed Beatrice, a housemaid. "We're not enough of us to clean and stoke and tend the whole place."

The housekeeper bristled, and then carefully crafted her response.

"You lack efficiency, Beatrice. There are enough hours in the day to run this house with time to spare, when time is not wasted, that is."

Mrs. Temmerton stood and the staff did the same. "Lady Pauncefote is visiting with the wife of the Chief Justice this morning, and His Lordship will host a luncheon for the Vice President, Mr. Stevenson, sharply at noon. I have posted the seating and dining arrangements for those assigned to this event. Sarah, bring me the chiffon tablecloth with the medallion pattern when Her Ladyship departs. That should work perfectly for this occasion."

Turning on her heel, Mrs. Temmerton swept from the room, pulling the tension out in her wake.

Feeling safer, Pauline whispered conspiratorially: "So which one of the others is dumping the sheets. Are you going tell the old girl?"

"Heavens, no. I want to get to the bottom of this mystery first. I think, though, I know who I'll find there."

"Who?"

"Let me ask this: Did Mrs. Temmerton instruct you to prepare the guest rooms?"

"No, got this one straight from his nibs," Pauline said, using a pejorative moniker the staff long ago pinned on Nigel Alderson.

Rushing back to the laundry room, Sarah made haste to examine the linens in question. She had worked at the embassy long enough to distinguish expensive perfume from cheap imitations. Other signs pointed to activity that gave Sarah pause as to whether these were, in fact, guests of the ambassador. Having lived and worked among all classes of people, Sarah knew how young, poor women were often convinced – by powerful men – that moral compromise would alleviate economic desperation. The signs were beginning to make sickening sense.

Dustin Boyle could not be in on it. The Spirit was prompting her to help this man, Sarah believed. She hoped her concern was, at least, in part spiritual, though she could not deny an attraction to the debonair southerner. He had a serious weakness, though. He clearly trusted Alderson.

13

Ezekiel Swanson hands shook with fury as he read the latest wire from Secretary Lamont. The order for the troops in his command to stay put for the next month was a knife in the back. Judging from the verbiage, he discerned that Lamont was not happy about issuing the directive. It no doubt came from the president. Looking across the breakfast table, he informed his wife, "Well, my dear, it looks like that old, porcine boar in the White House is getting cold in his cloven hooves!"

Madeline Swanson was used to her husband's derogatory remarks about his commander-in-chief. The substance of his remark is what troubled her. "Does that mean we're staying here?"

"For several more weeks, at least."

Swanson bound from his chair and let loose a barrage of expletives. His wife, grateful that their sons were boarding at school, tried to calm him.

"It does no good to curse, Zeke. Does he give an explanation for this change?"

"Just a bunch of political excrement about the 'delicate balance of negotiations at present.'"

When he was upset, Swanson's authoritative general's voice jumped an octave or two. Right now, he was a boy

soprano.

Madeline led him back to his chair and sat on his lap. "Zeke, you have always known how to take a bad situation and turn it around. There are hundreds – maybe thousands – of dead Sioux and Cheyenne around here to testify to that."

He always had a soft spot for her flattery and the magic her fingers worked in his hair. Returning to his usual baritone, he pecked her on the cheek and began ruminating. "You're right, of course. I just wish I knew what was going on in Washington. I feel like I have no…" He abruptly gazed straight ahead. "…leverage."

That very moment, the general had an epiphany. His downcast eyes were suddenly bright. His momentary rage swiftly dissipated. Of course he had leverage; he had it for two years.

"Remember when we got leave to visit your folks at Christmas in '93?"

"Oh Zeke," Madeline cried, joyfully, "you mean we can go back this year?"

"Out of the question. I'll be fighting Brits in South America."

"Oh," she said, dejectedly.

"That cotillion we attended in… What was the name of that lawyer?"

"Why?"

"Remember our conversation, when…"

"Ezekiel Swanson, look me in the eye, and tell me that you believed his far-fetched story about Mr. Cleveland."

"It was not so far-fetched, Madeline," Swanson countered. "Presidents are just men, after all, and men get…"

"Zeke, please!"

"Never you mind. If this solicitor's story is true, then Secretary Lamont was in on it. He knows everything about the president. I happen to think Grover Cleveland is so fat because he carries Lamont inside of his suit!!"

Madeline chuckled. He could always make her laugh.

"You see, my pretty New York debutante, if it's true, they are hiding the facts for a reason. If Dan Lamont knows that I know, he might just resume the troop consolidation to shut me up…which is fine with me."

Madeline loved playing political foil when her husband in such a mood. "Is the president going to go to war with Britain just to purchase the silence of General Ezekiel Swanson?"

"Perhaps not, Maddie. But if war is to come, I want to be the general who has the men and munitions in place to lead the way. I will not finish out my military career in this

God-forsaken territory, dodging tornadoes and picking off leftover Lakotas."

"On that, we are in agreement."

"We'll give the good secretary a few weeks. If I do not get the order to resume, I will have to pay him a visit in Washington, and share with him the idle gossip that has turned out to be my favorite Christmas present."

"You're an incredible woman, Bridgette," Nigel Alderson flattered, buttoning his coat with some difficulty. "I rue all the days I have not known you." It was a sincere statement from this habitually insincere man. He was on top of the world. She made him feel like the only man in the world that could hold her interest. But had he done so?

Lying in the bed, twirling her chestnut locks, she now said nothing.

"When can we next, say, share with one another?"

Bridgette finally spoke up: "I don't know, Nigel. My time is fairly well occupied in the weeks to come."

A shiver descended his spine, vertebra by vertebra, as an uncomfortable knot quickly formed in his stomach.

"Well, you certainly turn on a lark, my dear. Am I not pleasing to you?"

Bridgette's tone reeked of boredom. "You're not a bad fellow, Nigel. I get excited, though, by the powerful men of this city; the ones who make things happen. I thought you might be such a man, but it turns out you're more of a clerk."

That hurt. She was slipping away from him at the very time he was becoming dependent on her. He could feel it. Desperate measures might have to be employed. She would learn that Nigel Alderson mattered.

"Clerks do not broker issues of war and peace, Bridgette. Clerks don't set terms for negotiations, nor do they draw international boundaries. If these issues are too mundane for you, you best report to 1600 Pennsylvania Avenue. The Big One, as he is known in some quarters, may still have enough of the old alley cat in him to amuse and entertain you. Now," he bluffed, "I have business to which I must attend."

Bridgette Maher was no longer twirling her locks. She was sitting up, projecting all of her confident allure in her most winsome grin. "Come here."

Resistance melted as she stroked his sparsely covered scalp. Her attentions were unlike any those of any other woman. They consumed him. Furthermore, she did not want money. She wanted instead to be at the center of power. Alderson would prove to her that he could be found at that very hub. He would gain her love by taking her into his confidence. He could trust her. Clearly, she trusted him.

"You recognize these contraptions, no?" Patiño asked Mendoza impatiently.

The prisoner inspected the troughs and boxes configured crudely to perform an obvious function.

"I do, Captain, but..."

"How do they work, rat?!"

"They are jet elevators, otherwise known as pump sluices. They separate water from the mud and dirt of a ravine or gully and sift the solid for gold, to put it in a simple way."

"Don't patronize me!" Patiño roared. "Take them to the embankment and get them to work."

"Captain Patiño, the water flows too quickly in the Cuyuni to allow for significant accretions. This quest will be futile. And the river is full of..."

Patiño lifted the barrel of his German Empire Reichsrevolver to Mendoza's head, causing the latter to quiver. "Humor me, Rafael," he said quietly. "Just humor me."

It now made sense. The jaguar was chased away with a rapier because Patiño did not want the British to hear gunfire and use it as a pretext to shoot back. Since he sought to preserve his own life, it was evident he had not abandoned all reason. Mendoza and his comrades hauled the pump sluices to the bank of the river. They were burdensome and heavy charges for the seven malnourished and abused prisoners. The soldiers remained on their steeds, close enough to intimidate, far enough to make a quick getaway. Upon arrival at the bank, Mendoza whispered to the others:

"Take heart, amigos, the soldiers will not fire upon us. I have a plan to free us from Patiño and to stay alive, but you must do exactly as I say. Are you with me?"

The men nodded warily. "If we run, he will shoot us. Rafael. He can not return to Ciudad Bolivar if we escape."

"True, he can not. They can, though," Mendoza said, glancing at the distant soldiers on horseback. "His men will not fire on us for fear of arousing the English in that fort over there. We are in British Guiana, muchachos."

Their faces betrayed their fear. Mendoza reassured them: "Courage. Our lives will be more likely spared by British soldiers than by Crespo's henchmen."

"But what about the Captain, Rafael? Even if he does not shoot, he will chase us down and either hack us to pieces or trample us with his steed."

"Follow my directions carefully. It is our only hope."

Dustin could feel his eyelids drooping even as Alderson was talking. The all-night trip back from New York was sleepless and now fatigue enveloped him.

"Dustin, are you listening to me," Alderson protested. "After all, I'm here at your request."

The verdant beauty of Lafayette Square was just beginning to give way to the multiple shades of autumn as the two men stood by a massive oak tree. Acorns dropped about every 15 seconds, keeping Dustin from passing out.

"So sorry, Nigel. I am not well-rested this morning."

"Why, then, did you want to meet at this ghastly hour?"

Why indeed. The sun was just beginning to light up the eastern sky. Birds had only begun chirping. Not even servants were yet stirring in the darkened Executive Mansion across Pennsylvania Avenue.

"You know why. The embassy is going to be busier in the evenings with the social season approaching. We need to vary the times and places of our meetings so as not to engender curiosity." Dustin hoped he did not sound paranoid.

"Well, old chap, before you nodded off, I was telling you that the ambassador had forwarded your proposal to the PM in full, every jot and tiddle."

"Why is Lord Salisbury so slow in responding?"

"As I explained at our last conference, we British do not decide matters of import without examining the issue from all four corners."

Dustin looked crestfallen. "We do not have time for all four corners. Doesn't Lord Pauncefote have any pull in London?"

"A good deal of pull, Dustin, but he is an ocean away. My…the PM is talking every day to the Cabinet ministers, specifically Landsdowne and Goschen. They do not know either of us, so they will likely be skeptical of your offer. Whatever their advice, he will decide when he is satisfied that he has attained complete understanding."

Dustin was now fully awake. Alderson had dumped cold water on his head, so to speak.

"Are any of our old friends from the *Georgia* well-placed in the Admiralty?" He asked Alderson, hoping beyond hope.

"What do you think?"

Dustin looked up at the bronze statue of Andrew Jackson on horseback. The general made things happen in his day by the force of his own personality. He never flinched. Ever. The sculpture was a visible reminder to Dustin whenever his confidence flagged. But for the Battle of New Orleans, America came out the worse for wear in the War of 1812. Jackson made it a victory. Confidently doffing his cap astride a rampant stallion, the general was a testament to unshakable resolve.

"Nigel?" Dustin admonished, gathering himself up. "We will need to see each more frequently in the coming days."

"Whatever for? Things are at a standstill?"

"And will remain there if we do nothing."

"Very well, Dustin, but I can see no alternative now but to wait."

Dustin placed his hands on Alderson's now rounded shoulders. "There is always an alternative," he said, pointing to the statue. "Just ask my friend up there."

Mendoza worked rapidly, locating the drop-off where the shallow bench ended. It was exactly as he remembered: about five feet in before a steep underwater cliff. The captain had equipped the expedition well, considering the whole thing was doomed to fail. The landscape worked to his advantage, too. Digging to a clay layer along the bank, he deposited some in a large bucket found among the equipment. The prisoners set up the sluices to obstruct the captain's view of Mendoza, who sent another of them to scrape limestone from a nearby rock formation. Adding the limestone to the clay, the engineer strained to remember the next step from an article he had come across. Yes, that is it: apply heat.

"Captain," Mendoza beckoned. Patiño rode halfway to the bank, insisting that Mendoza meet him there.

"What is taking so long? Why are you wasting time?"

"Begging your pardon, sir, some of the components are old and rusted. May I have permission to build a fire to burn off some of the corrosion?"

Patiño glared at him in disbelief as Mendoza squirmed.

"You're the engineer here. Make a decision, yourself. Just get going!" The captain was clearly eager to depart. This fact would make the final step more difficult, but Mendoza would cross that bridge when the time came.

Moving the sluices to the edge of the water, the engineer took the strong cord from the equipment wagon, gauging its texture and resilience. It had to hold. It had to. Praying for protection from the carnivorous fish, he stepped onto the shallow bench as water immersed his legs.

Sarah was exhausted. Preparing tablecloths, pressing drapery and starching footman uniforms consumed the better part of her 13-hour day. The evening reception for the Governor General of Canada was now ensuing and her work was done. Shutting the door to her 14 by 10-foot bedroom, she quickly dropped to her knees. Giving praise and thanks to God for his provision, she then began her typically lengthy set of petitions on behalf of her co-workers, the ambassador's family, the staff, the president of the United States and all those in authority. As had been her custom for several weeks, she included Dustin Boyle and the work he was doing.

At that moment, a fearsome chill descended upon her. Something was afoot that would obstruct this man in his aims, she could sense it. She had experienced these impressions before, and they were always proven accurate. Had Dustin's goals been counter to the Divine will, she would not be suffering this disturbance, she was certain.

Warfare was upon her, as an obscure scripture verse from the Psalms flashed in her mind's eye.

"Let the sighing of the prisoner come before thee; according to the greatness of thy power preserve thou those that are appointed to die."

She lifted her voice to heaven: "Oh God, my Father, intervene mightily on behalf of Mr. Boyle. I know you have brought him into my life for a reason, and I pray that you will prepare the way for him to stand before you in surrender. Remove this threat to his hard work and effort, whatever it is. Thwart those who would thwart him, and grant him success. On this very day, at this very hour, make his obstacles fall by the wayside. Shed your grace upon him now, and rebuke the powers that would make vanity of his task. Save those from death who can come to his aid. I pray this in the name of Jesus Christ. Amen."

Slowly, the chill subsided and assurance filled her heart and mind. Getting into her nightclothes and slipping into bed, she knew that any threat to Dustin's project would soon be removed. Oddly, the more intensely she prayed for him, it seemed, the more she…

Sarah slept in sweet peace until dawn.

Mendoza was getting on Patiño's last nerve. There he was, down in the water on his hands and knees. He had been "preparing" the sluices for an hour and a half. His fellow prisoners were running back and forth, looking clueless. It was time to commence.

"Mendoza!" he bellowed, directing the prisoner to their established meeting place. Wet and tired, Mendoza nevertheless ran to the officer with all due deference.

"I want these pumps to start pumping. No more 'preparation'!"

"Only one thing prevents commencement, Captain Patiño. The men you have given me are weak in body and slow in wit. One of the sluices needs to be pulled to the very edge of the river, requiring enormous strength and competent judgment. Perhaps one of your men..."

"Enough!" Patiño looked at the sorry lot over which he had command. They would be here all day. "I will do it, as long as the pumps will begin."

"Thank you so much. We can start right after we put the sluice in place."

Patiño dismounted and walked the hundred or so yards to the river. Mendoza waded in and directed him to the sluice. The soldiers had their rifles trained on the other men, who stood at a distance from the pumps.

Plunging his boots into the water, the captain took hold of the machine and backed up so it was right at the edge of the river. Mendoza could barely breathe for fear, yet stood at the edge of the bench and—with great effort—kicked the cement-filled bucket off the bench into the seemingly bottomless channel. As the hardened clay-and-limestone concoction descended, the submerged rope to which it was tethered lost all of its slack. A noose closed around Patiño's ankle and the cement weight caused the officer to lose his footing and disappear beneath the surface with frightening suddenness. The same Añu foothold trap that foiled many a conquistador centuries earlier was now the fate of Captain Victor Patiño.

Mendoza knew that the captain would be furiously trying to work himself loose, yet hoped the accomplices would get to him first. He did not have long to wait. A crimson lagoon began forming at the surface within 30 seconds. The piranhas were nothing if not dependable.

The soldiers—at first frozen in horror—were now in a full panic, wailing and shouting at each other. Mendoza knew it was then or never, shouting to his own compatriots, "Vamoose, amigos, rapido!" As the ragtag crew began darting in the direction of the Union Jack, the engineer's suffered his first miscalculation of the day. The soldiers regrouped and took aim at the fleeing party. The open grasslands made them easy pickings. Exhausted, the prisoners would present no challenge.

The lieutenant, by virtue of rank, pulled the trigger first. The feeble sound of the iron hammer striking the flint was all that was heard. The other soldiers took their turns, only to suffer the same humiliation. A quick check of the stocks revealed that their weapons had been depleted of ammunition. Evidently believing his men did not possess the requisite discipline to hold their fire so close to a British post, Patiño felt safer being the only armed soldier on this mission, emptying their weapons of bullets before issuing them.

Without firepower so close to an enemy fortification, the soldiers decided that self-interest was the better part of valor. Turning their horses and escaping into the forest, they would devise an appropriate story before reaching Ciudad Bolivar.

Meanwhile, Mendoza and friends were dashing headlong across the plain toward the garrison. He spotted figures moving about the parapets, so took off his stained white shirt and began waving it frantically in surrender. The other men followed suit. In minutes, the red tunics and white helmets emerged from the fortress and began advancing on the approaching prisoners. The phalanx grew and then gave birth to smaller detachments as they got closer. Finally, five British soldiers emerged to make contact. Mendoza figured at least forty gleaming, repeating rifles were aimed at them, all well stocked with bullets, no doubt.

The five-man contingent drew within a few yards of the prisoners, ordering them to their knees. Their faces looked young, their complexions fair, but their eyes were all steely-blue and menacing. The one with the most blue-and-gold battle ribbons ordered them—in Spanish—to state their business. Panting from fatigue and anxiety, Mendoza hoarsely responded in the soldiers' own mother tongue, "I speak English, sir. I will tell you everything."

14

November, 1895

Dustin had not visited the Secretary's office since Gresham's death. Olney had not made many alterations…yet. The ostentatiously-carved wood, stenciled wall designs and oriental rugs reminded Dustin of the halcyon days when he and Secretary Gresham devised a more rational and sane foreign policy from that very chamber. Surprised and confused by the summons, he nonetheless appeared punctually, steeled for whatever abuse was to be heaped upon him.

"Good morning, Mr. Secretary. Mr. Oberstreet said you wanted to see me," he said, nodding toward the ubiquitous toady and bane of his existence.

"Good morning, Boyle," Olney responded. "We're having a visitor and I would like you here to answer any international legal charges he might level."

Olney had scores of diplomatic visitors every week. Strange that he would invite Dustin in on the proceedings now. Was the secretary of state warming up to his counselor or…?

"I know you've been researching these matters from your library activity and we will need an expert to respond to Pauncefote when he gets here."

A chill went up Dustin's spine. He shot a dirty look at the meddlesome spy, Oberstreet, who returned it with a triumphant grin. "This is about the boundary dispute?"

"What else of note is going on around here?" Olney laughed, hollowly. "He's got his nose out of joint about some new development and I don't want to be caught unawares. He is being escorted from the Diplomatic Reception Room as we speak."

Panic began to set in, as Dustin feared his entire enterprise would be exposed in a matter of minutes. Surely Alderson impressed upon the ambassador the need for discretion. Pauncefote was professional enough to know not to take terms from under-the-table negotiations into the secretary's office. Or did Alderson, in an attempt to inflate his importance, give the ambassador the impression that Secretary Olney was his counterpart in the surreptitious talks? If so, Justus Boyle's son would fail in his goal of southern vindication, and lose his job, to boot.

The office door swung open, admitting the Chief of Protocol, who announced: "Mr. Secretary, Her Majesty's Ambassador to the United States of America, the Lord Pauncefote."

The ambassador swept into the room with Cecil Rice, his bespectacled number two who looked like a young Sigmund Freud. Pauncefote looked to be in his 50s, and had thinning white hair on top that connected to out-of-style muttonchops on his otherwise hairless face. Both men sported gray suits when on diplomatic calls.

After introductions were made all around, the principals took seats while the aides stood around them. Dustin avoided looking directly at either Brit for fear that they might have seen him coming or going during a nocturnal visit. Pleasantries were exchanged before the ambassador got down to business.

"Mr. Secretary, I have come to protest in the strongest possible terms a violation of trust that will threaten the progress we have made on the boundary issue."

Olney shed his diplomatic face and revealed his inner-lawyer:"Your use of the word "progress" is extremely ironic, Lord Pauncefote. Since our remonstrance forwarded to your government last July, we have had no movement on this matter. In fact, I think it fair to say our overture has been effectively rebuffed."

"Your communication, sir, is receiving due attention, I assure you. Meanwhile, both Her Majesty and the United States are being undermined by surreptitious activity."

Feeling nauseous, Dustin looked down at his reflection in the black polished leather of his shoes, waiting for the final blow. How did Alderson manage to bungle this?

Olney was already impatient. This was just more stalling, as far as he was concerned. "Please be specific. Who are the parties involved and what are they doing?"

Taking a folder from Rice, Pauncefote began reading from a military transmission. A British Army detachment apprehended seven Venezuelans involved in an extraction operation along the southern bank of the Cuyuni River, over 200 miles southeast of Ciudad Bolivar. Among the impounded equipment were several makeshift jet elevator sluice boxes and bucket dredges, the purpose of which could be none other than to mine alluvial deposits. During interrogation, one prisoner—an educated man speaking competent English—told officers that the party was operating under the supervision of Venezuelan soldiers, who fled when their commander accidentally drowned during a preliminary stage of the operation.

"If their military was overseeing this theft," Pauncefote inquired drily, "does it not stand to reason that their government—a military junta—was the motivating force? You, Mr. Secretary, commend the Crespo regime as a legitimate party to arbitration. Where is the legitimacy when there is no rule of law?"

Dustin's relief at not being the subject of this meeting was immeasurable. At the same time, this episode clearly complicated things. The British would have no reason to believe Dustin's private assurances about arbitration if Olney dismissed the event as irrelevant. From the Secretary's tone and expression, that appeared to be the direction in which he was headed.

Oberstreet piped up: "Boyle, where is this location relative to the Schombürgk Linc?" Loath to show the toady any deference, Dustin looked to Olney, who wearily nodded assent.

"If I heard the coordinates correctly—6.5° latitude, 61° longitude?—that would place the apprehension east of Schombürgk's 1840 demarcation by 10 or 20 miles."

"Precisely!" Rice interjected. "The distance of the penetration into British Guiana can only mean this to be a deliberate attempt to abscond with our resources. The ambassador is here to request redress from the United States."

"On what grounds?" Oberstreet demanded. "We can point to scores of excursions by British personnel into the disputed region—well *west* of the Schombürgk Line, I might add. We never get as much as an explanation from your government."

Ignoring the assistant, Pauncefote spoke directly to Olney: "Mr. Secretary, the Prime Minister would like to address your position articulated July last in the most amicable manner applicable. That task becomes impossible when the Venezuelan regime acts in this way. This was not an exploratory expedition, sir. This was a mining enterprise by the admission of its participants."

"All that may be true, sir," Olney responded. "We can not be certain of all the facts, however, since the alleged soldiers withdrew and their commander is dead. Whether it was directed from Caracas or simply the opportunistic mischief of a few rogue officers is unknown."

Pauncefote and Rice were expressionless as Olney spoke. Consummate professionals, Dustin thought. How on earth do they work with the impulsive and somewhat immature Nigel Alderson?

"It underscores the core of this conflict," Olney continued. "Venezuela and Great Britain have two irreconcilable positions relative to the boundary. An honest third party must broker a compromise and the Monroe Doctrine dictates that it must be the United States."

The ambassador bristled at the mention of the Monroe Doctrine, but otherwise gave a polite audience. Finally, he stood, signaling Rice to do likewise. Pauncefote had ice in his voice: "If this doctrine accords the United States hemispheric paternity, as you assert, then the *pater familia* best take charge of his errant child lest there be discipline imposed from without."

"The president would view such a development very seriously, I assure you, Lord Pauncefote," Olney intoned with equal frigidity.

"Good morning, gentlemen," the ambassador concluded, departing with a resolute stride. Rice followed as if imitating Pauncefote. The room was silent for several seconds. Finally Oberstreet spoke.

"This tears it, sir. They have no intention of responding to the remonstrance, and are going to use this trifling incident to justify their foot-dragging. My recommendation is for you to advise the president and Lamont to give General Swanson the order to accelerate and mobilize."

Olney glared at Oberstreet, who suddenly remembered Dustin's presence and immediately bridled his own tongue. The secretary turned to Dustin amiably, if not sincerely: "I appreciate your input, Boyle. Thank you for coming."

Dustin nodded and cast a patronizing glance at Oberstreet, whose emotional outburst provided the counselor with needed political intelligence, if not any encouragement. Walking down the garishly ornate corridor to his own office, he tried to digest the new development. Given the equipment obtained for the aborted operation, he had trouble thinking that a few corrupt Venezuelan soldiers could have launched this effort. Moreover, the presence of an educated and English-speaking prisoner hinted that this was a political enemy of Joachin Crespo, a fact that might not be known to provincial military governors. His scientific know-how would not normally be shared with his jailers, but would be well known to the president of Venezuela.

How would Crespo expect to get away with it? Why, furthermore, would the mining party initiate dredging and pumping in full view of a British outpost? Dustin abruptly stopped in the middle of the hall, bureaucrats swerving around him on either side. The dread realization suddenly dawned on him that yet another component in the war engine was completely out of his control: Crespo was trying to provoke hostilities. Like the rest of Washington, Dustin bought into the belief that the dictator was a bit player in a grander drama. This event belied that presumption. Whatever his weaknesses, he had enough resources and guile to light the fuse of war.

Another troublesome fact was the existence of an additional British frontier station so close to the Schombürgk Line. Although he had stocked the department with the most updated maps, none showed any other garrison in the disputed region other than one at the mouth of the Rio Orinoco. Where there was one there could be more, indicating that the Brits might be better entrenched militarily than Lamont's War Department was anticipating. Oberstreet's loose lips regarding troop movements and who was in command revealed competing pressures on Lamont to order a full mobilization. Dustin's sly allusion to administration secrets might have temporarily stalled the secretary of war, but even Lamont could not defy the president. It made the urgency of Dustin's task all the more acute.

Finally, Dustin was most concerned that he did not see this coming. Why had Alderson not alerted him? Perhaps they could have strategized and prevented Paucefote from bringing the issue up with Olney in the first place. Alderson had seemed inordinately preoccupied of late. The man he saved from the London "bullies" in 1863 never quite managed to shed his penchant for making enemies. Dustin hoped his friend was not getting distracted from their common goal. Without Alderson's active cooperation, he thought, there would be bloodshed by winter. He would need another set of eyes and ears at the British Embassy, Dustin decided. The problem is that he had no history with any of the other diplomats on staff.

Arriving at his office, Dustin shut the door and stood, head bowed. Appearing to be in intense meditation, he was instead plotting a contingency. He would expand his circle by just a little. Alderson would prod Paucefote, who would, in turn, prod the Prime Minister to agree to arbitration. Dustin would cultivate a new source to make sure Alderson was on top of things. This source should raise no suspicions and be nearly invisible when gathering information. Raising his head, he walked to his favorite perch and again set his gaze on the White House.

Who better than the charmingly nosey Negro maid with the sparkling green eyes?

Laid upon a swamp by Pierre L'Enfant, Washington, D.C. remained unbearably humid well into the late weeks of autumn. His obesity aggravating his discomfort in such a climate, President Cleveland purchased a federal-style country home on higher ground, four miles northwest of the White House. Finding it easier to breathe and more private than the Executive Mansion, he would reside in the white clapboard home with black shutters with his wife and three daughters until the social season commenced in December, when living at the White House was more convenient. In the interim, he would travel to work, often in the company of a cabinet secretary or staff man in order to make maximum use of his time. Waiting for him to emerge from the house this morning was the Secretary of the Navy, Hilary Herbert.

Uncharacteristically late by seven minutes, Cleveland emerged from the dwelling. He descended the porch stairs in excruciating pain, hobbled by his recurring gout. The movement imposed sharp and stabbing pain in his big, and inflamed, toe. Herbert extended his hand to help his commander-in-chief up into the waiting carriage. Muttering oaths as he climbed in, the president then rested his girth and extended his leg to a custom-made footrest.

"Sorry for the language, Hil."

"No occasion to apologize, Mr. President," Herbert drawled. "I can see you're in some powerful pain, sir."

The driver set the horses apace and the presidential conveyance was off. After several minutes on the long trail leading to the thoroughfare, the carriage turned onto Connecticut Avenue, where the passengers had an unobstructed view of the city below. The 10-year old Washington Monument stretched brazenly toward the sky as if to puncture the heavens. The Capitol Dome gleamed in the early-morning bath of sunshine and the crispness in the air partially lifted Cleveland's spirits.

"So, where are we?" the president asked.

"We can move the Maine, Texas and Indiana to the mouth of the Orinoco by the first of the year," Herbert replied, referring to the arsenal of available battleships. "I would have liked time to make improvements to the Maine. She is a tinderbox."

"Aren't they all?" Cleveland returned knowingly. The United States was late getting into the modern world of naval warfare. Her fleet was slowly improving and expanding, although its readiness against a seafaring behemoth like the British fleet was dubious.

"Upon what is your schedule based?"

"Upon receiving the order at your earliest convenience, Mr. President."

The president became sullen again. The swelling number of government employees would not change the fact that all of the big decisions devolved on him. He hated to delegate even the most mundane matters yet, ironically, he often wished he could staff out the monumental ones.

Cleveland patted his walrus mustache for neatness. Two constables standing nearby doffed their hats in respect. The president nodded back, asking Herbert: "What is British capacity in the region?"

"They have three warships in the region left from their skirmish in Nicaragua. We are unsure how many soldiers are aboard. The question is, how many more vessels and men can they insert before we even get there?"

"Granted, but we need not vanquish them to win."

"No sir, just make them expend enough men and munitions until they decide the Schombürgk Line—or whatever their latest boundary claim is—is not worth the cost. Given their African troubles, that decision may arrive sooner than we think."

The president took in the scenery as woodlands and pastures gave way to homes and commercial buildings of brick and brownstone.

"At what cost to us, though?" he suddenly piped up. "I know beyond doubt that our prudence on fiscal matters will break this Depression eventually. It has to. As sure as I am that there is a God in heaven, I know that this economic crisis will lift. At the same time, just as we can not know his timing, I can not predict when recovery will set in. I just hate to see it interrupted by war."

Herbert sympathized with his boss. Like Cleveland, he was committed to a non-interventionist philosophy...up to a point. When that pivotal moment arrived, however, he understood the need for preparedness and ruthlessness. Wounded during the Battle of Shiloh, Herbert knew the physical, emotional and spiritual toll that war could inflict on victor and vanquished alike. Still, the fear of the damage could often be worse than the damage itself.

"Mr. President, this country will survive as long as we stand firm in defense of our interests. Giving the Queen a larger foothold in South America is an invitation to the other European powers to do as she has. Forgive me, sir, if I sound like a jingo but, you know, they are not wrong all the time."

Letting out a large sigh, Cleveland exclaimed, "That's what makes them so vexing, Hil. But, I agree with your position and Olney's remonstrance was the best thing I've ever read. The time that Salisbury is consuming before responding is infuriating and I will not let this drag into another year."

At that moment, the presidential party passed the Embassy of the United Kingdom of Great Britain and Ireland. The Union Jack was waving proudly, as if to mock the host country.

"Would it help for you to dine with Pauncefote and make our position clear?" Herbert inquired, hooking his thumb toward the embassy..

"Hardly," Cleveland answered, skeptically. "I can not imagine they ever do business informally."

15

Dressing like a tradesman did not come naturally to Dustin Boyle. Since he had returned from war to resume his studies, he prided himself on a dapper, professional wardrobe. Procuring a set of denim overalls, flannel shirt and work boots took him the better part of a day and, when he donned the spectacles he only wore in private, he detested the image in the mirror. For one thing, the clothes did not fit right, which may have worked to his advantage. The legs too short and shoes too tight gave the lawyer exactly the pedestrian look he was trying to affect. Nevertheless, he was anxious. Acting skills may have accounted for much of his rise in Washington but he was unsure of whether he could do justice to the role of laundry supply conveyor.

Having purchased several large canisters of ammonia, borax and potash, he then acquired a hand-pulled wagon and began the long trek up Connecticut Avenue. The boots began to hurt his feet after about 200 yards and he knew he would be in serious discomfort upon reaching his destination. His manner of walking already compromised by his war injury, he now imagined himself as a hobbling, unsightly troll out of Norse mythology. During his growing-up years, Caleb would sometimes be limping from one mishap or another. For all the foreman's capabilities, he was the most accident-prone slave Dustin could remember.

On one occasion streaks of blood were soaking through the back of his shirt when he was loading a wagon early in the morning.

"Daddy, Caleb's hurt!"

Watching nearby, Justus reassured his son, "Caleb is fine, Dusty. Go inside for breakfast."

Dusty ran to comfort the Negro who was a second father to him.

"Are you hurt, Caleb?" the wide-eyed, seven-year old redhead asked.

Wincing while lifting heavy barrels of rum, Caleb finished his task, and then hoisted the boy on the edge of the wagon.

"Your Daddy is speaking truth, Seedling. I just got sliced up by those mean old cane leaves. Remember I told you to be careful? They got blades like swords. I just got to be more careful is all."

Dusty looked at the man's kind face and knew everything would be fine. Caleb would be more careful and not get himself hurt. Daddy was telling the truth.

Justus had always been a man of his word. Dustin's present soreness was more bearable because it was for Justus' sake that he was in Washington in the first place. He would not fail. He would not disappoint Justus, no matter what the strain. Picking up his pace, Dustin lifted his head high while pulling his cargo toward the British embassy.

In the distance he spied mounted police officers flanking a carriage. Consternation seized him as he realized it was the president coming from Woodley and heading to the White House. How could he forget that detail? Cleveland would likely not recognize Dustin, especially given his attire, he reasoned. He would just keep his head down and continue his journey, letting the Chief Magistrate pass by.

Or not. Coming into view was President Cleveland's traveling companion, who definitely would recognize him regardless of clothing. Serving in battle side by side—and then as law partners and political actors for two decades—Dustin and Hilary Herbert knew one another intimately. Yet the Navy Secretary was not privy to Dustin's activities in recent days and would express vocal shock to see him on the street in the garb of a common laborer.

The street crowd took notice of the oncoming retinue and began tipping their hats and waving. Dangerously exposed, Dustin had little choice but to execute the most desperate measure available to him. He leaned forward degree by degree until gravity took over. His face hit the ground with punishing force but not enough to knock him cold. Listening to the footsteps rushing toward him, he hoped and prayed that the presidential carriage would proceed unabated.

"Sir? Sir? Can you hear me? Somebody get a doctor!" The crowd around him was pressing in as he continued to feign unconsciousness, listening to the hoof beats and carriage wheels. Growing louder, the telltale sounds reached a climax in volume and then slowly diminished without stopping. Cleveland and Herbert were gone. He was in the clear. Climbing to his knees, he accepted the assistance of onlookers in getting to his feet.

"Did you have a dizzy spell or something?" one well-dressed matron inquired.

"I suppose I must have fainted in all the excitement of seeing the president. I feel just fine now. Thank you."

"Let us get you some medical attention."

"Oh, no. You're very kind, but I am feeling tip top. Really. I must be on my way."

The crowd looked upon him with a mix of skepticism and concern. It did not matter. He was safe to proceed with the task at hand.

"Cabot, this blubasaurus is a waste of our time. Why should we pursue him? He is obviously a low man on the totem pole."

Full of nervous energy, Theodore Roosevelt was shouting into his long-stemmed candlestick telephone while reading his morning correspondence. Awake until three in the morning as a (unwelcome) tagalong on a stakeout for boat thieves along the East River, the police commissioner showed no signs of fatigue at 9:30am. From his office at 300 Mulberry Street, the drab if massive headquarters of the NYPD, Roosevelt could multi-task with the best of them. He read incoming letters while dictating those to be sent, practiced judo, received oral briefings and sat for a portrait all while conversing with his senatorial friend.

"He need not know everything, Theodore, just enough," Senator Lodge replied patiently.

"But even if he had significant information to share, how do we extract it?"

"By exploiting his vices. If his record with your police department is illustrative, he unquestionably lacks the character to withhold secrets when confronted with the appropriate temptations."

"Stop. I shall hear no more."

"Well, you asked."

"To my eternal regret. What do you think he knows?"

"My suspicion is that he at least knows who is coming and going, who Ambassador Pauncefote is meeting with and some knowledge of his correspondence."

"This helps us how?"

"If they're influencing Congressmen, we'll know. If they're preparing the Canadians for invasion, we'll know."

"We should take Canada when war is declared," Roosevelt declared with finality.

"You've made that abundantly clear, but first things first. If we can prove they are preparing for battle, Cleveland has no choice but to ask for a declaration. Then you can plant your flag in Ontario."

"Bully. What can I do in the mean time?"

"Clean up this filthy city. I have to catch the train to Boston."

"It was good of you to visit, Slim. I'll see you in Washington for the grand climax of this little adventure."

Later that night, Lodge was at his Boston home with his feet upon the desk of his handsome study. The cozy Beacon Hill neighborhood suited his Brahmin sensibilities, though he despaired at the number of Italians, Slavs and Poles beginning to occupy the community's North Slope. Those Statue of Liberty exhortations were carried too far, he decided.

Roosevelt may be exceedingly enthusiastic, Lodge acknowledged, but it is good to have a friend who doubles as a force of nature. That energy would be needed when they exposed the British plan to circumvent the United States, desecrate the Monroe Doctrine and seize the gold between the rivers. Key to the whole endeavor was to get their target to regurgitate an incriminating dossier against his mother country.

"We ordered no laundry supplies, so you can just turn around with that cart and go back to where you came from," spat Elizabeth, a downstairs maid and the Housekeeper's Number Two.

"Well, now, just let me check my purchase order. I'm certain you requested this," Dustin replied, feigning concentration as he looked at some blank papers. The two stood at a rear access to the embassy that Dustin thought would open to the laundry service. He did not expect to find the porcine domestic with a tight bun of raven-black hair.

"I order the provisions here, sir, and I would know whether or not a delivery is due. Good day."

"Uh, wait, perhaps your laundry maid could clear this up?"

"I told you that I order…"

"Elizabeth?" Sarah Corbett, also in unfamiliar garb, stood behind the forbidding Elizabeth, who turned to her with annoyance.

"Sarah, you are not authorized to order supplies. I'll handle this."

"Of course. I just thought you might like to know that the last delivery was short. We are not being charged for these items, are we sir?" she asked innocently.

"No. No, ma'am. This is to make up for our error." Grateful for both her quick save and feigned non-recognition, Dustin played along with the charade. She did not strike Dustin as the type to lie, but he would not judge her for it.

Elizabeth let her guard down. "You should have come out and said so. Sarah, please escort this man to the laundry room so he can deposit his goods and be off."

"Yes, ma'am. Right this way Mr. B_, uh, sir. Dustin followed Sarah through the labyrinth-like corridors of the embassy's ground floor, where he had several near-collisions with myriad footmen, cooks and maids. Finally, she brought him into a cavernous section where mountains of clean clothing awaited pick-up.

"It's a wonder you have time for what you do upstairs. Thank you for not identifying me. I had to come and talk to you."

"We were indeed short on the last delivery, in case you were wondering."

"I did not think you could pull that one out of thin air."

Sarah shook her head. "I wouldn't have, but seeing you in those overalls made me want to laugh out loud."

Dustin looked at himself, and back at Sarah sheepishly. "I don't play this very role well, do I?"

Grinning her trademark grin, she replied "Stay clear of Ford's Theater." Turning serious, she said, "Let's work while we talk. She began checking the heat on her irons while Dustin unloaded canisters.

"Is this about Mr. Alderson?" Sarah asked.

"How did you know?"

"He's a nice man, but I suspect somewhat sneaky."

"You're a sharp judge of character, Sarah."

"How do you know him?" she asked.

"I did some business in England some years ago. I met him then."

"Do you trust him?"

"Yes and no. Yes, because he is a loyal friend; no, because he lacks self-control."

"You're a loyal friend to him, too."

"Not as loyal as you think. That's why I'm here to see you."

She put the iron down and looked straight at Dustin. "You're losing faith in him?"

Dustin knew he was at a watershed moment when he would either jeopardize the operation or save it. He had to trust her.

"Sarah, Nigel Alderson and I are trying to prevent a war between our countries. I don't know if you are aware…"

"Mr. Boyle, I am an American working at the British embassy. I am well aware."

He had never felt chastened by a Negro before, yet her gentle tone gave him no cause to take offense.

"My apologies. I'm sure you are. Anyway, both Nigel and I are trying to persuade our superiors to restrain any haste in going to war. Up until recently, I thought we were making progress. Yet I fear Nigel has found other things to occupy his concentration and he failed to inform me about a critical development."

Sarah did a quick scan of the surroundings to make sure nobody came in. Turning back to him, she asked, "How can I help?"

With a barely perceptible twinkle in his eye, Dustin said, "You seem to have a knack for, shall we say, paying attention."

Sarah buried her head in towels to muffle her laughter. Coming up for air, she told him, "You can say it, Mr. Boyle. I'm a busybody. Everyone else says it, though without your southern grace."

She seemed to know how to affirm him without flattery. Few had that gift. Gresham and Caleb did, and Sarah did. He could never help but smile when he was with her.

"I need a busybody to keep watch on Nigel's comings and goings. He has a weakness when it comes to pleasure of all kinds. I have to make sure he remains invested in our partnership and performs his part of our agreement. Otherwise there is war."

"He is so blessed to have you as a friend."

"Thank you. Will you help? I'll compensate you for your trouble."

"You insult me, Mr. Boyle," she teased. "I'll just take the borax and potash and you can consider me paid in full."

Dustin laughed out loud and observed, "You're too gracious a lady to be toiling down here in anonymity. I've grown use to you as…"

Sarah cut him off: "Nobody is ever completely anonymous. There is one who always watches and neither slumbers nor sleeps."

Puzzled, Dustin continued to his point. "In any event, when this crisis passes, I would like to secure a better position for you."

"I am always open to promotion, Mr. Boyle," she rejoined, stepping close to him. "But at this moment, I can think of no place I would rather be."

The tall and slender figure sitting across from Lord Salisbury had ridiculously long sideburns for 1895, and a comb over of the few chestnut hairs he had left on his head. The two men sat in overstuffed chairs by the fireplace in a cramped study at 10 Downing Street, the prime minister reading a draft response to Olney's remonstrance from the previous summer. His audience, the secretary of state for war, listened attentively, interjecting occasionally with a suggested revision or clarification. The wording struck him as not nearly strong enough.

Henry Petty-Fitzmaurice was educated at Eton and Oxford. The great-grandson of a prime minister, he had already served as Viceroy in India and Governor General in Canada. He was born and bred to lead, and now held the title of Marquis of Landsdowne to burnish his credentials.

Although the Liberal Party sponsored his early career, he was entirely at home with his new Tory colleagues. He had one beef with many of them, however. Their preoccupation with the Boer conflict in Africa inhibited British influence in other parts of the world.

When Salisbury finished his recitation, he asked Lord Landsdowne for criticism.

"It's well-crafted, Prime Minister, perhaps too well."

"Explain that."

"It goes out of the way to justify British intentions, to show ourselves as benign neighbors."

"Exactly," the prime minister answered. "We are being branded in their newspapers as gold-diggers and ruffians."

"Yes, sir. This communication, by contrast, should answer Secretary Olney's points, not those expressed in American rags. I speak specifically of his references to this Monroe dogma business."

"Doctrine."

"Call it what you will: it expresses nothing more than American chauvinism, and we should give no expression—explicitly or implicitly—that we are in any way bound by it."

Salisbury looked into the roaring fire. "That is precisely why I called you here, Landsdowne, to whittle away the diplomatic finesse."

"At your service," Landsdowne proclaimed with confidence.

"What do you make of Pauncefote's contact in their State Department? Do you still think it's a diversion?"

"I do. Gammon and spinach, all of it, especially given the testimony of the Venezuelan political prisoners. That regime does not respect diplomatic protocols, quite obviously. The lack of U.S. outrage or even protest over this incident demonstrates that the two countries have locked arms. We do ourselves no favors by further entertainment of these privy overtures."

The prime minister sighed and began re-working his document. "The terms are quite generous, you know. It would seem we just send a few representatives on behalf of Her Majesty and we get much of what we ask for."

"Why should we have to ask for what is rightfully ours?"

"Why, indeed?" Salisbury said, continuing to scribble.

16

His two presidencies were devoted to the idea of America minding its own business. True to the founding fathers, President Grover Cleveland sought a comfortable buffer between the United States and the old European powers. Securing native control of Samoa, getting out of Hawaii and going slow on Cuba reflected his desire not to emulate the strong-arm tactics of the so-called civilized world. If the United States of America stood for anything abroad it would be for the rights of the weak against international predatory powers, each eager to plunder resources and impose their will. Otherwise, the president asserted, America should tend to the home fires. In this he was of one mind with Walter Gresham.

Venezuela posed a dilemma, however. Its forces were no match for British Guiana's mother country, to be sure. Her economy was heavily dependent on credit, with her primary creditor—Germany—acting no less arrogant than the U.K. Her own government symbolized the oppression of the weak by the strong. There were no heroes in this story, nobody with whom to sympathize. Nobody, that is, unless Cleveland asserted American interest in the region. Either way, it appearedl, the poor and powerless would bear the brunt of the battle. While Secretary Olney made an airtight case for the legitimacy of U.S. involvement, the president still approached the scenario with vague dread.

Until today.

Just returned from a duck-hunting excursion, Cleveland was greeted with Lord Salisbury's response to Olney's remonstrance. It may have been worth the long wait were it not for the patronizing tone, imperious declarations and complete tone-deafness to Olney's reasoning. Particularly annoying was Salisbury's assertion that the American government was misinterpreting the Monroe Doctrine beyond a very narrow issue of European overthrow of duly elected Latin American governments. The Prime Minister's message was clear: the U.S. had no right to call for an international tribunal; British claims were modest; and Venezuela must yield.

Not since contending with Tammany Hall as the governor of New York had Grover Cleveland encountered such naked arrogance. All of his caution, restraint and diplomacy had come to naught. The British had taken his patience for timidity. Their contempt for American military prowess was only exceeded by their disrespect for the president himself. No more olive branches, Cleveland decided. That boundary line would be drawn with or without British cooperation. If they object, they can eat American shot and shell.

At 10:15pm, the president summoned Olney and Lamont, who found him amending Olney's suggested rejoinder. He neither looked up from his work nor invited the two men to sit.

"Your draft is fine Dick, but I am revising it for a different recipient. It's going to Congress without delay."

"You're asking for the Commission?"

"I should have done this 10 years ago." Cleveland scrawled furiously for another two minutes before gesturing his subordinates to sit.

The blackness from the outside was held at bay by the bright electric lights while President James Buchanan looked down from above the mantle, as though to witness a momentous decision. The wind howled violently on this pre-winter evening, egging the president on.

Olney broke the silence. "The American people are behind you, Mr. President. They have no more patience for imperial swagger. The world will know we're not to be taken lightly."

Allowing himself a moment of light-heartedness, the president winked at Lamont and turned to Olney: "Careful, Dick, Your pince-nez spectacles are showing," referring to those worn by arch-jingo Teddy Roosevelt.

The Secretary of State could afford to laugh at himself with the others. This was the victory he savored. Knowing the Prime Minister would rebuff his summer communication eventually, Olney had allowed Dustin Boyle to craft the Venezuela section of the president's annual address that was delivered to Congress the week before. Boyle's language was polite and hopeful, as though expecting a miracle. The Secretary would make sure his Counselor received a complete copy of Salisbury's contemptuous response. Perhaps then Dustin Boyle would feel the sting of total repudiation and quietly depart.

Secretary Lamont, while normally aggressive when discussing Great Britain, was lost in thought. Cleveland did not know that knowledge of the 1893 surgery had breached the small, trusted circle in which it had been confined. Worse, the information was threatening to proliferate if the secretary of war did not keep tight rein on the military preparations. Once the commander-in-chief transmitted his wish for a boundary commission, Congress would pick up the baton and run with it. Inevitably, a senator or congressman or reporter would want to know why so many troops were still camped out on the southern plains. President Cleveland would want to know the same thing, perhaps sooner than Lamont thought.

"Dan, come by around one o'clock tomorrow. I want a progress report on mobilization. You know the Brits might just want to get the jump on all of that gold once the news of the Boundary Commission comes out."

"I'll be here, Mr. President."

"Good evening, gentlemen."

Lamont and Olney stepped out into the broad corridor, the plush new carpeting installed by President Harrison muffling their steps. They spoke in hushed tones.

"Finally, Dan, the Big One is on board! He's mad clean through. This is historic: the Brits getting humbled in South America by the U.S. And under a Democratic administration!"

"It won't be as easy as it sounds, Dick," Lamont answered despondently.

"With you running things, old man, they'll be lucky to field an army to fight the Boers when the time comes."

Olney was off on a lark and would not be dissuaded by military realities. Nevertheless, he could not ignore political ones.

"You're forgetting something, Dick. The little matter of your counselor's knowledge of the *Oneida* procedure," Lamont said, referring to the yacht aboard which the president's oral cancer was furtively removed. "I've mollified him so far by pulling back on the reins, but now…"

"Now, you have been ordered to make haste by the president himself," Olney finished the statement.

Olney suddenly shed all emotion, becoming coldly rational. "As far as I can tell, you have little choice, Dan. You simply must obey your commander-in-chief."

"Exposure of this secret will hurt the economy, Dick, and reflect badly on the president, on me and on you, too."

"You overestimate the ramifications. Dan, if we chase the Brits out of the Americas, nobody will remember that a healthy president was once ill and failed to tell the public. And let us be frank. War will stimulate the economy—and shut the jingoes up for good measure. All things considered, we come out ahead."

"You don't think I should tell the Big One about Boyle's threat, veiled as it was?" Lamont asked.

Olney was now smiling. This was actually a positive development. "Trust me. Boyle is neutered in this administration. That's why he approached you in the first place. He's probing. If he is serious about making this issue a matter of public record, let him take his threat to the president of the United States himself, and see if it gets him anywhere...other than fired."

Olney only hoped he could be in on such a meeting. "Besides, I think we have the goods on him that can completely void the president's commitment to Gresham to keep this man on."

"What goods?"

"Do I have to draw a picture? Who are the women in his life? None. A good-looking fellow like that? He should at least have a lady friend."

Lamont snorted: "You'll need more than that. You'll have to catch him in the act."

"Just a matter of time, Dan. Meanwhile, I guarantee you he will make no noise when he knows that the president has authorized mobilization. Not if he cares about his job."

The Secretary of War wished he shared the Secretary of State's unfounded confidence.

"Mr. President, I rise to address this body on a matter of the highest national urgency," Senator Lodge bellowed before his assembled colleagues, his tone dripping with gravitas.

"You will recall that last March I called your attention to the disturbing geographic pattern relative to British naval installations in the Atlantic, particularly those on this side of the ocean. I asked what the purpose could possibly be in placing naval vessels and supplies in Bermuda if none other than to dominate the Western hemisphere, particularly our South American neighbors, in stark defiance of the Monroe Doctrine. While my words received the strong support of most Americans, many—some here in this body—were contemptuous of my view that our hemispheric obligations are threatened by a European power with outsized ambition and inordinate lust for the plentiful resources of those countries in the equatorial region.

"I was labeled a *jingo* for my troubles, an instigator who simply wants war for war's sake. In response, I ignored these attacks, confident that events would vindicate my position. That day is upon us, brethren. The Salisbury government has revealed its true character. Britain alone, we are told, can properly apprehend the Monroe Doctrine; she alone will decide where boundaries are drawn; indeed, the United Kingdom has assumed sole authority over political divisions in South America, at least where her interests are affected."

Lodge paused for effect. Each man in the Senate chamber was now aware of the dismissive British response to Olney's remonstrance.

"Are we to be ignored? To be patronized? Is the United States of America but a bit player in the global drama? We all now know the contempt in which our beloved country is held by the government of the Marquis of Salisbury. We know it has no intention of good faith negotiation with Venezuela. We are all now one in opposing its international high-handedness. Indeed," Lodge drew out his last words for emphasis, "we are all jingoes now."

The thunderous applause from the gallery gave Henry Cabot Lodge no cause to exult. While he knew that the establishment of a boundary commission would sail through both houses of Congress, even Salisbury's arrogant reply to Olney did not guarantee all the votes needed for a full-fledged declaration of war. After all, appointment and formation of the commission may take up to two years. Only hard evidence of British preparations would bring the matter to a satisfactory boil.

Sitting after a falsely modest bow to his colleagues, Lodge was confident such intelligence was forthcoming.

17

The president's strong response to British indifference regarding Venezuela was mildly encouraging to General Ezekiel Swanson, but it was too little, too late. They should have been fighting by now—in South America, in Canada, or any place else that the Brits could be found. All this delay just strengthened Her Majesty's position. Hence, this long train ride to the nation's capital. He would request—and receive—the first available appointment on Secretary Lamont's calendar. In that meeting, he would demand orders to complete the consolidation and to mobilize. Did Lamont really think he could hide the fact of Cleveland's corruption in perpetuity? If the secretary of war valued secrets that much, he would have to redeem them for what they were worth.

The landscape began to take on a verdant and varied topography as his train lumbered eastward toward the capital city. Trees of all kinds—coniferous and deciduous—increased in number, as did bodies of water and outposts of civilization. Whitetails and turkeys soon replaced antelope and prairie dogs as the fauna most in evidence out of his window. Swanson—and Madeline, of course—were both eager to put their western life behind them. They needed the sights, sounds and stimulation of the eastern seaboard. Undoubtedly, his campaigns against the native populations had made possible the expansion of the

U.S. in fulfillment of its Manifest Destiny. Cities would rise up, commerce would thrive and culture would flourish. That, however, would take many years of fighting inhospitable terrain and often punishing climate. The Swansons had paid their dues. After the war with the U.K., they would settle in Washington permanently. This trip would hasten that future.

He was not sure how Lamont would respond. From his investigation into the matter, Swanson learned that Lamont's allies in the press had successfully squashed an enterprising reporter who had sniffed out a similar story. Would the secretary take a like form of vengeance on him? Swanson worked for Daniel Lamont, after all, and was subject to military discipline if the right charge could be leveled. Should the secretary call the general's bluff, the mere accusation of insubordination could end Swanson's career. He knew that Lamont was not one to be trifled with.

At the same time, Swanson believed his career to be at a virtual end if he could not secure a battlefield command abroad. With his wife's wealthy family and fat inheritance, the Swanson's would never be in want if he were to be dismissed. That alone gave him a stronger hand going in. Furthermore, President Cleveland was much less popular than he was in 1893, leaving fewer publishers willing to give him cover. These facts convinced the general that he had little to fear from a direct confrontation with his superior. Swanson was no pushover himself. If Lamont wanted a bare-knuckle brawl with the nation's premier Indian-fighter, he would have one.

Colleagues referred to Swanson as the "competent Custer." He possessed all of the swagger and charisma of the ill-fated warrior, yet reflected none of the impulsive bad judgment. As much as he lusted for high office, he would not leave himself vulnerable in attaining it. He made sure that if the Cleveland political operation tried to do him in, there would be another trusted general to resurrect the Maria Halpin affair with the public. And another. And another. As in conquering the Lakota, Swanson knew the keys to defeating an intransigent enemy were infinite waves of overwhelming force. Lamont would come to learn what the Lakota learned at the hands of General Ezekiel Swanson.

On this visit, Dustin—again in laborer's attire—met Sarah at the outside entrance to the laundry room, where fewer eyes and ears could bear witness.

"I think he's bringing women into the embassy for…"

"Go on, Sarah."

"Assignations."

Dustin was touched by Sarah's embarrassment. By now, he knew she was not ignorant of the ways of political men. She nevertheless had an intrinsic wholesomeness which would not reconcile itself to immorality.

"It does not surprise me. That's how we met," he told her.

Sarah looked back in shock. Dustin laughed.

"It's not what you think. Nigel was referred to me for navigator duty by a military officer. When I found him, he was about to be snuffed out by a gang of—let's call them 'peddlers'—for not paying his bill."

"So this is an old habit?"

"And, it seems, an enduring one. My problem is to make sure he is following up with the ambassador on our negotiations. The more time he spends with these women, the less he is engaged in our project. "

"What can I do?" she asked earnestly.

"Well, I can't confront him here. But, if I can find out where he goes to meet these girls, I can head him off at the pass, talk some sense into him and get him back to business."

"Should I follow him?"

"That might get you dismissed if he were to discover you. Just watch him coming and going, if you can. Let me know in what direction he heads most often. And continue to pay attention to his clothing. He may leave clues."

"Leave it to me, Mr. Boyle."

"You're my only hope, Sarah."

She beamed as she closed the door behind her.

Ben Tillman allowed the lid of the writing box atop his mahogany desk to drop loudly, rousing his more lethargic colleagues from slumber. He wanted full attention on his speech from its start to its conclusion. Positioned in the back row of the semi-circular desk arrangement, Tillman's location demanded strong vocal projection and a fair amount of theatrics—two skills he had in abundance—if his oration were to be heard and understood. Despite the rococo carvings and plush comfort of his furnishings, courtesy of cabinet maker Thomas Constantine after the destruction of the War of 1812, Tillman preferred having his own office to sharing the cavernous Senate chamber with his 90 colleagues. As a governor, he could receive visitors and conduct ceremonies at his spacious statehouse quarters. Here, he felt like a schoolboy waiting for teacher recognition.

"The chair recognizes the distinguished minority leader," intoned the gaunt and severe vice president of the United States, Adlai E. Stevenson. Tall and handsome, Senator Arthur P. Gorman rose to his feet at his front-row desk, looking unnaturally anxious. The Maryland pol had done his best to carry water for the unpopular administration, coming under heavy fire from his populists. Now, he had to throw them a bone, with the hope of future cooperation. What he was about to do left Gorman feeling helpless, like lighting a stick of dynamite with the fervent hope it will fizzle. Once a baseball player, Gorman later served various appointed roles in the Senate: Assistant Doorkeeper, Assistant Postmaster and Postmaster. The institution was present in every corpuscle running through his veins, and he detested novice Senators who diminished its majesty with hotheadedness. Political survival, however, warranted this indulgence, so little was gained by postponing it any longer.

His voice heavy with dread, Senator Gorman lit the fuse: "Mr. President, I yield to the distinguished Senator from South Carolina, Mr. Tillman."

Dustin was coming to enjoy his encounters with Sarah, but despaired over their absurd purpose: he had hired a spy to keep watch on his spy. Having drafted the Venezuela section of the president's annual message, he was satisfied that he had struck the right tone of non-aggression. More than that, he was extremely surprised neither Olney nor President Cleveland had revised his language. Still, he knew where both men stood on the matter. Further delay on the British end might invite a more assertive intervention by the United States.

Where was the bottleneck, he wondered as he changed into his regular suit and headed to his office. Was it between Alderson and Pauncefote? Pauncefote and Salisbury? Or Salisbury back to Pauncefote? As much as Dustin hated being left in the dark by Olney, being sidelined by Nigel Alderson was completely unacceptable. He had to talk to Alderson with much greater frequency; if it meant stalking the man, so be it.

When Dustin was very young, Justus Boyle had introduced his son to the workings of one of the busiest sugar plantations in the United States. Dustin came to know Caleb first as an apprentice knows a master. Spending hours together each day, the two would inspect plants at random during the course of the growing season. Caleb would show Dustin the signs of diseases like leaf scald; the presence of pests like moth borers; and the methods of harvest, including the proper use of a machete. As an early teen, the boy would work the fields with the rest of the hands—for two hours a day. He believed he gained much empathy for the Boyle workers through such daily toil amid the 18-foot high stalks of sugar cane.

As Dustin grew up, Caleb evolved from second father to loyal employee. He treated the young man as the heir he was, though the large foreman would occasionally slip and still refer to him as "Seedling." Among Justus and Caleb, Dustin felt a sense of belonging. In the years leading up to the War of Northern Aggression, all seemed right with the world and Dustin's position seemed assured.

Most importantly, he believed he had been given the keys to the kingdom: that nothing about the plantation was held back from him. It seemed to Dustin that he had been initiated into an elite triumvirate with his father and Caleb. It was the last time he had felt such elation, though his service to Secretary Gresham came close. Since the war, however, Dustin had to fight for every scrap of access he had. In the practice of law, in the halls of Congress and in the Cleveland Administration, his heritage was no longer a boon, but rather a bane. He was held at arm's length in so many environments and he despised the aura of exile. It was no surprise, then, that his British ally—Nigel Alderson—was vexing him greatly with his recent standoffish behavior.

Dustin approached the 17th Street entrance to the State, War and Navy Building with a crush of last-minute bureaucrats, each rushing to be at his desk by the appointed hour. Among the throng, he spotted a distinguished-looking military officer—a flag officer, no less—adorned in a dark blue full dress uniform with shoulder boards, gold frogs, rank trim, a braided aiguillette and myriad battle ribbons. The general moved his way effortlessly through the door, impervious to the jostling all around him. Although Dustin did not know the man, he had a familiar look to him. Very familiar.

Senator Tillman surveyed his surroundings. From the packed galleries to the Senate floor, all eyes and ears were peeled. He was no longer unknown quantity, but the farthest extent of his firebrand rhetoric was anyone's guess. Other than the random plink of senatorial saliva hitting a spittoon, the silence was optimal. The finely polished desks stood out in stark relief against the royal purple carpet with floral patterns. What Tillman loved most about the chamber was the high iron ceiling, displaying 21 striking glass panels that reflected light from the skylight and from the gas jets installed between the panes and the roof. Light and truth were of one substance, and he would speak truth while bathed in light.

"Mr. President, I rise this morning to express grave concern over the tensions now growing with Great Britain. Mind you, I am no advocate of the monetarists of the United Kingdom who—aided and abetted by this administration and many colleagues here gathered—have successfully crushed the initiative and hopes of the industrious Anglo-Saxons on this continent. Yea, the monopolization and gluttonous acquisition of gold, tethered to the ruthless suppression of a silver-backed currency, has left the farmers and wage-earners of my state beleaguered and without recourse. We can lay this injustice upon the British, yes. Many inhabitants of this city also bear blame for robbing farmers and laborers of their birthright as Americans. Will they ever know shame? Will they ever yield to conscience? Their behavior does not leave me hopeful."

Tillman's speeches always began with the same set of premises.

"Though deserving of unmitigated condemnation, the mother country is far from singular in her abuse of power. If we are sincere about protecting the weak; if we are without guile in a commitment to fairness; if, indeed, we seek to impose a standard of right upon all nations who conduct commerce in this hemisphere, we must begin within our borders. The criminal repeal of the Sherman Silver Purchase Act is part and parcel with the seed of the conflict we see brewing on the lower continent. The disputed region north and west of the Cuyuni River bears neither strategic value nor historical relationship to either party in this contention. Only the gold beneath its earthen crust bids them come. When one or the other contender has depleted this metal, it will no doubt recede, leaving it the uninhabited jungle hinterland it has thus far been."

This speech was different, thought Senator Lodge, seated on the Republican side toward the front. Aside from one brief reference to Anglo-Saxons, Tillman's usual racial bile was absent.

"The irony, nay tragedy, of this condition is that this administration—bowing prostrate to the golden calf—presumes itself an unbiased and reasonable source of arbitration when, in fact, it has fanned the flames it now wants to douse. I would suggest to our distinguished secretary of state that he consider the relationship between this government's monetary policy and British designs on Venezuela before he fires off another belligerent note to London. I would further suggest to the president of the United States, his secretary of war and his secretary of the navy that they examine the economic consequences of launching a war against the country upon whom they rely to back our currency, in support of a dictator who evinces neither integrity nor competence."

Lodge winced involuntarily. The less spoken of President Joachin Crespo, the better.

"Finally, I remind my colleagues in this body that declaring war is a congressional prerogative. Let war's advocates and their claims be examined with the same standard of rigor we hold to our potential adversaries. Let these guarantors of greedy and corrupt banks explain to this Congress why— apart from gold—this matter is in the purview of these

United States. Let them argue for spilling the blood of our sons on the premises of the Monroe Doctrine when, by their own argument, no boundary is yet established between Venezuela and British Guyana leaving none, therefore, to be breached.

"Do not agree, I implore you, to senseless bloodshed in order to appease a misguided minority that believes American authority and credibility is measured by the amount of carnage our soldiers can inflict…and, I would add, endure. Resist the pressure of boys who require a war to feel like men. Resist, also, the monied interests who have brought the world to this point, when only the rarest metal holds sway over men and nations for—I assure you, gentlemen—imposed violence in Venezuela, British Guiana or any other nation will lead to greater conflict elsewhere. And to what end? The acquisition of bullion that will depress credit and kill the aspirations of millions of our fellow citizens.

"May your oath of office, if not your conscience, guide you in this grave decision. Mr. President, I yield the floor to the distinguished minority leader."

What happened next was an anomaly: scattered applause and several murmurs of affirmation from senators on both sides of the aisle. Ben Tillman had—until now—never garnered any response from his colleagues other than stony silence. His proud record of violent acts and lynchings during Reconstruction, coupled with the unrepentant rhetoric of white supremacy, left none wanting to openly endorse him. Even those who agreed with him did so covertly. The muted plaudits he now received were, therefore, extraordinary.

Although poker-faced, Henry Cabot Lodge was in a significant panic. Tillman had managed to maintain his high oratorical intensity without letting the speech degenerate into an emotional, racial screed, as was his want. If this renovated senator can move the hearts and minds of their colleagues, Lodge reasoned, he had the power to disrupt the forward motion of American assertiveness. Clearly, somebody was advising Tillman on what to say and what to leave out, and doing an effective job, at that. The only way to counter this phenomenon would be with substantive information. Opening the box top to his desk, he pulled out a writing tablet to record an urgent reminder: "British Embassy!!!"

Senator Tillman took his seat without the usual satisfaction. Granted, he received at least some demonstrable support from other senators, but the gratification was fleeting. He was only really satisfied when he could vent his spleen and this speech, frustratingly, required all his powers of restraint. The reward would come later. Dustin Boyle was now obliged to him for delivering a forceful, if bland, assault on the warmongers. Ben Tillman would exploit that debt to the fullest extent possible.

18

"What of it? You find a check for 856 dollars and think you can push me around?"

Lamont was simmering to a slow boil. General Swanson sat confidently across from the desk, lighting a cigar as though the conversation were about the weather.

"No, Mr. Secretary. Intimidation is more the mark of a Cleveland man, wouldn't you agree?"

"I don't know what you're talking about," Lamont hissed back.

"The president paid the legal bill for a newspaper that libeled an opponent. He demonstrated that libel is an acceptable political tool in his arsenal."

"That paper was found innocent of the charges. George Ball smeared Cleveland in 1884 and the *New York Evening Post* was truthfully reporting his scheming."

Swanson smiled. "Politicians get smeared by opponents on a regular basis. Newspapers almost as frequently find themselves involved in litigation. Rare, however, are the instances of politicians who bankroll the journalists' lawyers."

"I might point out, General, that Mr. Cleveland was between terms during that trial. He was a private citizen, free to help a friend in need. I am curious to know why you left your post—without permission, mind you—to share such innocuous information with me."

"It's part of a larger problem, Mr. Secretary. This president, who presents himself as a man immune to political machinations, is actually knee-deep in them. He was not party to this lawsuit, yet involved himself to assure that Reverend Ball was destroyed and his own return to the presidency unimpeded."

Lamont was now red with fury. "George Ball destroyed himself!! How dare you come into this office and disparage your commander-in-chief!"

Swanson was unmoved. "I will finish my statement and then take my leave. If you ask for my resignation, I will readily comply."

Lamont was hoping that his anxiety would not be evident. "Just state your business."

"Gladly. I said this is part of a larger problem. I believe that the helter-skelter, proceed and delay commands regarding the troop consolidation are part and parcel with the political agenda of this administration. America's finest lads are out on the Plains, Mr. Secretary, ready to fight for their country. You, sir, have given them the instruction to prepare for this contingency only to reverse yourself in a matter of weeks. If I believed this to be an honest adjustment of policy, I would say nothing. Long experience, however, has taught me that those who are most ruthless with their political enemies at home, are often submissive to our real enemies abroad."

"The president will deal with our enemies honorably and without fear, I assure you. He will not, all the same, launch a bloody war precipitously just so the army can stretch its legs."

"I think this check for $856.82 to the firm of Rogers Locke Milburn on behalf of editor Edwin L. Godkin makes it clear that the president fears a great many things…in addition to military service."

"Get out."

"I will remain in Washington for the time being. At your request, I shall resign. Otherwise, I will await new orders. Obviously, there is little for me to do back in Oklahoma."

Tucking his Burnside-style hat under one arm, Ezekiel Swanson rose and smartly saluted the man he was blackmailing.

Lamont swiveled around to look out the window, the same pane he stared through after Dustin Boyle had strong-armed him with the suggestion of the president's secret surgery. He was now again being subject to another man in possession of embarrassing political information. Cleveland appreciated the *Post*'s vigorous defense of his character when the Maria Halpin story was raging, hence the favor of picking up the lawyer fees. That was the president's way, loyal to a fault. As successful as the president was, Lamont thought, his political sensibilities were often dull. True,

George Ball ran Cleveland's name through the mud when word of Maria Halpin's illegitimate son came out during the 1884 campaign. The *Post* was returning the favor on Cleveland's behalf. There was nothing sinister there.

Grover Cleveland failed to see, however, that his check could be easily misinterpreted to imply that the paper's attack on Ball may have been executed at the candidate's request. A fundamentally honest man, President Cleveland only once saw fit to conceal the facts—when news of his health may have prevented the repeal of the Sherman Silver Purchase Act. The Vice President was a known silver proponent and voted for repeal may have fallen away if legislators believed that Adlai Stevenson were soon to be president. Thus, the decision was made to cloak the surgery in secrecy. Not secret enough, it turned out. Dustin Boyle had confirmed that fact.

Ezekiel Swanson's new assertions not only complicated the issue of whether or not the war was advisable, but also promised to color the conduct of the war should the British stand their ground. Lamont hoped there might be something to Olney's belief that Dustin Boyle was bluffing. Swanson, on the other hand, had a reputation for saying exactly what he meant; in this instance, as in all others, he did not mince words.

The Secretary did not tell the general of Cleveland's decision to unilaterally establish a boundary between British Guiana and Venezuela. Keeping Swanson guessing was now Lamont's only leverage. For now, he would let the General believe he had forced the resumption of troop consolidation by means of his threat. The greater concern was that Swanson would want to prosecute the war on his own terms—and those of his sponsor and booster, Henry Cabot Lodge. An expanded war as envisioned by the jingoes would not only end in ignoble defeat, Lamont believed, but would also permanently taint the legacy of President Grover Cleveland.

At this point, Cleveland's long-time friend and advisor had to concede a change in the political calculus: the president could not run again. Between the possible exposure of the cancer surgery and the resuscitation of the Maria Halpin scandal, the risks were now much too high. They had weathered the illicit affair in the 1884 campaign due to a posture of straightforwardness and—admittedly—the public's fatigue with the Republicans after two decades. Now, however, that exhaustion worked against the Democrats. The old scandal would grow new and stronger legs as the Depression lingered. No, the political task now was to deliver Grover Cleveland into retirement with his reputation for honesty intact.

Both carrot and stick would have to be employed. Swanson would hold his tongue about the check when he learned consolidation was continuing apace. If necessary, Lamont would hold out the prospect of promotion as long as the general ran the war per the president's instructions. In the mean time, Lamont would wait and see what Dustin Boyle's next move would be. If the man were smart, he would accept the facts and get behind administration policy. Otherwise, Lamont may have to take Olney's suspicion about Dustin's personal life and—true or not—disseminate it widely as fact.

The letter from Tillman was waiting for Dustin as he arrived home at the Hotel Washington late in the evening. He left his coat on as he entered his rooms and sat at the small table upon which he had spent many hours outlining his future. At this stage of his scenario, contact with Tillman was supposed to be short and indiscernible, certainly not a matter of record. Written correspondence was risky and Dustin wondered what could be so urgent. Unlike most senators, Tillman did not invest in expensively embroidered stationery and Dustin was surprised by the crude paper and smudge-laden text. The letter began with reassurance:

> I have enclosed the text of my speech of 19 December. You will be gratified, I am sure, as to the message conveyed and the language used to convey it. It was received well among many colleagues and, without doubt, gave many of the undecided Senators pause for thought.

Dustin was indeed gratified. At this point, any doubts raised over a war with Britain were welcome. The fact that any legislators demonstrated open support for Tillman's, or Dustin's, call for restraint was cause for celebration. Shedding his coat, he remained fixed upon the encouraging note. All of a sudden, the positive tone changed quickly as Tillman came to his point:

> I am certain you agree that our platform must be built on a firmer foundation than

opposition to war over Venezuela. The profound social and economic consequences of Negro emancipation continue to wreak havoc upon the United States. While the destructive results of the War of Northern Aggression can not all be reversed, we can at the very least move to secure the racial purity of our culture and institutions.

Where was he going with this? Dustin knew Tillman's heart was set upon re-asserting the concept of white supremacy, but first things first. Tillman may have fired a salvo at the jingoes, but they were far from interred. This was no time to indulge in distractions.

I believe we can not stress a policy of humility abroad without fortifying our culture at home. I should therefore ask that you prepare some notations upon which I can base my next speeches, the content of which should assert the inferiority of Negroes in intellect and morality. You fought for these beliefs as a young man and are suited for the task of preparing compelling arguments to advance this cause.

Please Ben, Dustin thought, I do not need more to do. All of this can wait. Tillman then let the shoe drop.

Any further assistance I can lend on the boundary matter is ineffectual without

attention given to the central problem that
the unnatural elevation of the dark races
threatens our moral authority. I am
unable to render further aid without
inclusion of this issue in my public
addresses. I am moreover unable to
articulate this position without your
active participation.

Dustin sat with one arm still inside the sleeve of his
overcoat. There it was. Tillman would not lift another
finger unless Dustin committed his time and energies to the
Senator's racial agenda. He was giving notice that Dustin
would receive no help in the upper chamber unless he
signed on to the draconian philosophy that grew up in
Reconstruction and was manifest, briefly, in the violent
activities of the Ku Klux Klan in the 1870s.

Dustin hung up his coat and began his usual pacing. So
what if Tillman wanted to play up race? That had always
been his *raison detre*. Would it really take too much time to
write out some anti-Negro rhetoric for Tillman's benefit?
Justus' more tolerant views could be set aside in the service
of his commission to his son: to vindicate the South by
rising to the highest level of leadership. This request really
should present no challenge at all.

The Negro question was never what motivated Dustin
Boyle. Despite his plantation origins and military service to
the Confederacy, Dustin's resentments were against a
coercive and intrusive government more than about who
could vote for whom. But he was a political man. Throwing
Tillman a bone on race was certainly not beneath him. So,

216

what was the problem? Why did Tillman's scrawled message disturb him? Perhaps Dustin had conveyed too great a desire to enlist the Senator's help. Now Tillman could use the boundary issue as leverage with him, threatening to abandon it unless Dustin toed the line on race.

Dustin's concerns went deeper, though. What would Caleb's life be like had he survived the fire? Would he have been hunted down by the Klan? Harassed by self-proclaimed vigilantes like Tillman during Reconstruction? Without the Boyles to look after his interests, Caleb and his family may have known only fear and poverty. Dustin physically shivered at the thought of that robust and warm-hearted man being terrorized by hooded lunatics. Immersed in education, business and politics during the post-war years, Dustin paid scant attention to the cultural forces at work in the South. He had to admit that some of them were sinister.

How would Sarah's life differ if Ben Tillman got his way? In her, he detected light-heartedness and seriousness of purpose. She would do well for herself given her work ethic, friendliness and acute powers of observation. And yet, would those traits be enough to survive a Benjamin Tillman administration? Even a single term? The more Dustin chewed on the matter, the more he realized the danger of hitching his own political star to Tillman's wagon?

Dustin stood up and slammed the extortion-in-print down onto the table.

What choice did he have in the end? Tillman was the only southerner with half a chance, given the growing power of populism in the United States. As he had done throughout his career, Dustin would make the moral compromises necessary to bring Justus Boyle's dream to fruition.

19

"From the information we've been able to gather, he does little more than serve as an appointments secretary, his attaché status more an honor than a function."

In spite of his name, Miles Small was a large, muscular man who looked like a bare-knuckled boxer when walking the street. This day, however, seated at Senator Lodge's dining table with multiple reports before him, he gave the appearance of a small-town banker or bookkeeper conducting an audit. The glare from his thick spectacles concealed the dark circles under his brown eyes; his thick blond hair and waxed mustache softened a protruding forehead and severely chiseled jaw; and his voice spoke with quiet authority. Two decades as a private investigator – and a prior ten years with the Metropolitan Police – earned Small a following by those who wanted the inside skinny in the nation's capital.

"So he's useless is what you're saying," Lodge prompted.

"Hardly. This arrangement is with his hearty consent, because it suits his purposes."

Theodore Roosevelt piped up, having bounced in his chair for the duration of the briefing. "Of course it does. He's a degenerate in every other facet. Should it surprise anyone that the man is lazy?"

"Lazy in terms of official business," Small interjected, "but amazingly diligent in his alternate career."

"Debauchery is not a career, Small."

"No? Have you looked at your own department's arrest records, Commissioner? It is as huge an enterprise here as in New York."

"But this man is a...a...he's buying, not soliciting," Roosevelt persisted, uncomfortable with the direction of the conversation.

Small let the Commissioner's naïve observation hang out for several awkward seconds.

"He's operating a prostitution ring of his own?" Lodge inquired.

Small nodded slightly. "Right out of the embassy, where my former brother constables can not touch him."

"Clever. How does he conduct his hideous trade under the ambassador's nose?"

"You have just brought us back to his ignominious job, Senator. He's in charge of the calendar: he knows when social events take place and, more importantly, when they don't. He also knows when Pauncefote *et ux* will be out for the evening, which is often. He keeps close track of every other diplomat on that post, as well."

"What about the household staff?"

"My source informs me that he brings his "employees" in through a private entrance off the laundry service. Alderson engages the one laundress who keeps quarters there with other tasks on the nights that he conducts business, so he is able to scurry the women up the service stairs with no one else the wiser. The patrons are all government men with whom he could ostensibly have legitimate dealings, so they are welcomed at the formal entrance."

Lodge was about to pursue the issue further but, refined as he was, stopped short: "Mr. Small, we are trying to obtain important information regarding British government policy. Whether or not this man is knee-deep in the flesh trade is scintillating, but not especially helpful. What good is he to us if all he knows is the ambassador's physical whereabouts? We need to know the ambassador's mindset, and what messages he is getting from London."

The detective displayed no reaction, other than to continue his briefing. "It seems that Alderson is his own best customer, auditioning his women several times before releasing them to his circle of friends. He has – and this is key – a pathetic need to impress them with his position and knowledge. In so doing, he lacks discretion."

Lodge was getting irritated. "His position is lowly and his knowledge is nil, from everything you have said here."

"All true, Senator Lodge, except in one area. He has confidential knowledge of discord in the State Department over the Venezuelan boundary matter."

The senator froze: "Our State Department? How did you discover this?"

"Shall I tell you?"

"I retract the question," Lodge responded, thinking the better of it.

"Secretary Olney's posture on Venezuela is not, as the facts bear out, unanimously supported by his underlings. One official is petitioning Alderson to persuade the British government to agree to mediation, with the promise of favoritism at the table. This guarantee is made with the hope of putting a damper on American military preparations."

"Gutless coward!!" Roosevelt exclaimed. "Will our country forever snivel and appease the great powers?"

Lodge was shocked, but pressed forward: "Do you know who the traitor is?"

"This information is not easily drawn out in one fell swoop," Detective Small observed drily. "But I suspect I will have identified this person within 24 hours."

"Here we are trying to divine the intentions of Salisbury and the U.K., and our own people are undercutting us!" Roosevelt fumed. "Cabot, this traitor must be exposed, stripped of his position and prosecuted without mercy!"

Senator Lodge stood, clearing his throat. "Why don't we meet here again tomorrow evening for an update, Small. Theodore, can you postpone your return to New York?"

"As long as I'm home by Christmas Eve, I can. I must. We're at a momentous crossroad here."

Looking to the silent figure silhouetted against his front window, Lodge asked, "Is that acceptable to you, Mr. Yarrington?"

William Yarrington had not spoken during Small's discourse. The diminutive man with thinning gray hair, and unsightly dark freckles nodded affirmatively, turning to the detective. "Make it worth our while, Mr. Small. That's what I pay you for."

Sarah finished arranging Lady Pauncefote's undergarments for drying, and took a seat while carefully placing hot coals in the flatiron for the 26 holiday-themed napkins before her. She was uncharacteristically exhausted, but pleased about the reason why. Dustin Boyle had arrived the previous evening for a scheduled meeting with Alderson at 11pm, waiting until midnight for the attaché, who never showed. It was not the first time Alderson had been away from the embassy all night. In fact, his absences had grown in frequency the last few weeks. Dustin, however, was visibly upset by the unexpected adjournment. Sarah tried to keep his mind at ease as the hour grew later...and later.

"Having visited your daytime workplace, I can see why you are so cheerful when you can venture out of the dungeon," he said.

Sarah smiled, knowingly. "If it were just a matter of surroundings, Mr. Boyle, I would think you should always exhibit good cheer. Yet, you are preoccupied and worried. On the other hand, a contented person can be so amid a pile of soiled linens or behind the bench at the Supreme Court. It makes little difference in the end."

Dustin laughed heartily at her naïve outlook. "I wish we had more like you where I come from."

"That makes two of us."

He suppressed a smile that wanted desperately to be flashed.

While he always professed to adhere to Justus' benevolent views regarding Negroes, Dustin had to admit – if only to himself – that he had not really been close to any, other than Caleb. Sarah talked to him like Caleb had, as a friend and companion. He did not have to appeal to his status or position with her. For some frustratingly unknowable reason, she liked him just as he was.

"Are you hoping for a permanent position upstairs?"

"I would like it, absolutely, but do not set my heart on things like that. If, ten years from now, I am still a laundry maid, I aim to be ten years better at it than I am now."

"Is that enough incentive to keep yourself going? I mean, what is there to look forward to?"

Sarah looked him straight in the eye. "Everything...in this life, and the next. Don't you feel that way?"

She was beautiful, he had to admit. She needed a man to provide for her and give her children. There was too much love in her heart to be wasting her life with bluing and soda crystals. Exuding curiosity, strength and nurturing instincts, this woman deserved better in life. Maybe he should find a Negro man with a secure position to court her. Dustin was warmed by the thought of her personal fulfillment.

"Well, Mr. Boyle, don't you?"

"Uh, I'm not sure, actually." She startled him. He had actually allowed himself to think about something other than the matter that brought him there. For a few precious moments, he had forgotten himself, his political plans and the accursed Venezuela Boundary Dispute.

"Well take my word for it: good things are in store for Mr. Dustin Boyle."

He wanted to bask in her smile, but the clock sounded the midnight toll.

"Sarah, will you tell Mr. Alderson to get a message to me as soon as he can? I hope he's alright. He, of all people, should be wary of the danger of that business if our suspicions are correct"

"Leave it to me. I suspect he just lost track of time. You'll hear from him soon."

Dustin struggled into his overcoat, only to sense her capable assistance behind him. He wished, for a moment, at least...

Turning back as he was leaving, he told her, "You take care of yourself. Good things will come your way, too, if there is a God."

She placed her hand on his forearm. "There is. You'll know that for yourself soon enough."

Sarah basked in the memory of that seemingly inconsequential exchange until an unexpected guest broke her trance.

"Sarah, would you kindly oblige me, and remove the stain from this lapel?"

Nigel Alderson was down in the laundry room, unheard of for one of the ambassador's men. Household staffers were peering around the corner to satiate their curiosity. Sarah peered at the silk fabric, looked up at Alderson and whispered, "Did you forget your appointment with Mr. Boyle last night, sir?"

His voice dropped to barely audible. "I was detained by other matters, unfortunately."

"He wants to hear from you."

"I'll manage Mr. Boyle, Sarah. Just have this ready for me in two hours at the latest. There's a good girl."

As he left, she could see his mind was as far from Dustin Boyle as the east is from the west. She placed his coat over her arm, but heard the rustle of paper in the pocket. Before she was inundated by gossipy colleagues, she darted into her bedroom and shut the door. This could be confidential correspondence. She had no business looking at it. Still, she was concerned for Dustin's welfare, and worried about Alderson's increasingly frequent absences.

Sarah removed the folded paper and opened it with some trepidation. To her relief, it was not a diplomatic document, only some scribbled names with dates following. They were first names only, all women. In fresher ink at the bottom was a full name and address:

Bridgette Maher
1206 U Street, N.W.
3rd Floor

It could all be legitimate, Sarah reasoned. But Alderson's erratic behavior of late was likely related to this address…or at least to this Maher woman. Did any of this relate to Dustin? She dropped to her knees beside the bed. What could she do? What should she do? Obviously, Dustin was unaware of Alderson's whereabouts the prior evening. He was depending on Alderson to keep their appointment. No, he was not privy to the goings on at 1206 U Street or the activities of Miss Bridgette Maher. Still, if those activities were undermining the partnership of the two men, she had a duty to tell him what she knew. Either her head or her heart was at that moment loudly echoing prophetic wisdom: "These are the things that ye shall do; Speak ye every man the truth to his neighbor…" If it was good enough for the prophet Zechariah…

Sarah opened the door and returned to her duties, praying for a word of knowledge. Waiting for her by a large pile of dirty uniforms worn by the household staff was Nelson, one of the embassy's couriers. Of medium height and olive complexion, the man was nervously running a hand through his curly brown hair. Although he gave every indication of being British, he could easily pass for Italian.

"Sarah, thank heaven I caught you. Did you happen to run across…"

She pulled a letter from her apron. "This invitation? Of course, my friend," she informed the relieved messenger. "I go through every pocket before anything gets washed." Her warm smile helped to relax him.

"I would have been sacked if I had lost it, what with how her Ladyship likes to hobnob. You're a peach, girl!" He pinched her cheek, and returned her grin. "Gotta run, love."

"Oh, Nelson?"

Nelson halted the momentum of his mad dash and turned to face her. "I'm late already, Sarah."

"I just wanted to know, do you take messages to the State Department?"

"Practically every day. Why?"

She began to copy the information on Miss Bridgette Maher onto a torn piece of butcher's paper that she would use to protect delicate fabrics when pressing. She added: *Our absentee host carries this address. For whatever it is worth, Sarah.* Folding it twice, she wrote Dustin's name on the outside. "Can you deliver it to this gentleman?"

"Everything that goes to State is delivered in a diplomatic pouch, Sarah. Their people sort it all out."

"I happen to know that you have many pockets, Mr. Hardwick. This little note could travel in one of them, while you find out in which office Mr. Boyle works. I really need your help, Nelson."

His body slouched in full surrender. "If you weren't so bloody nice, I'd tell you where to put your note," he teased. "OK, my dear. Done." He slipped the note into his coat pocket, patting it for confirmation. "I won't forget *this* one."

"Oh, and can we keep this little favor between us? You may just be helping to bring peace to the world."

"I'll be happy just to get some peace from Lady Pauncefote. See you later."

<u>20</u>

As president of the Northern Plains Hardware Corporation, William Yarrington was one of the first to exploit the discovery of metallic ores in Minnesota. Extracting huge amounts ahead of his competitors, he immediately employed several-hundred low-paid tradesmen to manufacture all manner of steel vessels, tools and other implements. A veteran of the Mexican War, he combined warrior aggression with business savvy to achieve his ends – namely, to dominate the emerging trading markets in South America. Though rich in metals themselves, his target countries were unsophisticated in mass production, and were beginning to enrich Northern Plains beyond Yarrington's wildest dreams. Now that Venezuela had come into a small fortune between the Orinoco and Essequibo rivers, he was not about to let the English grab what was destined for his coiffures. He called the rump session to order.

"Are we all here? Begin, Mr. Small."

"As you wish, Mr. Yarrington. The last 24 hours have yielded just what we were waiting for, gentlemen. Our operative," he said, glancing at a blushing Roosevelt, "has extracted the name and status of Alderson's contact in the State Department. It goes to the highest tier of authority."

"Olney?!" Lodge asked, incredulously.

"Not quite, thank Heaven, but close. Secretary Olney has a roving legal counselor, who was previously serving Secretary Gresham. This man was retained by Olney at the president's direction, though his influence is somewhat diminished. His name is Dustin Boyle."

"I should have known!" Senator Lodge exploded. "He was the lawyer who Gresham used to scuttle the Hawaii annexation. Of all the underhanded machinations, he now dares to broker an agreement, one by which the United States will doubtless be weakened?"

"Exactly, Cabot! When they are weak in the Pacific, they will be weak in the Atlantic. That sort is always for surrender. Cleveland must dismiss him immediately!" Roosevelt intoned, his voice rising to a squeaky pitch.

"We don't know, Teddy, if Mr. Cleveland knows about Boyle's activities," Lodge cautioned." His sentimental attachment to Gresham's memory may cause him to dig in his heels."

"But the remonstrance from Olney received a presidential accolade, I'm told. Why would he undermine his own secretary of state now?"

"I don't know, but we can not make assumptions."

Small chose the short pause to interject: "There's more, gentlemen, much more."

"Proceed," Yarrington calmly directed.

"Mr. Boyle served for two years in the Confederate army, rising to the rank of Major."

"What of it?" Lodge countered. "Most of the southerners in Cleveland's administration wore the gray. It's immaterial."

"It would be, Senator" Small said, "if that were all. He distinguished himself – and was wounded in the process – at Shiloh, Tennessee with the 17th Louisiana Infantry Regiment; and at Seven Pines, Virginia, with the Alabama 8th Infantry Regiment, both in 1862. Several months after that last battle he appeared in his home state of Louisiana and surrendered. He then attended the Louisiana State Seminary of Learning and Military Institute. Upon completion, he moved to New Orleans to study law at Tulane College. From there, he joined the Alabama law practice of Hilary A. Herbert, with whom I believe he served at Seven Pines. Although CSA records were poorly maintained, it seems that his name was placed on the Confederate Roll of Honor in 1864. Shall I continue?"

Impatient, Lodge answered, "Are you going to tell us anything we could not know by calling the Civil Service Commission?" He looked at Roosevelt, who had become suddenly docile.

Small continued: "Herbert, as you know, was elected to Congress in 1876. Boyle served as his confidential secretary when the House was in session, and Herbert brought him to Washington permanently when the congressman was named secretary of the navy."

"And not a bad one, either," Lodge conceded thoughtfully, stroking his beard.

"Within just a few months, he gained the favor of Walter Gresham, who requested that Boyle be transferred to his employ at State. That is where we find him today."

Lodge sighed loudly.

Small again pretended not to notice, and went to his point: "You recall that I mentioned an interlude of a few months between Boyle's last active military engagement and his surrender in Louisiana?"

Nods all around.

"Well, my source reports that our Mr. Boyle doffed his gray uniform and donned civilian garb, traveling to Jolly Old England on a mission for Jeff Davis. Specifically, he was recruiting British naval officers to fill in the blanks on boats where the Rebs were short. If you recall, the South built a small, but effective, navy. Many of their ships were launched from London and Liverpool, under the supervision of their spymaster, James Bulloch."

Yarrington burst out in laughter. "Well, Senator, try getting that information from the Civil Service Commission."

Lodge appeared agitated, but Roosevelt grew sullen.

"Among his recruits," Small pressed on, "was one Lieutenant Nigel Alderson of the Royal Navy. Alderson had been restricted to shore pending a hearing related to a disciplinary infraction. Apparently, Bulloch endowed

Boyle with a considerable sum to lure young, unassigned officers to serve on the CSS *Georgia,* an iron hull vessel that ended up sinking three Union ships and capturing another six."

"So that's how they met," Lodge said. "They corresponded after the war, then?"

"With great frequency," Small asserted. "As an attorney, Boyle shrewdly solicited clients who transacted large shipments from the Port of Mobile, Alabama. In this capacity, he made numerous contacts in foreign trade ministries, and exploited his relationship with Alderson, who then had a low-tier assignment in the British Foreign Office. While the circumstances are unclear, my agent believes Alderson owes Boyle some form of obligation. I reason that he is now fulfilling it."

Yarrington was excited. "Well, gentlemen, it seems we have enough information to put this man in irons, if not a noose!"

Theodore Roosevelt was, by now, nearly frozen in deep thought. The mention of James Bulloch, the legendary Confederate espionage leader and ship builder, changed everything. Only Lodge knew that Bulloch was Roosevelt's uncle – his mother's brother – and his favorite uncle at that. Remaining in England after the war, Uncle Jimmie would accommodate the Roosevelts when they traveled to Europe, and visit the family in the U.S., *in cognito*, of course. He taught young Teddy everything he knew about ships and sailing, and inspired the lad's authorship of the tome, *The Naval War of 1812*. The volume made a name – and a tidy nest egg – for young Roosevelt, who still aspired to become secretary of the navy. As angry as he was at the State Department counselor, he could not countenance Uncle Jimmie's name being slandered in a federal prosecution. He would derail this effort now.

"The aim, my good fellows, is to neutralize this parallel diplomacy. Boyle must be fired, and the Brit must be recalled. However, we have neither the time nor the cause to engage in a legal rigamaroll. What do you think, Cabot?" Roosevelt asked his friend, with a plaintive undertone.

"I concur, Commissioner," Lodge answered knowingly and empathetically. "This boundary conflict must be resolved above board, without subordinates and secret deals. We'll notify Secretary Olney of Boyle's scheming, and inform Cecil Rice of this attaché and his brothel. The president can then cut his ties to Gresham completely with a clear conscience. Those actions should be satisfactory."

For several long seconds, Yarrington stared at the pair, slackjawed. "My friends, this will simply not do," he protested upon regaining his wits. "This matter has gone too far for half-measures. Do you know what these ex-rebels think about, day and night, hour upon hour? Revenge. Do you think they returned to federal service out of patriotism? Politics is war by other means and – I promise you – they are still at war. Letting Hawaii go, ignoring the Spanish atrocities in Cuba, now rolling over for the Queen in Venezuela: it's all part of preventing this country from assuming her rightful place in the world."

Yarrington was warming to his subject, his voice rising accordingly. "The Democrats are leaning toward a policy of international irrelevancy and Dixie is providing the gravity!"

Lodge began decanting wine in crystal goblets. "I'm not certain of that, Mr. Yarrington. Many southerners in the House support our position on Venezuela. William Scruggs himself is from Georgia."

"I speak of the hardened veterans, Senator. The ones who had to make do with raggedy uniforms and mediocre weaponry, and watch their friends die in a losing war. The ones who had to return to conquered homes in humiliation. It will never be over for them. This man, Boyle, must stand trial for treason. Small, here, has assured me that the Confederate spies in London and Liverpool did not fall under the amnesties issued by Presidents Johnson and Grant. If Boyle has an assemblage of international friends, as Small indicates, he can still make an enormous stench for us abroad. He must not be left to his own devices."

Roosevelt stood and turned on Yarrington, getting in his face. "Sir, the purpose of our inquiry was to discern the intentions of the British government, not to launch time-wasting trials. We can, from all the evidence, determine that they are intent on absorbing the disputed territory. This secret diplomacy among underlings means that the principals are still wedded to their opposing positions. We need to mobilize! Pursuing a bureaucrat – particularly after his dismissal – is a superfluous and self-defeating use of our time."

The industrialist was by now red in the face. "Did you not, Commissioner, just yesterday call for prosecution without mercy? What in blazes is going on here?!"

Yarrington turned plaintively to Lodge, who simply shook his head and handed him a goblet. "Don't worry. Bill. We will keep the Brits from stealing Venezuelan land. Your interests are secure. Shall we have dinner?"

As Roosevelt and Lodge headed for the dining room, a dazed and confused Yarrington pulled his detective aside. Practically panting, he stated, "This is a bazaar turn of events. They are good men, but naïve. We have to resolve this matter so Boyle is held accountable for his crimes. He can actually pose greater danger as a private citizen, I'll be bound."

"Information and operations are two distinct services, Mr. Yarrington, the latter coming at a higher price," Small advised.

"Pennies compared to what I stand to lose if Her Majesty seizes that gold between the rivers," Yarrington concluded grimly.

The eggnog had a powerful kick and Dustin was already tired from waiting up for Alderson the previous evening. Though largely excluded from the administration's official parties, this Christmas Eve gathering was a tradition set by the secretary of the navy years before. Although his law partner and protégé had, in seafaring terms, jumped ship for the State Department, Hilary Herbert was not about to let

Dustin spend the holiday alone. He would dine with the Herberts' family and friends this night, and they would all attend church at St. John's at midnight.

As seemingly indifferent as Dustin behaved, his loneliness hurt most at this time of year. He was grateful for the hospitality of his old boss. He returned the kindness, always bearing many gifts for the ladies and grandchildren, and summoning his suppressed—but never forsaken— southern chivalry. It was the one time of year he could put aside Justus' expectations and simply be one among many. For days afterward, he would carry the warmth and friendship of the evening with him.

This year was different. For all of Dustin's shuttling and cajoling, for all of his careful planning, events were overtaking him and war was imminent. The British dismissal of Olney's remonstrance infuriated the president, who issued an uncharacteristically bellicose addendum to his Annual Message to Congress:

> I am nevertheless firm in my conviction
> that while it is a grievous thing to
> contemplate the two great English-
> speaking peoples of the world as being
> otherwise than friendly competitors in the
> onward march of civilization and
> strenuous and worthy rivals in the arts of
> peace, there is no calamity which a great
> nation can invite which equals that which
> follows a supine submission to wrong
> and injustice and the consequent loss of
> national self-respect and honor, beneath

which are shielded and defended a
people's safety and greatness.

He was forming a boundary commission without British
input and daring them to defy him. What had gone wrong?
He knew Alderson had forwarded his offer to the highest
levels of the British government. Was the president right?
Were the Brits only interested in supine submission? Dustin
was giving them an out—a crucial out in lieu of their other
conflicts simmering around the world. They should have
jumped at the terms he advanced through Nigel Alderson.
Now it looked as though Dustin had only one avenue left,
an unlikely one given the president's fury. Worse, Sarah's
note seemed to indicate that whatever good Alderson had
been to him was now being dissipated by his pathological
womanizing.

If that were not enough, his one redoubt in Congress was
going to collapse unless Dustin drafted orations for
Benjamin Tillman that were replete with accusations of
shiftlessness, promiscuity and genetic inferiority against
Negroes. He had spent the last few nights trying to
compose something, yet could not bring himself to
approach the intensity of loathing that Tillman demanded.
Of late, it seemed, whatever Dustin touched was turning to
ashes.

A friendly arm was suddenly slung over Dustin's shoulder.
"You diplomatic folk are always ruminating. Had you stuck
with me you could have left your work at the office, son.
Cheer up. It's Christmas!" Secretary Herbert had long been
a father figure to Dustin, leading him in battle and
sponsoring him at the bar. Dustin knew they had become

more distant since he went to work for Gresham. Herbert likely felt abandoned and Dustin was riddled with guilt over it. But his grand political plan was better served by a sinecure at State. One day, Hilary Herbert would appreciate why Dustin had to jump ship. He would be proud of Dustin, as Justus would have been.

"I'm sorry, Colonel. I am prone to daydream sometimes."

Herbert's trousers and frock were bottle green, contrasting seasonally with his red vest. Though Dustin never saw him take a drink or smoke a cigar, the Secretary always exuded a comforting southern aroma of tobacco and whiskey. He was always hospitable despite the parting of their professional ways. Dustin almost felt like burying his head on the man's shoulder and crying in remorse.

The act would be futile, of course. Aside from the fact that men of their station did not engage in emotional displays, Dustin would not have found a sympathetic ear. Herbert was in perfect accord with the Olney policy on Venezuela. Any overseas hostilities played into his strategy of securing healthier appropriations for the Navy. It went beyond that, though. Like many other southerners in Washington, Herbert inexplicably made his peace with the United States. Not just legally and politically, but in his heart. He, of course, did not have to bear the posthumous charge of Justus Boyle.

"Not me," Herbert replied. "Too much to do these days." He scooped a running toddler up in his arms and kissed the little blonde boy on a chubby cheek. Under his Dutch-boy haircut, the child beamed through blue saucer eyes at his grandfather, earning another kiss and a big hug.

"This is why I do what I do, Dustin," he continued, releasing the boy to his cousins. "It's for that generation that we need to build a great and powerful navy. When we practiced law we were in the thick of world trade, but we never needed muscle. The world has changed, son, and our commercial interests need safe passage on the high seas. Many countries can stifle our commerce absent the threat of our gunships." He paused. "You're worried about the Boundary Dispute."

"Begging your pardon, Colonel, but I believe that to intervene is tantamount to the invasion of our lands back in '61. How can we be party to this?"

Herbert stepped back and surveyed his one-time protégé. He knew Dustin was smarter than that and wondered what force was compelling his stubborn pacifism. "You don't believe that, Dustin. You know that any action our forces take would be to repel an invasion." Lowering his voice, he continued: "More than any man in this administration, you know how lethal British warships are. The Venezuelans can not mount an effective resistance. What, then, is their recourse?"

"Diplomacy," Dustin intoned, somewhat piously.

Herbert could see through Dustin Boyle, who spent so much of his energies trying to be opaque. He offered a father's embrace to his prodigal son, whispering in his ear:

"Your day will come, Dustin. Just don't hold a small country hostage to hasten that day."

Dustin looked at the secretary. Like Gresham, Herbert loved him. Neither man, however, truly knew him. To know Dustin Boyle, one had to know Justus. The son was but a penumbra, an afterglow of the great man himself. Herbert may have suspected Dustin's enormous ambitions. But he would never know the hows or the whys. Even Dustin was not certain of the whys.

"Let us dine, my boy. Soon it will be time for church." Leading Dustin to an elegant buffet of Beef Wellington, breast of goose and pecan pie—among other delicacies— Hilary Herbert burst out into a rousing rendition of "Good King Wenceslas," cheering, for a little while, even the dour Dustin Boyle.

<u>21</u>

January, 1896

The buttery-yellow silk upholstery added to the elegant appearance of Dustin's office, but the modest length of the federal-style sofa made for a fitful and uncomfortable night of sleep. He wanted to get in the reception line early, hence stayed overnight to position himself toward the front of a line that normally extended into the thousands. Given a coveted and luxurious corner office by Gresham, Dustin had windows facing east as well as south. Stiffly rising from the couch, he walked to the eastern window from which he could view the South Lawn. Drawing open the royal blue drapes, he felt instantly encouraged. Frost on the windows and a howling wind confirmed that the long wait to enter the Executive Mansion would not be for the frail. So much the better, he thought, since the violence of the elements would probably depress the turnout.

The southern pane, however, revealed a stunning refutation of that hope. The line of New Year well-wishers was already wrapped around the south side of the State, War and Navy Building. Having originated at the northeast gate of the White House, it extended down past the State, War and Navy Building to 17th Street , then snaking to the south. Hundreds were out there already. How long did he sleep? The clock read fifteen minutes past seven o'clock. This would be a long, miserable day, he thought, as he entered the small lavatory to clean and groom. His anger at Lane had subsided somewhat. How would he have known that Dustin was not included among administration officials that were invited to greet the president and his wife ahead of the general public? It was a forgivable oversight on the part of his guilt-ridden war comrade. Lane came through for him as best he could. He was a loyal friend. And he was not a coward. Confederate officers were not cowards.

The fact remained, however, that he would have to make his introduction to Mrs. Cleveland during the public reception, as opposed to the earlier, closed event for administration bigwigs. She would be tired and, worse, her husband would be right beside her. Given his rumored temperament, he would doubtless be grouchy by this time, wondering why a strangely familiar looking man was whispering to his wife. Approaching the president directly was out of the question. This was not an occasion to talk business in any event. Moreover, Dustin was counting on the First Lady to soften the chief executive up for an unscheduled talk with "a friend of a friend." He would, therefore, ask for an appointment as quickly and unobtrusively as possible, give a quick greeting to President Cleveland and then exit with all due haste. Nevertheless, the long wait in line seemed a colossal waste of Dustin's time.

Having lived away from the sub-tropical Louisiana climate for many years, Dustin was still unable to reconcile his body to mid-Atlantic winters. Hanging a hot water bottle around his neck, he finished dressing and wrapped two scarves around himself before slipping into his long, black overcoat. Memorizing a few trivial facts about Wells

College, he left his office to begin a wintry vigil, followed by a snail-paced procession to the Executive Mansion.

Frances Cleveland looked out the window of her sitting room at the uniformed men—generals and admirals all—entering at the South Portico with their wives on their arms. Decked out in finery alternating between elegant and gaudy, these women were excited to be among the first to wish the First Family a happy New Year. She would not disappoint them, but she never knew what her husband would do. He had always believed his senior commanders bore him a grudge because of his draft avoidance. Yes, they always saluted, calling him "sir" and doing his bidding. Regardless of etiquette, though, he could sense the resentment thick in the air whenever he would meet with them. It made him mad. He was not going to spend his presidency apologizing for paying a proxy to take his place in war. He had his responsibilities, he handled it legally. The rest was none of their affair. Frances had heard this rant before and she was always sympathetic. She just preferred that he keep it between the two of them.

"Well, Frank, the locusts are invading the house again. Are we prepared for the onslaught?"

She turned to find her husband standing in the doorway. The absence of his cane indicated that his gout was not bothering him, a sign that her post-Christmas project had worked. Limiting his intake of food and liquor for six whole days, and making him walk for one-half hour each of those days, brought him to the brink of divorcing her. The results, though, were worth it. His complexion was ruddy; his eyes were clear, blue and sparkling. Best of all, he was standing on his own two feet with enough stamina to get through the next several hours.

He strode across the floor and swept her up in his arms: "Happy New Year, my dear," he greeted, planting a passionate kiss on her mouth. She loved it, even as she wondered whether all men tasted like cigars. Since her childhood, he had always been there, strong and reassuring.

"Cleve, you make me feel so old!" she joked, as she stroked his graying mustache. "You're as forward as a school boy."

"Those college sissies have nothing on me," he rejoined, then turned serious. "Thank you, Frank, for enduring my bad humor this last week."

Pecking him on his jowl, she answered, "You will be glad for the extra strength you have by the afternoon. Getting those extra hours of sleep this week also seems to have given you a boost."

"Perhaps, but the extra hours yielded extra nightmares."

"About?"

"Jungles. Shooting. Warships. Death."

"What is that all about?"

Helping her clasp the simple gold pendant he had given her for Christmas, the president told his wife, "Be grateful, Frank. You are very lucky not to know what you do not know." Taking her hand, he continued, "Let's go down and greet those brass hats. But if one of them so much as gives me the snake eye, so help me…"

"Cleve!" she scolded.

Winking at her, he led the way to the private elevator that would convey them to the state floor. The couple would greet the guests in the Blue Room, the very room in which they were married a decade before. She was still as captivating, even after giving him three daughters. He knew she had endured more than she deserved: her image appeared on all kinds of products from licorice to laxatives; political enemies ran outrageous stories of how he would beat her; and the newspapers were constantly prying. She bore it all with a stronger stoicism than he could command. That is what he always loved about her. Her youth and beauty attracted the entire country, but he alone could apprehend her inner joy and spiritual strength. Who else— besides his beloved late mother— could make him start going to church again every Sunday?

As the elevator descended, he summoned every bit of romantic eloquence in his repertory to sweep her off her feet: "Frank, you are truly a sensible, domestic American wife!"

Smiling wryly, Frances responded, "Oh, my silver-tongued Ovid," referring to the ancient Roman poet, "my heart can only melt at such a stirring ode. If it pleases you, though, we will read through the Song of Solomon before prayers tonight."

She would expand his repertory, she decided, before 1897 dawned.

Although it was now close to two o'clock, the ice and frost coating the sturdy wrought-iron fence surrounding the Executive Mansion were as thick and dense as in the early morning. Though the sun was shining brightly, it was distant—as distant, it seemed, as the likelihood of Dustin's political dreams coming to fruition. Positioned by now at the northwest gate, he could see a long line ahead of him before he reached the northeast gate, and an even longer one snaking up the driveway to the North Portico. Peering at the house's majestic façade, he wondered if he would make it inside before the president and first lady retired for the day.

The cacophony of conversation around him took his mind off the numbness of his extremities. On hundreds of lips— or so it seemed—the words "Venezuela," "lousy Brits," "it's about time" and "war" were repeated constantly throughout the morning and into the afternoon. Even the women were spoiling for a fight. Dustin would not, nevertheless, fall prey to anxiety. Those who have no chance of experiencing the gore and grief of war see only its romance, he concluded.

"Ever met the president before, friend?"

Dustin turned to see the man behind him, dressed in a tan frock, striped trousers and turquoise ascot. His glossy black dress shoes looked like they had come from Paris or other exotic international city. Yet, for all his finery, the man had no overcoat, an absence that did not appear to affect his good humor or healthy visage.

"A time or two," Dustin responded, grateful for the conversation to divert his brooding mind. "How about you?"

"Many times, many times. He has a lot on his mind these days, I can assure you."

Dustin looked closely at the man. He was not part of the administration as far as he could tell. A thick shock of white hair covered his forehead under the rim of his top hat. His face, however, showed barely a wrinkle. Strangely, the color of his eyes kept changing from blue to hazel to brown to green and back to blue. The bright sun must be playing optical tricks, Dustin reasoned.

"How do you know President Cleveland?" he asked the dapper man.

"We go back to his days in Caldwell, New Jersey."

"But…he was just an infant."

"That he was, son, that he was."

"Well, if you know him so intimately, why are you waiting out here with the general public?"

"I can do more good here than inside, I suppose."

"You must be freezing."

"And yet you are the one who is shivering. What brings you to the White House on this wintry holiday afternoon?"

"I am just extending Mr. and Mrs. Cleveland the compliments of the season, like everyone else." Dustin was shivering, indeed, less from the cold and more from this man's serene presence amid the jostling line and icy climate. It was disconcerting.

"Oh, that's a great relief, my friend," the amiable stranger exhaled.

"Relief? You do not convey an air of anxiety about you, sir. What are you relieved about?"

"A very long time ago the president's mother said a prayer for him. She thanked God for his hardy physical constitution and his diligent work ethic."

Who is this man, Dustin silently pondered, and what on earth is he talking about?

"Mind you, she had many children, all of them loved and each of them talented. Steve, though, was different."

The happy bystander was now recounting a memory with ease, using a diminutive of the president's given first name, which Cleveland dropped in adulthood.

"He was big and stout and strong. He was completely dependable, and depend on him they did. With two brothers off to war and the others out of the country, his widowed mother and three sisters had no other means of support during the War Between the States…" he said, then looking into Dustin's eyes, "...or however *you* wish to characterize it."

There was no way the man could finger Dustin as a southerner. He had polished his speech to perfection and revealed nothing of his background. This individual, while open and engaging, was beginning to spook Dustin with his apparent familiarity.

"Anyway, the burdens weighed heavily on the young man. He is much more sensitive than people realize. He did not always carry his troubles nobly in his early manhood, giving in to one indulgence or another. Still, he never gave up on faith. Nor did Ann Cleveland. She prayed that the Lord would send angels to ease her son's burdens, to carry him while he was carrying others. To fortify his strength when so many others were sapping it."

Dustin had never heard anyone speak in human terms about Grover Cleveland. Faith? Cleveland was a man of rational self-interest, like every other successful politician. It was hard to imagine him kneeling by his bedside; harder, still, to imagine him standing up afterward. Religious vocabulary was employed by every president since the founding; part of public ceremony, yes, but irrelevant when making hard-nosed decisions. Like many ambitious Washingtonians, Dustin believed the presidency itself cloaked all the supernatural power upon its occupants, all they would ever need.

Oddly enough, however, this new companion possessed a presence that conveyed invincible strength against the cold—today, very cold—cruel world. "From rejected pensioners to insistent office-seekers to offended diplomats, he is buffeted daily with requests and demands. Your simple act of courtesy will do wonders for him," the gracious man added. "It will do you a world of good, too, young man. This city takes its toll: politics, vindictiveness, getting even, they seem like the means to a happy end. But, like the old proverb says, 'There is a way which seemeth right unto a man, but the end thereof are the ways of death.'"

Another reminder of childhood Bible lessons. Where was this man then?

"So my New Year greeting is an answer to his mother's prayer?"

"You may have spent your entire life answering prayers and not knowing it."

It was so other-worldly. Dustin was there to enlist Mrs. Cleveland in the cause. His rehearsed and cordial salutation would be purely pro forma. The stranger, seemingly omniscient, was nonetheless clueless about Dustin's real designs. Perhaps his targeted statements just reflected heightened perception.

"Oh, and another proverb comes to mind, my friend: 'A man's heart deviseth his way: but the LORD directeth his steps.'"

It was positively dumbfounding. Was this gentleman some kind of hypnotist or spiritualist? He seemed to be reading Dustin's every thought. In spite of the innovations of Samuel Morse and the emerging theories of Charles

Darwin, the last century had been rife with ghost stories, superstitions, witches and other mediums conducting séances to summon the dead. Even Dustin was seeing the Grim Reaper on occasion. This visitor was different, though. He was not selling anything. Whether he spoke of the president or quoted the Bible, he spoke with…authority.

And it came to pass, when Jesus had ended these sayings, the people were astonished at his doctrine: for he taught them as one having authority, and not as the scribes.

The verses that had been drilled into his brain in his boyhood were now pouring out of a hidden attic in Dustin's mind. The stranger made them come to life, but Dustin had no clue as to their relevancy. His curiosity was sparked and he turned to face the mystic to ask his name. All that stood in his vision was a waifish woman with an oversized bustle and a Kelly green Boater hat.

"Where did he go?" Dustin asked her incredulously.

"Who?" she countered.

"That fellow behind me with whom I was chatting."

She stared at him blankly. "I have been behind you for the last five hours. And I do not chat with lunatics!" With that she turned to the side to fix her gaze on Lafayette Park.

Nigel Alderson thought he understood Bridgette. She knew what she wanted out of life and went for it. If he could not help her climb the social ladder, he knew, she would discard him like a rotten Irish potato. A mature man, he conceded to himself, would have nothing to do with such an egotist. Yet it was her very self-promotion that attracted him. He saw some of himself in her, save the excess poundage and complete lack of discipline. In fact, Bridgette Maher was his perfect complement: the two saw life much the same. Whereas she had the self-possession and wits to get to her destination, he had the vision to make her so much more than she could be. Yes, he knew she was dangerous, but in a thrilling way. The two of them saw love and war as one. He might be conquering her territory or— as happened to Napoleon's troops in Russia in 1812—she could be luring him to a chilly and isolated demise, a strategy only discernible when too late. It did not matter. Little else mattered to him but her intoxicating ways.

With no business pending at the embassy on New Year's Day, Alderson bounded up Connecticut Avenue to see the object of his infatuation. Normally one to hop a street car, his excitement propelled the sedentary civil servant around Dupont Circle and up New Hampshire Avenue, making U Street in a matter of minutes. He had long concluded that she was not a working girl like his other women. She was, nevertheless, vague about how she made a living. She dressed immaculately, if somewhat invitingly. Her rooms were tastefully furnished and located just a few blocks from the embassy. She had pretty well tamed her native brogue, and her pronunciation and grammar would put English linguists to shame. For a moment, he thought of how his friend Dustin Boyle had slain the drawl Alderson remembered he had when they met. Stopping momentarily, he pondered. Was he supposed to speak with Dustin recently? Not to worry, he would contact him later. If their alliance bore fruit with regard to South America, Bridgette would know that Nigel Alderson was a force to be reckoned with.

Gripping the key she gave him tightly between his index finger and thumb, he entered her building and, with considerable wheezing, climbed the three flights of stairs. Waiting outside her door to catch his breath, he then inserted the key and opened it in excited anticipation. He halted. It was Bridgette's abode, alright, but none of the inhabitants were Bridgette.

"I'm terribly sorry, chaps. Forgive the intrusion; I'll just let you get on..." Prior to losing consciousness, Alderson muttered to himself: "I have a weakness for the ladies."

<u>22</u>

A sharp gust of south-southeasterly made a wind tunnel of the North Portico, where Dustin now found himself after an hour of vainly trying to discern where the elusive, coatless alien had retreated. He could now feel warmth emanating from the open doors to the house, calculating arrival in the Blue Room to be about a half-hour away. Concentrate, he told himself as he watched the men ahead doffing their hats and the women primping in anticipation of the three-second presidential audience. The stranger had told him how much Cleveland needed this greeting, from Dustin specifically. It made no sense. Dustin's presence in Cleveland's government was a testament to the president's love for Gresham and nothing else. If he even recognized Dustin, his reaction would—in all probability—be a cocktail of awkwardness, annoyance and impatience.

Fortunately, Dustin was not there to curry Cleveland's favor, not today at least. As the warm air of the Entrance Hall embraced him, he began to run his lines for his encounter with the president's wife. She was the conduit through which he would make his case. As Grover Cleveland would have inevitably listened to Walter Gresham, he would certainly pay heed to his lovely Frances. She, reportedly, was smart enough not to offer him direct advice, but also very successful at neutralizing the presidential pique. If she could cool him off about

Venezuela and arrange an appointment for Dustin, the State Department counselor-without-portfolio could remind the president of Gresham's distrust of the Venezuelan dictator and suggest some back-channel diplomacy (which, of course, he had been fruitlessly conducting for six months). Perhaps if that impressive old man had remained in line with him, Dustin could have gleaned some advice on what approach to take with Cleveland. His Bible quotations notwithstanding, the man might have had some practical wisdom to share.

The simple elegance of this receiving area was—to Dustin—marred by outsized oil paintings of Presidents Martin Van Buren, Ulysses S. Grant and Chester A. Arthur. One Democrat, two Republicans and not a southerner among them. Hanging in the Cross Hall—flanking the Blue Room entrance—were portraits of John Tyler and Rutherford B. Hayes. This was the Cleveland White House? It suddenly donned on Dustin that he had never entered the Executive Mansion from its formal entrance. The stately receptacle for honored guests and the general public gave no evidence that a southerner ever occupied this house. He was not sure whether he was warmed by the house or by his gradually boiling blood.

It was during this slow march to the Blue Room that Dustin's spirits began to revive, fueled by the bitter resentment that kept him charging ahead all his adult life. Justus had commissioned him to reclaim this mansion for the South and he would do just that. Unlike the barbaric Ben Tillman, Dustin would do it with class, courtesy and, if necessary, deception. One way or the other, his thousands of dead compatriots would be vindicated. And Justus Boyle, whose progressive views were ignored by Union invaders, would have the last word. Since the ultimatum from Tillman, Dustin had fallen into a deep sulk. Alderson seemed to be checking out of their joint venture; the discovery of mining equipment on the Rio Cuyuni made the Brits all the more truculent; Olney was working overtime to discredit him; and, hardest of all, he was beginning to sense strong feelings for Sarah Corbett. Even if she were white, he could never be a complete husband to her. Vexation oppressed him on every side.

So be it, Dustin decided. He had a job to do and would not be dissuaded by melancholy. He would get an audience with the First Lady and give Cleveland a quick "Happy New Year, Mr. President." Short and sweet. The president will appreciate the brevity without realizing they would soon meet again. Dustin began mouthing the salutation with the speed of an auctioneer. Already, he could see Cleveland's protruding belly framed by the doorway to the Blue Room. His five-month wait for the pivotal moment was drawing to a close.

"He really is sweet. Please don't hurt him, if you can help it," she said, counting her cash.

"That is none of your concern. Your job is done. For that, we thank you."

"What else do you have for me?"

"Please," he responded, "This should provide well enough for the coming weeks. Don't get greedy."

"Age comes upon a girl quickly, Mr. Small. I have a nest egg to build, you know."

Seated on Empire-style chairs at a small round table, William Small and Bridgette Maher had developed a familiar routine as they met in the dining room of the Willard Hotel.

"Rest assured, Bridgette, when suitable assignments avail themselves, we call you before any other."

"I count on that, Mr. Small. He was a funny little elf, though. Harmless really. I hope you will not do anything extreme."

"All I can divulge to you is that Alderson is not our target. Satisfied?"

"I suppose I have to be, Mr. Small." With that, Bridgette rose from the table and exited the dining room to a ballet of turning heads and open mouths.

Standing just feet away from the president and his wife, Dustin surveyed the couple. He was about as Dustin remembered: gray, thinning hair, piercing blue eyes, a walrus mustache and generous girth. At the same time, Dustin could not help but remember Cleveland's first inauguration in 1885. Attending with his boss, Congressman Herbert, the ex-Confederate soldier was glad to see a Democrat, albeit a New Yorker, finally assuming the highest office. The Grover Cleveland of that day had a thicker mane of dark brown hair, though still quite fat. His facial expression was much more severe; his demeanor, more forbidding. Married life obviously agreed with the Chief Magistrate, Dustin thought with a trace of envy.

Frances Folsom Cleveland stood alongside her husband, radiating youth and charm. Her brown hair was styled in the manner typical of the times, but she wore no bustle, setting a new tone for ladies' fashion throughout the country. In fact, she had all the attractiveness of the flame of Dustin's youth, Priscilla Girard, though Mrs. Cleveland appeared savvy in the ways of the world whereas Priscilla evinced adorable naïveté. He indulged his imagination for a moment, placing himself where the president stood and Sarah where Frances stood…no, not Sarah. Priscilla. Where was Priscilla?

It occurred to Dustin that Priscilla, whom he had thought about every day for the last thirty years, had been absent from his mind for nearly five months. Sarah had supplanted Priscilla, but neither relationship was possible. After the war, Dustin avoided contact with Priscilla because he was ashamed of his condition. He hoped she would find a man who could be a suitable husband to her in every aspect. The issues with Sarah exceeded his personal problems to include legal penalties should the two ever attempt to simulate a marriage. At the same time, he knew he would dread the prospect—his nobler intentions notwithstanding—of Sarah finding love with another. The only thing that salved his anguish was the idea of fulfilling his father's vision. He had to focus on politics.

A pat on his shoulder caused Dustin to turn to the rear where the white-haired fellow in the tan frock stood.

"He needs to know how his mother was praying. Please let him know," the man implored with passion.

"Where did you disappear to?" Dustin whispered. "Why don't you tell him?"

"Too late, friend."

Dustin turned about to find the President of the United States staring right at him.

"Good afternoon," he said brusquely.

"Uh, yes, Mr. President. Good afternoon to you, and a very Happy New Year. Dustin Boyle at your service, sir."

Cleveland registered recognition, but did not smile. "Ah, yes, Boyle from the State Department. I haven't seen you since the funeral for Walt Gresham."

For a moment the two men looked into each other's eyes in shared pain. Dustin was suddenly gripped by a need to continue talking to Cleveland, despite his rehearsed scenario of a quick exit. He opened his mouth without knowing his lines.

"Mr. President, my mother always comes to mind on New Year's Day. I was only 18 when she died, but she was a praying woman."

Where is this coming from, he thought to himself. Cleveland looked puzzled, but not annoyed. Dustin glanced back at the old man for affirmation but, again, he had vanished.

"There is something comforting about a mother that prays," he said, following up with a long pause; and then: "Your mother prayed for you, and you have overcome many obstacles to get where you are. You worked hard, but her prayers brought you here."

Knock off the gibberish, Dustin, he frantically told himself. *Stop talking. Now.*

The president was still unsmiling yet he was also transfixed on this foreign policy aide with whom he should not be seen speaking.

"That's getting mighty familiar, Boyle."

"I beg your pardon, sir. I mean no disrespect. I will take my leave. Good day."

He turned to greet a gracious Mrs. Cleveland when the president called after him.

"Boyle, would you be so kind as to pay me a visit at nine-o'clock sharp on Monday next?"

Dustin was flabbergasted. After all his scheming with Henry Lane to get an entrée with the first lady, he had just leapfrogged over her to land a presidential appointment. He silently thanked the disappearing leprechaun who told him what to say to Grover Cleveland.

"Nine-o'clock it will be. Thank you, sir."

Pleased, Dustin then cultivated Frances Cleveland, using a pre-composed speech about Henry Lane and Wells College. It was good enough to get 15 minutes with her before his meeting with the president. She could be a useful ally if he could earn her trust.

Lord Salisbury stared out at the carriage traffic on King Charles Street. Going about their mundane tasks and making their routine visits, most Londoners, the prime minister realized, had no idea of the import of the next few minutes. Would that he could be likewise so blissfully ignorant.

"Send him in," he commanded his secretary wearily.

Ambassador Thomas Bayard entered the elegantly paneled office of the Foreign Secretary, arrayed in his ever-present mourning coat with black cape. A consummate professional, no diplomat would ever had suspected that Bayard himself had served as his country's foreign minister in the first administration of President Cleveland. He possessed all of the deference, restraint and empathy of an ambassador without any of the sniveling. For the most part, Bayard was a pleasure to deal with but even he could not blunt the impact of President Cleveland's message on the boundary dispute.

"Happy New Year, Prime Minister."

An overhanging forehead and flat, graying hair gave the ambassador—now pushing 70—an even older appearance. Slight tremors in his hands also gave evidence of frailty.

"Thank you Ambassador. 1896 is bound to be better, I hope."

To that Bayard gave no reply as the two men took oversized leather chairs by the crackling fire that Salisbury ordered perpetually stoked throughout the winter months.

"I asked you here, Mr. Bayard, because, in all candor and confidence, the messages transmitted by our own embassy in Washington are of questionable authority."

Bayard arched one eyebrow: "In what aspect, your Lordship?"

Salisbury would not go into the details of a smoldering scandal that required a swift and silent response. A family problem that he had tried to resolve by exporting it to America was about to blow up in his face.

"Nothing to concern your government," the prime minister continued. "Some organizational changes are in process and communication is mildly affected. Still, the president's addendum to his annual message to your Congress calls for a precise and unmistakable response. I am hoping to transmit that through you."

"I am at your service, Lord Salisbury, but must advise that the president has—upon my recommendation—adopted a very patient approach to the conflict between your government and that of Venezuela, and done so over his two terms. Both he and Secretary Olney believe this latest pronouncement to be an effective means of breaking the circular arguments that have kept this issue boiling for decades."

"It makes two arrogant assumptions, Bayard. The first is that Caracas is a reliable and honest party to proposed mediation. The recent Cuyuni stunt gives lie to that belief. Second, it demands that the United Kingdom, vested in Guiana since 1814, abide by a unilateral doctrine not articulated until 1823."

"Your Lordship," Bayard said softly but seriously, "I have known every president since Ulysses Grant. I can assure you that the least arrogant among them is Grover Cleveland. In fact, his humility is reflected in his willingness to abide by this time-honored virtue of protecting our South American neighbors. Otherwise, he would go with his natural bent and stay away from the issue altogether. Yet, I can guarantee that he would be equally resolute in opposing favoritism toward the Crespo regime if your government will cooperate. Rest assured, sir, that any guile on the part of the Venezuelans will be exposed in arbitration and certainly work to their detriment."

"Is Mr. Cleveland serious about forming a boundary commission?"

"He is of one character with you, Prime Minister. Neither of you bluster."

Salisbury stood and walked over to his massive desk. Upon it were two dispatches from southern Africa. One was an estimate of diamond deposits in the Transvaal region. The second was an intelligence report on the military strength of Dutch Afrikaner populations in the same area. Each dispatch, Salisbury believed, seriously undervalued its subject matter. He sat down at his desk in a dejected posture. He was now withdrawn into his own interior, hearing the competing, antiphonal voices of Landsdowne and Goschen.

Bayard turned his head in the prime minister's direction, confused by the change in juxtaposition. Salisbury sat staring for a long while.

"Are we through, Prime Minister?" the ambassador finally inquired.

Salisbury snapped out of his gloom and stared at Bayard with earnest intent: "'Work to their detriment,' you say?"

23

Sarah emerged in the embassy's grand entry hall stunned to find the ambassador himself waiting for her. "Lord Pauncefote, I…I believe I am assigned to the main floor this evening."

"That will be fine, Sarah. I should like you to bring Mr. Rice and me some refreshment, as we will be meeting late tonight. There's a good girl."

His condescension notwithstanding, the ambassador held a special place in Sarah's heart. He took care to learn his servant's names and, as best any diplomat could, fostered a family feel among the household staff. She raced through the cavernous dining room to the kitchen, where a cook was arranging finger sandwiches on a platter.

"Way ahead of you, dearie," Margaret Tuckford announced in her strong cockney dialect. "These should hold them over for a time."

"How did you know, Maggie?"

"I got me a pair of big ears, same as you. Lord Pauncefote and Mr. Rice were squawking on about Mr. Alderson. I think they finally know what he's been up to."

"And what's that?"

"Hmmph. Church-going girl like you won't get it, not at all. Let's just say he's been selling without a peddler's license, and got nabbed by the bobbies. Take this tray and come back for the tea…and tell me everything you hear."

Sarah dutifully took the tray of cucumber and watercress tea sandwiches into the same sitting room in which Alderson caucused with Dustin Boyle. This time, Lord Pauncefote sat in Alderson's chair while Cecil Rice occupied the ornate love seat.

"How long do you think it will be before we hear from London on this?" the Ambassador asked.

"Long. Nigel's blood ties complicate matters immeasurably. Otherwise, he would be gone by now."

Sarah placed the platter down. "Will there be anything else, your Lordship?"

"No thank you, Sarah."

She pulled out a clean cloth, turned to the mantel and began to polish the brass plating.

"Excuse me, Sarah, but His Lordship and I will require some privacy. I'm sure there are other rooms in need of your attendance?" Rice suggested.

"As you wish, Mr. Rice. Good evening," she bade both men, closing the heavy mahogany door by its large, shiny brass knob. This was serious. First, Alderson missed another meeting with Dustin the previous evening, and now this. The usually self-possessed southerner reacted with surprising emotion at the attaché's last broken promise. Resolving to "settle things within the next 24 hours," he gave the unmistakable impression of willingness to follow Alderson to his den of iniquity. She was praying incessantly for his safety.

"You know this nullifies our efforts to slow the velocity of this impending war, don't you? I will lose all credibility with the PM, and the belligerents in this country will push him into a corner. He will have to shoot his way out," Pauncefote declared gloomily.

Rice changed the subject. "Did you know Nigel was the PM's nephew?"

"I suppose I should have. We had no real use for an additional attaché on this post, after all. When the head of government asks me to keep Alderson occupied, I salute and try to make a go of it. What will become of the American?"

"Secretary Olney is being informed this very evening, I am told, and Senator Lodge will apprise him of his lawyer's independent activities. He seems to believe that this affair will be sufficient cause for the president to authorize Boyle's dismissal. How can Cleveland refuse? As the PM had no choice but to recall his shameful nephew, so the president must terminate this man."

"…and seal the fate of nations in the process."

"Respectfully, this was the wrong way to conduct foreign policy, my Lord. We have protocols in place under which we negotiate. Alderson and Boyle scoffed at longstanding procedure. With the utmost deference to your position, you should never have entertained any overtures that did not originate with Olney. The only good to come of it is that we discovered Nigel's desecration of our embassy with common whores. The PM has no choice but to take him back. Yes, we will suffer some embarrassment, but should consider the whole episode a healthy cleansing."

"As long as it does not turn into a public bath, Cecil," the ambassador said, lighting his pipe. He knew he could trust his secretary to resolve matters expeditiously and quietly. Although Rice had the maddening quality of always being right, he also possessed the comforting attribute of never being wrong. While Alderson was out – doubtless seeking out female companionship for himself and others – Rice had arranged the logistics and transportation that would put Alderson back in London in but a few days. The man would then be the PM's problem, once again.

"You're right, though. I should never have let Nigel talk me into arguing for arbitration. I end up looking like an American stooge." Lord Pauncefote shifted his weight, adding, "Still, how many wars can we fight at one time? Rome fell due to overreach, you know. I wonder if Boyle could have delivered on his promise."

"It was not his promise to give, Ambassador. Let us clean house for now, and await Lord Salisbury's instructions on Venezuela. Nigel's belongings are packed and we will only once more have to lay eyes on this dishonest libertine." Rice then rose, gathering his papers.

"Yes, I suppose one blessing has arisen from this cursed affair," Pauncefote conceded, walking to the door."Where is the blasted tea?" Leaving the room, he called for Sarah, who was nowhere to be found. He was nearly blinded, however, by the exterior door knob.

It was polished to the most brilliant sheen he had ever seen.

His Grim Reaper hallucinations were getting more frequent, as he swore the specter was again dogging his footsteps through the night. But nothing could dissuade him from catching up with Alderson. If the whole clandestine enterprise was unraveling at Connecticut Avenue, he may at least convince the tubby Englishman to keep make a last-ditch effort for peace. Dustin brought with him a small lantern, assuming that Alderson would be engaged in activity normally conducted under the cover of darkness.

Where was Alderson? Dustin, out of breath and panting, arrived at the reddish brownstone bearing the scrawled address given to him by Sarah. She may just be his best friend, he considered as he entered the building. He quietly padded up the soft carpeted stairs to the third floor, occupied entirely by a single unit, only to find the door ajar. He recoiled at the scene inside. Broken glass and upended furniture covered the cramped sitting room, but a separate bedroom adjacent to the far side of the room beckoned. A cold sweat informed Dustin that the boudoir would hold no good tidings, yet he advanced to the doorway nevertheless.

Yellow chintz curtains and floral wallpaper adorned the small chamber. Lying bound and gagged on the bed was Nigel Alderson, his balding head exhibiting minor bludgeoning. Dustin thought he was accustomed to brutality like this, but he felt nauseous outrage at the scene. Nigel Alderson was weak and self-absorbed, but he did not deserve such violent and ignominious treatment. In many ways, he was like a small child looking for love. For an indiscernible reason, Dustin identified with this troubled whoremonger. Perhaps, had he been physically able, Dustin would have pursued women as irresponsibly as Alderson. What the London pimps could not do to the young navigator in 1862, their American counterparts would apparently attempt to bring to fruition in 1896.

"Nigel, I'll have you free in minutes," Dustin reassured, placing his lantern on the dresser. Alderson, his eyes bulging in alarm, shook his head vigorously.

The lantern suddenly went dark and Dustin was scooped up into a bear hug from behind by two arms with the strength of a boa constrictor. In the darkness, a silhouetted figure approached him with what looked like a steel piece of pipe, the instrument that doubtless injured Alderson. Shifting into survival mode, the old combat warrior lifted his left knee and dug his boot heel into the shin of his restrainer, who elicited a loud cry and dropped his arms. Before the pipe-wielder could land a blow, Dustin caught his arm, locked his elbow – forcing the man to drop the pipe – and head-butted the attacker on his left temple, causing him to fall to the floor.

Making out a third assailant, amid metallic flashes that suggested a gun, Dustin leapt at the man – causing himself considerable sharp pain where the old Union bullet remained lodged – and tackled him. The gun dropped from the man's hand and Dustin reached into his own coat pocket to retrieve his pistol and dispatch the rogue. It was too late. The bear-hugging thug was back, lifting Dustin into the air with incredible strength. Realizing his spine was about to be snapped against the bear-hugger's knee, Dustin turned his head, summoned as much saliva as he could, and projected it down toward the strong man's face. Reflexively, the beast dropped his victim to wipe his eyes, and Dustin again reached for his weapon.

The two other assaulters were on him before he could succeed, punching him about the head and face. The large man again grabbed him and hoisted him against the wall. By now, the adrenaline was slowing and Dustin could feel himself weakening. The third hoodlum had recovered his gun and Dustin could hear the cock of the pistol, feeling the cold, steel barrel against his forehead. This was how his quest for Southern vindication would end: shot by pimps in a case of mistaken identity. He hoped Justus would understand how hard he had tried.

Something was amiss, however, even for a murder scene. The loud thud he just heard was not a bullet, since the gun and its owner had suddenly fallen to the floor. THUD. Now bear-hugger had dropped to the floor, while the rapid footsteps indicated that the remaining attacker was fleeing. He was free…and alive! An eerie figure moved in the darkness toward the dresser, relighting Dustin's lantern. His heart nearly stopped with terror: the Grim Reaper!!!

Years before, many of Dustin's troops thought him unbalanced for his lack of fear. They would be proud of him now. Death had never been so chilling as its ghoulish image stood before him. Its shadow loomed immense in the glow of the lantern, and in its hand it wielded the awful…clothes iron?

"Mr. Boyle?" the hooded figure effeminately asked. "Are you OK, sir?"

It was Sarah. She wore a broad black cloak with an oversized hood, but that was Sarah's voice. Her lovely, winning, confident voice.

Doffing her hood, she moved close to Dustin with great concern, helping him to regain his footing. "We need to get you home, Mr. Boyle. You may be seriously hurt."

He was dizzy, but coming to. "How did you find me? Why did you find me? What are you doing here, Sarah?"

"I will explain everything, but you need some attention right now. I can help you walk and..ohhhh," the laundress gasped. She put her open hand to her mouth in horror, gazing upon the bundled image of her embassy patron, Nigel Alderson. "What happened?!?!" she cried.

Dustin drew himself up and picked up the gun that nearly ended his life. "I thought that he was attacked by common hoodlums. I now believe, though, that there are some powerful forces at play here. These men are dressed too well to be pimps. And this pistol they were going to use on me is more common among soldiers. They were waiting for me, using Nigel as bait. I may be in danger, Sarah. And now you are, too."

Retrieving a kitchen knife from what appeared to be a considerable, if home spun, arsenal in her cloak, Sarah began to cut Alderson's binding. The diplomat was whimpering and hurting, but otherwise intact. Dustin removed the gag.

"They had it in for both of us, Dustin! I was to call you tomorrow for a meeting where they would have undoubtedly ambushed you. We would both be fish feasts on the floor of the Potomac had our young heroine not arrived straightaway. Sarah, you will receive higher wages speedily if I have anything to say about it," Alderson praised.

Sarah delivered the bad news. "I don't think you will have much to say, Mr. Alderson. Your activities have become known to the ambassador, and you are being recalled tonight."

"You told him?!?!"

"He told *me*. Well, not exactly. I overheard Mr. Rice tell Lord Pauncefote everything. Your bags are already packed." She turned to Dustin. "They know everything."

Dustin felt chilled to the bone. "Who told them?"

"I heard something about Senator Lodge."

Alderson sagged on the bed, dejected. "I loved it here. I truly loved it here." Beginning to shake and weep uncontrollably, he accepted a handkerchief from Sarah's bottomless pit of supplies. "I am not much of a public servant, you know. Not good at very much, at all. Were my uncle not the PM, I would probably be begging for throppins in Grosvenor Square right now."

"The prime minister is your uncle? Well, Nigel, that explains a lot of things."

Alderson blew his nose as though sounding a fanfare for Queen Victoria. "My aunt's husband, actually. I thought at the embassy, at least, I was making a contribution, small though it was. Why did this happen? I truly loved it here," he concluded, dissolving into tears.

Sarah softened. "Maybe too much, sir. Influential men throughout history have fallen serving the idols of money, power and women. You still have the chance to turn around and live righteously…back home, of course. I gather you will never be in want of a position."

"I am well-connected, that is true," he said, composing himself and standing to his feet. "Here, though, I am out of Uncle Robert's shadow. I can make my own way, as you Americans say. Or could have." Alderson hung his head in silence for several long seconds, as if to make peace with the inevitable. "Dustin, I tried to help you. I fear this last consort of mine has some inconvenient friends, perhaps in your government. This scenario has come to an end. I'm so sorry, old boy, this was all my doing."

His mind racing to process all that he had just heard, Dustin nevertheless could not be angry at his old friend, particularly after the news he had just received. "I know that when I sought you out in July I was taking a gamble, Nigel. Don't worry about Venezuela," he reassured him. "I have one trump card left to play. Just take Sarah's advice: find yourself a nice bride and live in peace."

Alderson was dabbing at his puffy eyes. "Funny that you never married, Dustin. You're a good-looking chap, and would make an excellent provider."

"I think all I would provide is misery. No, political animals like me should stick to bachelorhood."

"Didn't Mr. Cleveland hold to that view...until he was smitten?"

Dustin's eyes met Sarah's. "I do not know about smitten, Nigel, but these two men have been resoundingly smote by your laundry maid here. I think we should all depart before reinforcements show up."

"You go on home, friends. I will require some refreshment before facing the reception committee on Connecticut Avenue."

Sarah stepped forward and kissed Alderson on the forehead. "I am praying for you, you silly, sinful man."

Alderson blushed while Dustin again stood amazed at her familiarity. Who was she to pray for him? She was unlike any woman, white or Negro, he had ever come across. He would have many questions for her before the night was over.

24

"We'll return to my rooms. I need to talk to you." She had lent him physical support as they descended the steps from Bridgette Maher's lair. As soon as they reached the street, however, she dropped back behind him by about ten paces. Culture and physical safety dictated it. Her heart broke to watch this brave man limp nine city blocks, all the while wiping blood from his nose, ear and mouth.

Arriving at the Hotel Washington, where he maintained his chambers, she again assumed some of his weight as they ascended a seldom-used staircase. Finally arriving at his rooms, she opened the door for him and took charge. The chilly night air had cooled Dustin's dwelling considerably, so Sarah was surprised to see him despondently sit down without lighting the hearth.

"Mr. Boyle, you'll never recover in this deep freeze. May I?" She motioned to the fireplace. Dustin nodded warily: "I'm fine, but if you're cold, have at it."

The coals filled the modest, silver urn to capacity as though freshly replenished…or never used. Sarah quickly placed several in the hearth, striking the nearby flint (also suspiciously new) and filling the chamber with orange glow and soothing heat. Yet it became apparent to her that Dustin's spirit was considerably agitated by her activity. Though the room had not yet warmed, beads of sweat dotted his forehead as his eyes darted nervously back and forth from the fire to the correspondence he began to examine. At last, he arose and limped quickly to the far side of the room, sitting back down and examining the pistol he had recovered from his assailants.

"Let me clean those cuts," Sarah offered helpfully. She immediately located his wash cloths and an unopened bottle of bourbon, coaxing him with some difficulty to sit closer to the fire. The heat threatened and his wounds stung as she gently applied the libation, but – moved by her care and nurture – he calmed down considerably. The fear he would only admit to himself was lessened by her capable hands, good will and tender manner. It was hard for him to believe that minutes before she had flattened two thugs with a clothes iron. Accompanying the external warmth from the hearth was a comfort filling his inward parts, a feeling that the outside world was banished for a while and, if he dared, he could safely lower his guard with another human being.

"Sarah, why did you help me tonight?"

"Because you needed help, Mr. Boyle."

"So you would do that for anyone?"

"No."

"You didn't know how many goons would be there to jump me. You may have been seriously hurt or killed."

Sarah smiled her winning smile, then turning serious. "You were a warrior, sir. You saw the horror of bloodshed and smelled the stench of death. When you speak of war, you do so with authority. The jingoes have passion, but little knowledge. You're voice should not be silenced."

"All that is true," Dustin replied. "But you didn't risk everything to serve a cause. In the end people fight for their families, their friends, their land…and their loved ones. Causes can whip people up, but they can't keep men on the bloody fields of battle day after bitter day. I didn't take up arms for states' rights. My father was against secession. I fought then only to protect what was ours." He let his words sink in before continuing. "You fought this evening, but for what?"

Sarah rinsed the blood-stained cloths in the wash basin, then returning to her ministrations. How could she explain it to him? She, too, fought for what was hers, if only in her heart. Changing the subject, she asked, "So, you didn't fight to continue human slavery, did you?"

"No indeed, I did not. We were preparing for the day when our Negroes would be emancipated, but by the hand of progress, and not by aggression. I'm for sound and long-lasting emancipation. One achieved by guns and cannons will be short-lived, I assure you."

"I don't know, Mr. Boyle. General Washington seemed to liberate many through the force of arms, did he not?"

Dustin wanted to return to the present. "It sounds to me like you think our defeat was well-deserved. Which brings me back to my original question: why did you save the life of a one-time slaveholder?"

"Is that how you define yourself, Mr. Boyle? I suppose if I just saw you as a slaveholder, I would have no use for you."

"What have I done to earn your respect?"

"You visited the embassy on a hot summer night."

He stared blankly as she looked deeply into his eyes.

"It's not really a question of doing, sir, but of being."

Dustin was flummoxed by this philosopher-laundress, who moonlighted by performing hazardous feats of derring-do. Without a solid record of achievement, he was raised to believe, "being" was meaningless.

"Sarah, you have earned the respect of the embassy staff by doing a good job, by rendering exceptional service to your employer. You can't get that by simply 'being'."

"I do work hard, sir, because work is a blessing to me. As I've told you, praise from my superiors is simply gravy. This is how I am created. It's who I am." She added, "Same as you."

From their first meeting, Dustin noticed Sarah's respectful impertinence, acting as though she was equal to him, without a hint of self-consciousness. Against every cultivated instinct in his Southern body, he was beginning to believe that she was.

"I've worked hard my whole life, too, Sarah, *in spite* of who I am."

Dustin instantly regretted voicing that remark. It smacked of self-loathing. He didn't mean it, of course. He was a proud son of the Confederacy. His destiny was to bring about her total vindication. He was now losing his discipline around Sarah, and it scared him.

Sarah realized right then that her own destiny was beckoning, that the same Creator that made her so industrious had also summoned her for this moment. She carefully pretended not to notice Dustin's slip of self-revelation, finishing her task as an amateur nurse.

"You surely do apply yourself to your tasks, Mr. Boyle. You must have some powerful inspiration."

He nodded. "My father, of course. His words of guidance and direction remain with me today. And Caleb set an incredible example for me." Forgetting himself yet again, he blurted out, "I miss that man awfully sometimes."

Sarah's spirit was stirred at that moment, as though entering a realm of cosmic warfare. She stepped in without hesitation. "How did Caleb die?" she asked him.

"He was caught in a house fire," Dustin answered too quickly, startled and wishing to dispose of the issue. "It happened suddenly, the day I left for the war. We were too late to save him."

She looked at the floor, thoughtfully. "Who is 'we'?"

Dustin fidgeted with the newly-acquired pistol, wondering why Sarah was so interested in a slave she had never known. "Well…me…and Trueblood, I guess. He was the overseer, officially, but looked after himself mostly."

A period of tense silence passed between them, until she broke it: "How do you think it happened?"

"I've always suspected Trueblood of starting it out of jealousy, but I can't prove anything," he conceded, somewhat annoyed. "The fact is that I had to report for service, so did not have much time to grieve, or even think about the circumstances. When we saw that all was lost, I mounted my horse for training camp, and Lizzie and the children went back into the house, leaving Trueblood and his men to put out the fire."

"Lizzie?"

"His wife. She and the young ones witnessed the whole thing, the whole house burning to the ground." Dustin hoped beyond hope that would end the discussion… to no avail.

Sarah loved him in spite of herself. The prince of the plantation had won the heart of a daughter of slavery. Since she met him, she had known that he was more than just an embittered veteran. His spirit was honorable, charitable and strong. He had rebuked his own history to allow her into his life. Yet one critical vestige remained in control of him. Having risked her life once for him, she would die, if necessary, to liberate him from his own vicious master.

"Dustin?" she asked, rattling him with the casual use of his first name. "Tell me one more thing."

Up until now, he had been grateful for her company, but this line of questioning was disturbing.

"Why did you just say his wife and children went back into the house? Wasn't it engulfed in flames?"

Dustin halted. "It burned to the ground, I just said that."

"So, what house did they go into?" Sarah persisted, knowing the answer.

"I don't understand what you're asking." Fear and hatred were beginning to call out to him from his deepest recesses.

"They could not have entered a house that was burned to the ground, Dustin."

"They went into the house! I saw them!" Dustin repeated, his voice preemptory.

An uncomfortable silence passed between them.

"Mmm mmm mmm, I don't think that's the way it happened," Sarah observed, matter-of-factly. Dustin began to feel an awful rage – one that he had not indulged since the war – rising in him. She had been so comforting up until now, but was now meddling in personal affairs of which she had no part. He hated the ghoulish insecurity that was filling his spirit. He snapped.

"So, the little bed sheet cleaner is now an expert on infernos!" he said scornfully. "You weren't there! Keep your opinions to yourself!!"

Though nervous, Sarah kept probing. She lapsed into dialect, hoping he would reveal more: "Ain't no opinion to say you can't find shelter in a fireball, all I'm saying."

Dustin was suddenly seeing red. After decades of channeling his fury into his work, it felt good to unleash it on this suddenly annoying scrub-woman. "This is what freedom has done for you people! Too dumb and lazy to do an honest day's work, so you moonlight as a detective!! Let me tell you something, Sarah. If this country had not lost its sanity, you would be too tired from planting seed-cane stems to play sleuth! Now leave me alone!!"

"There was no cabin fire, was there?"

Like a man possessed, Dustin grabbed Sarah by the throat, shoved her against the wall, and raised the pistol butt to strike a devastating blow to her temple. Sarah gasped for air, but remained composed. Unlike the plantation slaves he had known, she did not cower under the lash, but stared straight at him. As their green eyes met, Dustin suddenly observed the reflected flames from the hearth flicker and dance in hers. Though keeping his large left hand firmly clamped on Sarah's neck, he lowered the gun, getting lost in the terrible fiery images.

They worked their murderous magic on their victim as he screamed. Bound to a pole, the victim screamed for life, screamed to be free of pain, to remain with his wife and children…and his Seedling, Dusty. His voice weakened as his figure shrunk, consumed by the orange and yellow shroud. No, the house did not burn down. Caleb was burned alive at the stake! But Trueblood, the overseer, was standing far off, himself taken aback by the grisly scene.

Off beyond the inferno was the perpetrator. While once a reassuring visage, the white mane and green eyes now appeared demonic as he held the flaming torch in hand. The rock upon which Dustin had built his life had morphed into an enraged lunatic. "I own you, boy. You and your manhood. If you can't learn your place here, you'll learn it in hell!" Justus Boyle shouted at the consumed corpse. The voice was possessed by a heinous fury, far from the soothing and even tones that his son had known so well.

The fury had a jealous overtone, as though betrayed. Dustin realized he himself had set these events in motion earlier in the day:

"I stopped down at the cabins first. Sanford told me that Caleb and Lizzie were having some 'married' time. Well, I know what that means, so I told them I would visit with them before I left tonight."

As if run through with a Union saber, Dustin now felt a searing pain in his gut, as all of his strength left him and waves of grief and dread besieged him. What he had seen that night had been too ghastly to live with. "My God! Why?! He could never...they were friends!" Shaking uncontrollably, he collapsed to the floor, releasing tears that would not cease. "Daddy loved Caleb, he would never..." Sarah descended to the floor alongside him, her left hand stroking his back. She used the right hand to caress her own assaulted neck.

At this point, Dustin's sobs had graduated to bellows, even howls, so great was his grief. Tears filled his eyes enough to blind him. Concerned that his crying be heard by other tenants, she buried his head in her chest, repeatedly whispering "It's not your fault".

"He killed him! My father killed him! He didn't just kill him: he tortured him to death!" Dustin cried. "And Caleb admired Daddy so much. We all did, I more than any." He grabbed Sarah again, but this time in an embrace, as if hanging onto a life preserver. "I loved him, Sarah. I loved them both. What manner of God allows this kind of cruelty?!?!" She would answer that in due course. The present, however, called for simple presence. For several hours, Dustin continued weeping and pleading to divinity for understanding. His spirit had fallen to a nadir he had never imagined, as if he himself were burning in perdition's flames.

In his excruciating suffering, however, a hidden, healing hand began its surgery on his spirit.

As agonizing as this recovered memory was, Dustin – with each and every tear – strangely began to feel whole again. He felt like a living soul, albeit extremely flawed. For the first time since the war, he understood himself. He was neither soldier nor spy; neither was he the southern political messiah of his own grand plan. His family's progressive stance on managing slaves had been pure pretense. As with their neighbors and plantations beyond, the Boyles viewed their Negroes as expendable goods. Justus did in fact keep a concubine – a male concubine. Signs of the relationship were always evident if not acknowledged: Justus' insistence that Caleb keep separate quarters; Trueblood's smirk when Justus would ask Caleb to remain at the house to complete "a special task"; and the unlikely stripes on his back which Caleb ascribed to the sharp cane leaves in the fields. Odd how they appeared only on his back – rather than on his arms – and only after Justus had expressed displeasure with Caleb's associations.

Dustin was the son of shame and hypocrisy, no more fit to lead a great nation than a son of the Emperor Caligula. Worse, he was a coward. Standing frozen at the awful conflagration set by his father, Dustin became an accomplice to the vicious murder of a loyal slave. Such acts were illegal in Louisiana, but perpetrators were seldom prosecuted. Caleb was doubtless libeled as an insurrectionist, killer or rapist. Thus portrayed, his death merited no investigation; his life, no remembrance. His family, too, would be forever scarred by the violent spectacle that ran its full course because Dustin was too afraid to defy his father.

He had always hated the North for its interference in affairs of which it had no part. He loved Gresham for his rigid adherence to the international doctrine of non-intervention. Even the vicious beating he recently received had reminded him of the ultimate importance of staying out of other people's business.

Until now.

Dustin's entire worldview was an attempt – strenuous in effort, yet feeble in result – to validate those few pivotal moments of inaction. His so-called heroics in battle amounted to nothing more than a death wish, a desire to find cover in the coward's last refuge – suicide. Likewise his service in England was motivated by a drive to seek danger and eat of its fatal fruit. Morally faint of heart, Dustin's outward physical courage masked his inner fecklessness. His adult life was like that of a child: Dustin Boyle had spent decades running away from home. His lack of emotion upon hearing of his parents' deaths evidenced his relief over never again having to face Justus. He saw it all now. As his tears fell, he gradually parted company with his demons.

Yet he could do so only now, he realized, because he was loved. He was loved by someone who had little reason to even like him. She was principled; he, pragmatic. Where he was cynical, she exuded idealism. He fled from a murder scene. She waded in to prevent one. She was even willing to die at his hands to help him understand himself. He had lived a privileged life because of the grueling labor of others. Hers was simply a life of grueling labor. Until now, Dustin thought of love as something to be earned, to be paid for. If truth be told, he saw little difference between love and obligation.

Sarah was youth, grace and beauty personified whereas Dustin was a middle-aged bureaucrat who walked funny. She was svelte and feminine, yet had the stamina of a soldier. Perhaps modestly endowed, she was nonetheless fetching at a less superficial level. He was always drawn to her since their first meeting. Now, her attractiveness suddenly and vigorously arrested him at the level of…instinct.

With unmistakable energy, Dustin's own youth – in a very important manifestation – returned to him as his hands caressed her face and her fingers ran through his hair. Their green eyes met again, not in rage but in desire. Upon facing up to his guilt and shame, he experienced the healing of what he thought was a battle wound. For the first time in decades, Dustin Boyle was made whole.

Her body quaked as he kissed her on the mouth. She could say it now: "I love you, Dusty. I have from the first day."

Dustin shed what was left of his hardened reserve. "You saved me, Sarah. You saved me from getting killed. You also saved me from a cold and bitter existence. How could I respond to such love without loving you back? Let me love you now."

She kissed him again, passionately…and then pulled back. "I can't save anyone. But the day of your salvation is at hand. Do you believe in God, Dusty?"

"Pardon me?"

"God. Do you believe in God?"

His re-asserted powers interrupted, Dustin leaned back, panting. It seemed an odd question in the throes of passion. He thought momentarily, then answered:

"I always believed God is there, somewhere. I guess I've done my best to ignore him."

"Well, we have to talk, because I can't ignore him. He freed my mother from slavery to men, and freed me from slavery to sin. I can't ignore him, even for you." Her strength amazed him –overheated though he was – yet again. He was at once enamored and embarrassed.

"Oh, you sweet, wonderful girl. I must beg your pardon. You see, I haven't been stirred like this since…"

"Before the fire?"

Dustin nodded, his eyes welling up again.

She took his hand. "It was all for a purpose, my love."

"I thought I knew my purpose, Sarah. Now…"

What purpose, indeed? How could he love Sarah in the sight of God and men when law and culture worked against them?

"You were intended for greatness, Dusty. You just need a lesson on love."

"I was trying to get just that."

Sarah laughed and kissed him again. "Not lust, Dusty. Love." Quoting from John 15:13, she spoke as though the words were from her own heart to his: "Greater love hath no man than this, that a man lay down his life for his friends."

"From the Bible," Dustin recalled. "I remember that verse from my lessons growing up."

"Jesus spoke it to his disciples. What does it mean to you now?"

"Obviously, I did not love Caleb enough," Dustin said, his voice cracking.

"You loved him all you could, Dusty."

"But you risked your life to save me. You had that greater love."

"Only because it was given to me by the Lord. You see, Jesus Christ is not a symbol or allegory. He is real, and his Spirit lives inside of me. You saw my Lord at work tonight. He was the one who saved your temporal life. He did this so he can save you for eternity."

"From what?"

"Your sins."

"Sarah, I have always strived to be a good person," Dustin said, lamely.

She let his protest hang there. He knew that he had not been good when he let Caleb burn. He had not been good when he tried to bypass the legal officials in charge of U.S. foreign policy. Mostly, he had not been good for 30 years as he harbored hateful plans of revenge in his heart. If he were to inventory all of the attitudes in his heart, he realized, his assertion of goodness would be exposed as a lie.

"I suppose you're right," he conceded. "I have little good to show for my life."

"None of us do. The apostle Paul wrote that none of us are righteous. It's not about the good we do; it's about the good God has in store for us."

God had revealed a glimpse of that good when he brought Sarah into Dustin's life. As Sarah could love him – in spite of who he was – perhaps God Almighty could love him, too. It was a liberating idea, if he could but believe it.

"I so want God to love me, Sarah. My life is a mess as it now stands."

She took hold of his hands. "'God so loved the world' – that means you, too, Dusty – 'that he gave his only begotten Son, that whosoever believeth in him should not perish, but have everlasting life.' Jesus suffered unspeakable agony on the Cross for Mr. Dustin Boyle. Accept him, now, as your Lord and Savior. For the sake of your very soul." Tears welled in her eyes. "There is no other way."

That was what she had all along, why her nominal superiors never intimidated her. Sarah Corbett spoke with authority. She was inviting him to be included—not in a political arrangement—but in a chosen race, a royal priesthood, a holy nation from which he would never be left out. Dustin realized that God was speaking to him at that moment. He stroked her cheek and bowed his head: "Lord Jesus, I…",

Dustin choked up. Beginning again,

"Lord Jesus, you have watched my life from birth, and all I can say is that I am so sorry for the manner in which I have lived. Forgive me, please, for thinking I am superior to others by virtue of race; for disobeying my superiors in the government; for allowing hate to rule my heart; and…for letting my dear friend die without helping him. For these transgressions, and countless others, I pray that your blood will wash them away, and that God will be my Father from this day forward."

Sarah was looking at him now, amazed. The Holy Spirit was praying through him. He, too, was amazed to hear himself, as the Bible lessons he learned by rote as a boy were now becoming life and truth.

"Thank you for setting your face toward Jerusalem, for your miracles and teaching, for enduring ridicule, humiliation, scourging and crucifixion. Thank you for rising on Easter morning and rolling the stone away."

Dustin paused. "As you forgive me, Lord, I forgive Daddy for what he did. As you forgive me, Lord, I renounce any claim on this country, praying that you will always place wise and righteous men at her helm. I turn from sin and pray for your Spirit to strive with me forever more. Amen."

Sarah embraced him for a long while, the two wondering where it would all lead. She then reached into her Grim Reaper cloak.

"You followed me home that first night I visited Nigel, didn't you?" Dustin realized.

"God told me to keep an eye on you."

"I am so glad you did. What are we going to do, you and I?"

Sarah pulled out her well-worn Bible. "We should consult the Master on matters of the heart."

The two would-be lovers shared from their histories until nearly dawn. Before the sun rose, the trajectory of Dustin's life would be forever altered.

25

After an incredible, if emotionally draining, night, Dustin
had caught some needed sleep before the momentous
meeting. In truth, the most important meeting had already
passed the prior evening, when Dustin gave his heart to
Jesus Christ, and experienced a joy that had been absent
from his life even in the golden days on the plantation.
Sarah had shared with him the secret of her strength, and he
came to realize that his surrender to fear on the awful night
of Caleb's murder was only one manifestation of a corrupt
heart. As noble as he had believed himself to be, he was
bonded to a fallen and dying world. Teaching him from the
scriptures, Sarah showed him that guilt had been his own
vicious overseer; fear, his ever-present foreman. Only a
new Master could free him from those oppressors.

Miraculously, the beating he had received only hours
earlier was hardly evident now. He washed, groomed and
dressed in his best, black cheviot suit, and arrived at the
south entrance to the White House right at the appointed
hour. Clerks and visitors shuffled past him as he ascended
marble stairs to the state floor where he had greeted the
Clevelands a few days before. Never having been invited
upstairs prior to this day, he loitered in the Cross Hall for
several minutes before climbing the Grand Staircase,
alighting at the spacious Center Hall. There he found

Frances Cleveland, wearing a simple cream-colored morning dress atop a silk skirt, awaiting him.

"Mr. Boyle, I am so glad to see you this morning. I know you have business with Mr. Cleveland, so I'll only take a few minutes of your time," the First Lady assured him. The superficial observer might think she was her husband's polar opposite: young, graceful and glamorous. Still, Dustin was beginning to realize that there was more than meets the eye to both of them.

She led him into a large, oval sitting room that had once—before children—served as President Cleveland's study. The nearly floor-to-ceiling windows provided a spectacular view of the Washington Monument. The recently dredged Tidal Basin, awaiting the development of adjacent park land, served as an unsightly backdrop to the marble obelisk. The room was tastefully furnished with Chippendale, Federal and Queen Anne pieces. Dustin sat on a Federal-style chair with red and gold-embroidered upholstery on the seat. Mrs. Cleveland rested on a simple walnut armchair directly across from him.

"Professor Lane spoke so highly of you, Mr. Boyle, I just had to meet you. He considers you, and I quote him, 'the embodiment of courage and grace.'"

Until the previous night, Dustin had no grasp on either virtue. He was only beginning to understand their connection.

"Henry Lane flatters me, Mrs. Cleveland. I only wish I had reflected those traits more in my life."

"Modesty becomes you, Mr. Boyle, but I think the professor is a superior judge of character."

"He is a man of deep conviction and loyalty. I have, perhaps, taken his strong character for granted."

"Not to hear him tell it, sir. Now, you have something you wish to tell me, he says."

Without warning, Dustin was struck dumb. He could not now articulate words, and knew it. Frances Cleveland began to look concerned as he sputtered. What was happening to him?

"Mr. Boyle, would you like some water? Are you feeling unwell?"

Dustin stopped trying and simply bowed his head. *Thy will be done*, he prayed. Immediately these words came to his mind:

> And when they bring you unto the synagogues, and *unto* magistrates, and powers, take ye no thought how or what thing ye shall answer, or what ye shall say: For the Holy Ghost shall teach you in the same hour what ye ought to say.

Dustin's power of speech instantly returned. He looked up at the First Lady and smiled. Relieved by his recovery, she smiled in response.

"These United States should be grateful to have such an intelligent and vivacious First Lady. You have adorned your office with dignity and liveliness. God has blessed you mightily, ma'am, and the rest of us through you."

She looked down at the floor with genuine humility. Since assuming her role in 1886, she was often flattered with words. This, however, was unique from the usual politicking. He was not dumping empty praise upon her. This man was praising God *for* her.

"Why are you telling me this?"

"When your time here is done and you return to a more conventional existence, you must do without the distractions and attention that your present life affords," Dustin explained, not knowing where he was going next.

"Indeed."

"We live in a fallen world, Mrs. Cleveland, where danger, evil and grief play no favorites with former First Ladies. I know you are a Christian woman."

"I am, Mr. Boyle. The truths of scripture give me constant comfort and strength for living."

"I know someone very much like you, but with fewer advantages. She has struggled for all she has and yet she relies on God as her provider. When all of the trappings of this office are no longer yours, I implore you to seek the face of your Creator. He can guide you through all hardship and he loves you as his very own."

He was now receiving incredible, even painful, insight into this beautiful young woman seated before him. Yes, the grief of a widow was ahead of her, he knew, but she was prepared for that. Marrying a man 27 years her senior—one in poor health, at that—doubtless implies a young widowhood. There was more, however. Dustin's spirit could hear the wailing of a young mother bereft of her little girl. He would not share that with Frances Cleveland today. Instead, he would leave her with words of hope.

"I hope you do not find my counsel impertinent. I only wish to impart that God will provide all you need if you will but cling to him."

Frances Cleveland did not register extreme emotions, but her expression softened and she spoke reflectively. "You seem to have read my mind of late, Mr. Boyle. The political obligations and social calendar have very much taken me from the devotions I have practiced since childhood. I've had little time to "taste and see" as the psalmist advises. Honesty bids me to confess that I've made little time to do so. I feel like I have just received a convicting message from my Lord this morning."

"Convicting, perhaps; but definitely promising."

"Living at the hub of American politics changes a person, not always for the better. I'm glad we will leave next year. My children will benefit from private life and my husband will be relieved of his crushing burdens. Yet you indicate our troubles will not leave us?"

Dustin closed his eyes to recall a verse: "In the world ye shall have tribulation: but be of good cheer; I have overcome the world."

Mrs. Cleveland perked up. "John 16:33."

"Hold fast to that, ma'am, and your years in private life will be sweet, indeed."

"And that is why you are here?"

Dustin felt sudden and profound satisfaction at the thought. "I suppose it is."

The First Lady rose and Dustin did likewise.

"I promised my children an outing this morning and I know you have business with the president."

As if on cue, four-year old Ruth and two-year old Esther came scurrying in, followed by a nurse carrying baby Marion. The two older girls were wrapped in so many scarves as to resemble Bedouins.

"This is Mr. Boyle. He works for Papa."

The little ones said hello politely, Esther articulating with great difficulty.

"I am honored to meet you both," Dustin said, kneeling to greet them. "And where are you off to today?"

Esther answered unintelligibly and her sister interpreted: "Sleigh-riding at Woodley!!"

"Oh, you'll have all kinds of fun. I wish I could join you." Dustin got to his feet and faced Mrs. Cleveland.

"I can not tell you how much I appreciate our brief chat, Mr. Boyle," she said with a youthful smile. "I will not forget your words to me…or, if you will, his words."

"It has been my genuine pleasure, Mrs. Cleveland."

"Where has my husband been hiding you?"

"I fear I was the one doing the hiding."

She nodded as if she knew. As Frances Cleveland escorted her children out, Ruth looked back at Dustin, ran to him and wrapped her little arms around his legs. He knelt again and stroked her smooth, pristine cheek.

"You're a very special little girl, Ruth. You have a wonderful day."

She started back to her mother, but turned her head while leaving: "God bless you, Mr. Boyle."

Left alone in the large oval sitting room, Dustin was fighting back tears. He did not know the year, day or hour, but knew it would be Ruth. As he healed Dustin in spirit, soul and body, so too would the Lord heal the Cleveland's pain. He stood in prayer for Ruth when he heard a throat clear loudly behind him.

Dustin turned to find Henry Thurber in a beige tweed Jacket and charcoal trousers. His green bow tie barely made a knot around his thick neck. The president's private secretary looked annoyed and suspicious.

"He's ready for you, Boyle. Follow me, and don't take up too much of the president's time."

"That is entirely up to the president, Mr. Thurber," Dustin replied without malice.

The two men hooked a right at the Center Hall and entered the president's office at the far end. Whatever insight God had given him for the First Lady's benefit, Dustin was now dreadfully clueless about this impending conversation.

After putting an exhausted Dustin Boyle to bed, Sarah had returned to the embassy to find Lord Pauncefote still up and about. Apologizing profusely for her absence—and subsequently reassured by the ambassador—she went to sleep for a total of 90 minutes before she had to begin her day. Now, after a night of intrigue, danger, romance and a miraculous spiritual conversion, she stood amidst a pile of dress shirts and detachable collars. Laughing softly, she marveled at how God called her to the front line of spiritual warfare one day, and back to the somewhat mundane life of a laundress the next. He never let Sarah get bored, but also never let her get too swell-headed for honest labor.

It appeared as though the ambassador had recovered his good humor, surprising after just having ejected Nigel Alderson. Not only had he pardoned Sarah for her disappearance—no questions asked—he also apologized to her for the former attaché's manipulative use of her services as he conducted his illicit trade. Reading and re-reading a transmission that arrived over night, he lit a pipe and sat on a stair, looking as though the weight of the world had left him. Sarah determined that his quick action in the Alderson matter had earned him a 'well done" from London.

At the same time, Sarah was hurting because she was in love with a man she could not marry. Truth be told, she would never have imagined herself with a white man, let alone one from Dustin's stock. She truly believed that God had designed their paths to intersect. Where, though, could they go from here? Anti-miscegenation laws prohibited marriage or intimate relations across the races (though that did not stop Sarah's father) and she refused to live as a concubine. As joyful as she was over Dustin's transformation, she ached over the idea of never seeing him again. Whole in body and restored in heart, he may seek to marry and leave Sarah to memory.

The cuffs and collars bore more stains than usual, until she realized that those stains were from her falling tears.

<u>26</u>

Dustin sat quietly across from President Cleveland as he signed what looked like an officer's commission and handed it to an attending military aide. He had never been in the president's inner sanctum before and was struck by the disconnect of the surroundings. Were it not for the stately portraits and massive desk—gifted by none other than Queen Victoria—Dustin would have thought he was in the office of a trial lawyer. Binders, folders and loose documents adorned almost every available space. While the president's work ethic was legendary, the appearance of his chambers gave the impression that he operated the United States government single-handedly.

"You made a curious statement to me on New Year's Day, Boyle," the president stated, dismissing the soldier." You spoke of my mother praying for me. How did you know that? Or did you simply assume?"

Dustin could think of no way to talk about his visiting angel in the receiving line, though he now thoroughly believed that the ruddy gentleman was just that.

"I imagine an acceptable way of putting it would be to say I felt it in my bones."

"Your bones are honest enough. She had many children, but she prayed for each individually, as if she only had one."

"She must have loved you all very much to seek God's ear so often, Mr. President."

"We had a hard life, especially after my father passed. But she kept right on praying..." The president paused, looking away for several seconds. For Grover Cleveland, Dustin knew, that was the equivalent of getting all choked up.

"...and I could feel those prayers. Whether I was struggling financially, down in the dumps, being smeared by politicians or what have you, I knew when she was praying."

Dustin sat transfixed, no longer distracted by Cleveland's jowls or multiple chins. He now saw an archetype of King David—a flawed man, but a man after God's own heart. No more was he the remote, curmudgeon to be dealt with through intermediaries. Dustin needed to see this, even if it was all prelude to his dismissal.

"Then came a day when I had to execute a man. I was the Sheriff and it had to be done. I was dreading it and nauseous, but when the time came, I felt peace blanket me. I knew she had been praying."

"Why did you go into politics, sir, if I may ask," Dustin inquired, somewhat impulsively.

Without blinking, President Cleveland answered, "To protect the weak from the strong. Simple as that."

It was ironic how so many—Ben Tillman among the throng—painted the president as an enabler of the powerful against the interests of the poor. How easily first impressions can take hold, Dustin pondered.

With considerable effort, the president lifted his bulk from the undersized chair and walked to the window. "You have a strong reputation, Boyle, albeit infamous. You get the job done, you have your facts straight, you improve the time and you tell the truth. The government makes a wise investment now and then, and you're one such venture." Still gazing down on the south entrance, Cleveland smiled beneath the walrus mustache. "But that is not why I agreed to see you. As much as I hate bowing to political realities, you're still a liability, son."

Dustin felt tense again, and started breathing deeply from the diaphragm.

"Come over here and take a look at that young lady who shares my name." Dustin approached the window as the presidential girth receded. Through the glass were Frances and the children boarding the carriage. Secretary of War Daniel Lamont was pacing furiously nearby as the Army captain approached him with the signed commission.

"I waited many years for that girl," Cleveland continued, "enduring constant and annoying hectoring from my sisters – all except Rose. She followed her own drum major most of the time. Anyway, they spared neither time nor expense in finding the oldest, ugliest bitties to parade before me as prospective brides. Boyle, I assure you, even I was prettier than these Medusas. Yet, the astonishing thing is that these ladies never had trouble finding suitable spouses. In retrospect, they *were* attractive women, and most of them younger than I. The problem was that nobody could hold a candle to Frank. I was in love with a young girl and could tell no one – least of all Frank – if I was ever to have a chance."

Dustin shifted his stance uneasily so to avoid looking directly at a president on the verge of spilling his guts. The First Lady's carriage made its way down the seemingly endless pathway, finally disappearing through the gate at E Street.

"She had heard all the stories," the president resumed, "those factual and those fabricated."

Dustin had heard them all, too. Even if only a quarter of them were true, Cleveland came off as a boorish, self-indulgent ogre. And yet…

"I've tried very hard to do right, but have learned the hard way that right does not cancel out wrong any more than castor oil cures the dread disease." The president immediately regretted the analogy. Cleveland knew that Dustin was well-informed, but saw no use in discussing his own medical cover-up as long as the possibility of blissful ignorance remained. "Were I to make every sick man whole, every poor one rich, every evil deed punished and every noble one rewarded, still my record would forever be stained."

Funny how Cleveland was paraphrasing the biblical verses that Sarah had showed him the night before. Not that

Dustin needed confirmation of their truth, but it seemed the president had indeed learned of their wisdom the hard way. Either that, or…

Is the president going to dismiss me because I have been a confederate operative? Or does he know about Sarah and me?

"Do you know what the problem with this government is?" Cleveland continued.

"Is there just one, sir?"

"At bottom, yes. Yes, indeed. The problem is that your federal government has become the vessel into which people pour their fondest ambitions. Jobs, money, power, even women. That's why I ran for this office, to stifle this impulse. But there is one ambition I am powerless to frustrate." Looking straight at Dustin with a steely-blue gaze, the president was looking into his soul, or so he felt. "Redemption. Too many are looking for something no man-made institution can grant."

President Cleveland motioned Dustin to have a chair and then shoehorned himself back into his desk chair. "Yes, as a governor and as a president I have granted pardons. But that is not redemption. A pardoned criminal knows he is a criminal. People still look upon him as a criminal. He is shunned as a criminal. Perhaps, he falls victim to unofficial justice."

An interesting phrase. Dustin's whole adult life had been about unofficial justice: receiving it and exacting it.

"Yet if you are ever blessed to be looked upon by another as though you had never erred, never indulged, never failed…maybe then will you understand redemption."

Before the previous evening, Cleveland's words would have rung hollow to Dustin Boyle. There was no distinction between justice and redemption. Redemption was achieved by delivering justice to the enemy. Turning the tables on the foe – getting the better of him – would provide sweet satisfaction. Then he could die in peace, he had believed. Sarah changed all that. She did not see him as a slaveholder or rebel soldier. Nor did she hold the barbarism of Justus Boyle against him. Instead she saw the teenager who liked working in the fields and who got excited about growing things; who had unconsciously repudiated his father by denying him further posterity; and who himself risked his own life and limb to save an ungrateful reprobate. Sarah did not weigh assets and liabilities with Dustin. She simply loved him, reflecting the Savior who had loved him from the beginning. When he realized that, his grand political plan – his feeble attempt at redemption – was instantly rendered inoperative.

More importantly, she was acting as Jesus would. She saw Dustin as God saw him. The would-be president of the United States realized that she was the Lord's instrument and gift to him, though he could not at the moment see how they could be together.

Cleveland broke into his reverie: "Poor girl lost her father at such a young age. But she never lost her winsome spirit. That's what got to me. I was Oscar Folsom's law partner and boon companion. I had a duty to look after her and her mother. But I needed no obligation to move me. Frank has the divine spark, always had. Being in her presence convinces me that all my father's sermons were right. God's grace is real, but I had to see it in flesh and bone to believe it."

Dustin felt a special kinship with Cleveland at that moment. He had found his own Frances. But how could they …?

"This Venezuela issue has provided an illustration. Two sides – war and no war – battle with each other as though the issue were war."

"It isn't?" Dustin asked.

"No. The real issue is redemption, brought about either by goodness or greatness. One side wants the world to fear us whereas the other wants the world to like us. My position is that we should like ourselves, fear God and let the world take care of itself. Sometimes war is necessary and other times not. My father would often preach from Ecclesiastes: 'A time to love, and a time to hate; a time of war, and a time of peace.'"

Convicted by divine authority, Dustin piped up: "Mr. President, I came here today to persuade you to drop the Venezuelan dispute altogether, whatever the British response. I realize now that I was pursuing the redemption you speak of, a false redemption. While I have my doubts about pursuing a policy of confrontation, you have led me to trust your judgment in this matter."

Dustin surprised even himself with this declaration. Months of effort, planning and angst had been spent to arrive at this meeting. Here he was now, telling the president to proceed without even a few words of protest.

Grover Cleveland looked bored by Dustin's show of support. "That's gratifying, Boyle. But you will be pleased to learn that I only this morning received Lord Pauncefote in this very office, where he proceeded to transmit his government's consent to arbitration by the United States. So, we can put this crisis behind us, at least for now."

Dustin was already too excited about his relationship with God to gin up any additional enthusiasm about this admittedly positive development. He smiled, nevertheless, leaning forward and extending his hand: "Congratulations, Mr. President."

Cleveland waved him off, unable to reciprocate since he was so solidly wedged in his desk chair. "None warranted. I think we should silently thank the South African Boers and their German backers for this happy news," the president observed, puffing away contentedly on his cigar. "And hats off to the British for wanting diamonds more than gold."

Dustin rose from his chair. "I've taken up too much of your time, sir. I'll take my leave."

Cleveland's visage became stern. "Not just yet, Boyle. Take a seat. We have an outstanding issue to deal with," the president intoned, removing a thick envelope from his desk drawer. Olney's frantic writing was visible on the outside.

Dustin realized that the president knew everything: his past espionage, his furtive negotiations, everything. He was willing to admit all of it. "Mr. President…"

"You were close to Walt Gresham?" Cleveland interrupted.

"Uh, yes, I was, sir."

"He spoke very highly of you, which – you must know – is the reason a man of your background was retained in your present position."

"I'm grateful, to him and to you."

"Well, I think a change is now going to be necessary."

Dustin steeled himself for the fall of the axe. He was at peace with God and himself, but the old pride dies hard. Dismissal was going to hurt.

"It appears from some reports that your gifts extend beyond legal and political analyses to active diplomacy. Am I wrong?"

"Sir, I admit that…"

"The reason I ask," the large man went on, "is because I need a dependable man to monitor the disputed parcel between the Orinoco and Essequibo rivers while the arbitration is ongoing. I thought about Ambassador Scruggs, but he may be too partial and, as is evident, has his price. Are you interested?"

Twenty-four hours prior, Dustin would have turned the president down flat. But now?

"There is one problem," Cleveland resumed, "of a personal nature." Peeking into the envelope again, he proceeded carefully. "It is regarding relationships between colored people and whites."

He does know about Sarah, Dustin thought.

"Venezuela has a very different history from ours, and the people's standards diverge from ours in some ways. As a native southerner especially, you may be offended by the mingling of whites, Indians and Negroes, inter-marrying and having children. This is not uncommon in that part of the world and you must have a sturdy constitution to abide this phenomenon."

Blessings now seemed to be falling on him from every direction. "I will exercise all due tolerance for the duration of my assignment, Mr. President," Dustin promised, suddenly overjoyed.

"Very well. You will be working directly for me in this capacity, so I'll inform Olney that you are no longer on his staff." Cleveland paused to shudder. "The fire is getting low; would you feed it for me?"

"My pleasure, sir."

Dustin leapt from his chair and began to select some choice kindling when the president cleared his throat with noticeable effort. Looking back, Dustin found him hoisted into standing position and holding out the thick, incriminating envelope.

"Use this," Cleveland said, without expression.

Ezekiel Swanson, now a Lieutenant General, was descending the steps of the State, War and Navy Building, exuding joy over a personal triumph. The cold January climate was offset by a brilliant sunny morning. He would not have his war with the Brits, but he could sense the political winds gathering force, and his chance for greatness was not far off. In the mean time, he had muscled Lamont into a promotion, making a significant command even more likely when the opportunity availed itself. That was likely to be soon with the Democrats is disarray.

Cuba beckoned, he was sure.

His mood was ebullient and his confidence soaring as he reached the bottom of the steps, and saw a similarly contented black-suited official – green eyes gleaming – approaching from the White House.

"Good morning, sir. Fine day, is it not?"

"Indeed it is, General. From your demeanor, I assume you just received that third star."

"Just by looking at me? You must be omniscient."

"Not me," Dustin Boyle said. "I'm privileged, though, to know somebody who is."

Just then, the crew responsible for the upkeep of the Executive Mansion – and getting a very late start – appeared on its roof and began lifting Old Glory to the top of its august and imposing pole, drawing the attention of the two men. The uniformed man snapped to attention, smartly lifting his right hand in salute. Neither had the old spit and polish left Dustin Boyle, who did likewise – for the first time in his life – in respect for the flag of the United States of America.

Sarah opened the service entrance door to find Dustin—in business attire, this time, and carrying a bouquet of flowers.

"Dusty! What in the world?"

"Have you ever thought you might like to travel south, Sarah?"

Thinking she was being teased, she shot back: "Louisiana has too many alligators, four-legged and two-legged."

"I was thinking a little farther south. There are beautiful mountains and rivers and—from what I hear—plenty of gold."

Dustin grabbed Sarah by the waist and kissed her with gentle gusto. "Come with me."

Running her hand through his hair, she replied as only Sarah Corbett would.

"I don't like heights and I can't swim. As for gold, I can wait for the paved streets when I see the Kingdom."

He stared at her wide-eyed, until she added, "But if you're there, I'll go."

Epilogue

Dustin loved this weekly ritual like no other. Each worker would come into his modest office near his home to collect his wages. Dustin disbursed the envelope—usually with more money than contracted—and asked about children, wives and health. His only requirement is that his employees allowed him to pray for them before departing. Some were deeply moved by the prayers; others, indifferent. Still, he had commanded the respect of all of them through a combination of competence and compassion. Although his farm was small in comparison to the other sugar concerns in South America, he had established strong partnerships with commodity traders in the region, and was able to move his crop every season at a comfortable profit.

Walking back to his nearby house—an unassuming white clapboard structure—he was greeted with hugs and kisses by his twins, Ruth and Caleb. Their curly brown hair had a burnt orange look in the sun while their freckles were unmistakably Boyle trademarks. At seven years of age, they were a handful for a man in his 50s, no matter how vigorous. Flanked by each one, he proceeded to his front porch to kiss a waiting Sarah. She threw her arms around him, asking "Is everybody happy?"

"Why not? Everyone likes a few extra bolivars for a week's work."

Since the resolution of the Venezuelan Boundary Dispute, Dustin—who was retained by the administration of President William McKinley until the final agreement was reached—labored hard to build his business. A civil war ousted Joaquin Crespo from power, but also brought German, Italian and, yes, British warships back to the region to collect the former dictator's massive and outstanding debts. Given the European firepower, there was some doubt that sugar exports would continue unimpeded, until President Theodore Roosevelt rattled the American saber. Dustin relished the irony of the jingo president keeping Walter Gresham's protégé financially secure.

The return of the Republicans to the White House followed the implosion of Ben Tillman's candidacy and William Jennings Bryan's capture of the Democratic nomination in 1896. Both Democratic contenders were largely viewed as repudiating President Cleveland's policies and rumors abounded that the president was actually hoping McKinley would succeed him, if only to knock some sense into the Democratic Party. In the interim, the jingoes had their war with Spain and an assassin's bullet brought Roosevelt to the Executive Mansion.

"Well, wife, did the post arrive? After all, we can't cut off all contact with our native soil."

Sarah sat on his lap, scratching the back of his head, as he rested on a rattan chair. "It's right here," she whispered emotionally.

He looked back at her with concern. "What should I look at first?"

She handed him a three-week old *New York Times*, pointing to the lower right corner.

RUTH CLEVELAND DEAD.

Eldest Child of Ex-President Cleveland Dies Suddenly at Princeton Home.

Since exhorting Frances Cleveland to renew her faith in God, Dustin and Sarah had covenanted to pray for the Cleveland family. He was beginning to believe he might have misinterpreted the Holy Spirit's prompting with regard to Ruth. After all, eight years had passed with no sign that this loss was impending. Yet, it was all too true. A mild case of diphtheria brought on sudden heart failure. The little four-year old who hugged him in the oval sitting room at the White House was now enjoying a far grander residence. Dustin was certain, furthermore, that President and Mrs. Cleveland—although doubtless grief-stricken— were being ministered to by God's Spirit and his angels. Would that be the case had the Lord not taken a man full of vain, vengeful ambition and turned him into a messenger of divine love?

Dustin Boyle stood and embraced his wife, Sarah, for a long while. She was the same as when he met her: serene and exciting, nurturing and strong, alluring yet adoringly wholesome. He could not imagine life without her yet he knew his Lord's grace would be sufficient come what may.

"She was a lovely child, Sarah, and she would have loved you, too," Dustin said with a heavy heart.

"I'm sure that's true, Dusty. I pray that we'll never lose either of these two little ones."

"Heaven forbid," he said, scooping his two wriggling offspring in his arms, much as Secretary Hilary Herbert had done with his grandchild many Christmases ago. "But Ruth Cleveland is not lost, and neither would ours be lost."

"You're right, of course. Still, the separation would be awfully hard to bear. We can counsel people to lean on the Lord, but that counsel can sound hollow when tragedy hits."

Dustin nodded. "I think that's why he brought me into the Cleveland's presence back in '96. It may take that long to grow adequately sensitive to God's presence and comfort."

"So, do you think they are drawing now from that sensitivity?"

"I have to believe it, Sarah. What we went through was prelude to all of this, I believe."

The little family sat for a little while on their little porch, thanking God for one another, and petitioning him on behalf of President and Mrs. Cleveland.

As was his custom since retirement, Grover Cleveland finished breakfast and entered his first-floor study of his home, Westland, at Princeton, New Jersey. As a trustee of Princeton University, he had held many meetings in this room trying to reconcile the disputes between faculty members and the university president, Woodrow Wilson. Lately, though, the house was quieter. In increasingly ill health as the years went on, the corpulent former president had lost some of his excess poundage. His suit hung baggily upon him and the lines in his face were deep.

He opened his diary and gazed at his last entry:

January 8, 1904

> I had a season of great trouble in keeping out of my mind the idea that Ruth was in the cold, cheerless grave instead of the arms of her Savior.

Dipping his pen in the small jar of black ink, the 22nd and 24th president of the United States updated his spiritual condition:

January 12, 1904

God has come to my help and I am able
to adjust my thought to dear Ruth's death
with as much comfort as selfish humanity
will permit.

Returning the pen to its holder, Cleveland leaned back in
his chair and closed his eyes. Slowly but surely, he and
Frances were gathering the strength and faith necessary to
live and raise their remaining four children, the youngest
only six months of age. In no way would selfish humanity
get the better of them. They would cherish their 12 years
with Ruth and take none of their offspring for granted.
They would raise them in the fear and admonition of the
Lord…and the love and nurture of doting parents.

He had tried so hard to do right, he would tell intimates,
knowing that in the sight of heaven it may not have been
good enough. He would now trust the God to whom his
mother prayed to make up the difference.

Author's Note

This work actually began as an attempted biography of President Grover Cleveland. I believed the existing works were time-worn and needed a fresh perspective. As I was actively researching for this task, two volumes were published by authors who were less charitable to the 22nd and 24th president than those biographers of old. While their accusations were not ironclad, neither could they be easily dismissed. Since I had neither the means of—nor the interest in—proving or disproving scandalous charges, I decided to accept Cleveland as he depicted himself in his own correspondence: a sinner saved by grace who, for the most part, tried to do what is right. Somehow, a straightforward profile of the man was not sufficient to this task.

The genre of historical fiction (heretofore known as hist-fic) can be a tricky one to navigate for both writers and readers. While the era and locales should be scrupulously researched, the plot and characters that stem from the author's mind might require flexibility to fit comfortably into the setting. *The Schombürgk Line* incorporates national and world leaders from the late 19th century—Cleveland, Lamont, Olney, Lodge, Roosevelt, Tillman, Salisbury, Pauncefote et al—and places them alongside fictitious characters who advance the plot. Obviously, any interactions between the historical and the fictitious will be, well, fictitious.

In such activity and dialogue, my consistent aim is to convey the beliefs and temperaments of the historical figures as recorded by authoritative sources. As this work evolved, it became easier to convey Cleveland from an outsider's perspective, specifically that of someone who knew him, albeit not very well. Thus, while President Cleveland is the 300-pound centerpiece of this hist-fic narrative, Grover Cleveland, the man, serves more as a supporting character. My hope is that giving readers a small taste of his personality will induce them to pursue him as a pivotal, if unappreciated, political figure in American history.

One of my favorite references for this novel is Alyn Brodsky's *Grover Cleveland: A Study in Character*. Published in 2000, the opinionated biographer occasionally compares modern presidents unfavorably to Cleveland. However, I must take issue with his portrayal of Grover Cleveland as a Deist. He was not. Nothing in his correspondence or the commentary of his contemporaries will accurately lead a person to that conclusion, I believe. Granted, we all like to project our own preferences onto our heroes. All the same, his letters allude to the blessings of prayer, the comfort of the Savior and the depravity of the human condition, doctrines more akin to the revivalist Jonathan Edwards than to Thomas Paine or Thomas Jefferson. All scripture, incidentally, is quoted from the 1611 Authorized King James Version of the Bible.

At bottom, my message in *The Schombürgk Line* is about the futility of politics as an agent for the redemption of countries or individuals. Much of the vitriol between and within political parties is rooted in such vanity. Grover Cleveland, a lifelong pol, nevertheless believed that the pursuit of happiness (redemption, if you will) was only possible if government was constrained by strict parameters, making political mischief much less dangerous. A longtime political junkie myself, I have learned this truth from hard experience…and from the wise Mr. Cleveland. Time will tell if hist-fic can similarly teach this lesson.

About the Author

JOHN CLIFFORD GREGORY is a New York/New Jersey-based independent writer specializing in agriculture and public policy. He is currently at work on a second novel—set during the administration of Rutherford B. Hayes—and a non-fiction history focusing on American farm policy in the 1960s. In addition, he edits and contributes to non-profit newsletters, and serves as a copywriter for numerous online and print outlets. His widely-read blog, *Life, Library and the Pursuit of Temperance,* is published several times each week, and reflects on literature, history, culture and politics.

Made in the USA
Lexington, KY
01 March 2014